Situation Critical

Amanda Knight

Copyright Page from the Original Book

ISBN: 9781489241009

Title: Situation Critical

www.escapepublishing.com.au

TABLE OF CONTENTS

About the author	iii
Acknowledgements	iv
Chapter 1	1
Chapter 2	13
Chapter 3	28
Chapter 4	33
Chapter 5	42
Chapter 6	48
Chapter 7	57
Chapter 8	74
Chapter 9	82
Chapter 10	97
Chapter 11	108
Chapter 12	115
Chapter 13	123
Chapter 14	152
Chapter 15	160
Chapter 16	171
Chapter 17	178
Chapter 18	194
Chapter 19	215
Chapter 20	223
Chapter 21	234
Chapter 22	243
Chapter 23	252
Chapter 24	259
Chapter 25	268
Chapter 26	270
Chapter 27	280

Chapter 28 297
Chapter 29 301
Chapter 30 307
BESTSELLING TITLES BY ESCAPE PUBLISHING... 322

Situation Critical
Amanda Knight

A taut debut novel about a wounded soldier, a courageous doctor, and a dog in desperate need of a rescue.

Soldier, surgeon, traitor, dog...

When Sergeant Nate Calloway is carried into the field hospital with no memory of how he got there or where the other members of his unit are, Australian army surgeon, Captain Beth Harper cares only about repairing his broken body. But it's clear that something went terribly wrong on the other side of the wire, and as Nate slowly recovers, he becomes more and more anxious to return to duty, go back into the field, and rescue his friends, his unit, and the bomb detection dog that he loves.

The only way Nate can be released to active duty is if a doctor agrees to accompany him, and Beth surprises everyone by volunteering. Her role is to monitor Nate and take him right back to hospital the instant that his health deteriorates enough to put their rescue operation at risk. But as she stays close, she finds herself inexplicably drawn to his courage, his determination, and his commitment to his fellow soldiers.

Instead of a straightforward recovery, however, Nate and Beth soon realise they've stumbled on a tangled web of deceit and danger, and the enemy is no longer outside the wire. He is one of their own, a traitor, and he has them in his scope.

About the author

Raised in suburban Sydney, as a child, **AMANDA** loved to escape the bright lights and bustle, and visit the home of her mother's rural roots, deep in Sydney's Blue Mountains or historical Bathurst, the dusty cattle country her father's family hails from. The ramshackle farmhouses, and wonderfully unique characters (both animal and human!) along with paddocks fringed with mysterious bushland, provided an endless canvas of sensory delights, and unending fodder for her writerly imagination ... and still does!

Intrigued by the machinations that motivate human behaviour, particularly crime, for as long as she can remember, and a little partial to a man in uniform, it seemed only natural Amanda study psychology and marry said man in uniform!

When she's not writing about psychopaths, soldiers and police officers, or love and loss in small town communities, Amanda fills her cup in the field of people and culture development.

Amanda resides in a beautiful beachside suburb in Sydney with her husband and children, a cranky (but lovable) Ragdoll cat and the most gorgeous Golden Retriever dog that ever lived.

Acknowledgements

To the many and varied uniformed men and women (and their patient loved ones) who dedicate their lives to a greater cause, and to the amazing animals that support them, my heartfelt and ongoing thanks to you all. And to Sarbi, canine war hero, and my inspiration for Finnegan ... may you be enjoying a glorious life over the rainbow bridge.

To Kate Cuthbert, without your belief in Situation Critical, I wouldn't be here! And to the delightful and ever supportive Brooke Moody, and the Escape and Harlequin teams, thank you for helping me to make this the very best book it can be.

Lisa Ireland ... there aren't words enough to express how very grateful I am to you. Without your friendship and steadfast support, in all things writing and life, especially during those darkest times, I simply would not have achieved this dream. Thank you with all of my heart.

Emily Madden, Beck Nicholas, Rachael Johns and Lisa Ireland—my on tap support crew who are strewn across four far flung states of this wide, brown land! Your encouragement, the kicks in the butt, and inevitable laugh-out-loud moments we share most every day in our 'writer's camp' has been invaluable. And to Shannean Moncrieff ... with astute insight and unwavering encouragement, you helped me find my path (and stay on it!) all those years ago ... to you I am forever thankful.

Helene Young and Bronwyn Parry, genre trailblazers and women of substance whom I am so very lucky to call friend. For your support and insight, especially during life's ups and downs that had nothing at all to do with writing, thank you so much. And to Georgina Penny, thank you for your thoughts and 'life-experience' suggestions—you provided the vital (and perfect!) missing pieces right when I needed them!

To Lyndall, my deepest thanks for your words of wisdom and endless support when the writing faded into the background, and life's trials took over. And then, with your courage and determination to face every new challenge, and get on with moving forward, as hard as each step was, you inspired me to make this happen, more than you know ... btw—welcome to the land of criers—(isn't it the best place?!)

Nicole and Brad Blumberg, for your patience and detailed answers to my endless (and endless) military questions, and hearty cheering on the sidelines, thank you! All errors herein are completely mine.

To my beta readers—Suzanne Whitfield and Leanne Lambert. You waded your way through drafts and rewrites without complaint—the end result has your stamp on it too! My deepest gratitude to you both.

There've been many people—including extended family, dear friends and wonderful work colleagues, who've shared various moments of this journey with me, and who've spurred me on with blind faith that I 'could do it'. To every single person who has encouraged me, your support has carried me when I most needed it ... thank you.

To the women and men I've been so lucky to meet through Romance Writers of Australia—there's quite a few of you who've been supporting me on this road since the beginning—the journey wouldn't have been anywhere near as much fun, or the achievement as satisfying, without each and every one of you along for the ride ... thank you.

Mum, my one-woman cheer squad, I love you. Amongst many other tasks, you've read every version of this book and sat through endless (and endless!) conversations about it—you're the best—the gold medal is in the mail! Auntie Sue, your eye for detail was immensely helpful during those early drafts! And to my grandma, I hope you're beaming wherever you are. You said I could be anything if I worked hard enough, and here I am.

To the Smith crew, thank you for celebrating my success at each step (even if you weren't quite sure what they were!), and particularly to Katrina. Your encouragement and pearls of wisdom during those conversations that stretched into the late hours of the night, when I wondered how I'd find the way ... they made a difference. Thank you with all my heart (and we really better nail that time management stuff now!)

To my treasures ... T, C and D, your whispered words of encouragement at the oddest of times spurred me on and filled my heart. And to my very own man in uniform, M ... for holding the fort when I needed it, and making it work. This journey's been a long and winding road, one that's been a little fraught at times, but we made it! I love you ttthhhiiissss much.

To my dad, a deeply complicated man ... I so wish you could've been here to see this. My heart is a little broken that you're not, even though I reckon all I'd get out of you is *'well I'll be buggered, she actually did it.'*

My darling T, C and D,
May this, my first published book, always remind you that no matter how hard the road, or how long the journey, it is worth chasing that which speaks to your heart ... because even the darkest hour fades, and is forgotten, in that glorious moment when you realise you've finally achieved your dream.

I love you.
XXX

Inside each of us, there is the seed of both good and evil.
It's a constant struggle as to which one will win.
And one cannot exist without the other.
Eric Burdon

Chapter 1

Doctor Beth Harper tossed her boots and army-issue woollen socks through the hospital's service exit and followed them out the door and onto the dirt. She dug her toes, her heels, the entire length of her feet into the gritty Afghani sand and exhaled. A far cry from the lush soil at her mum and dad's farm, the loose earth was still sensation enough to reground her. Calm her. Centre her.

Almost.

She closed her eyes and welcomed the chilled night air into her lungs. Sharp and crisp, it helped clear the aching tension burning deep in her chest.

She'd almost lost him. Twice.

Death happened here, it was part of the deal for an army trauma surgeon in the field, but she'd long ago reconciled the fact that no matter how hard she worked, or wished or wanted, she'd never save everyone. But today, more than any other day, she just couldn't—wouldn't be responsible for the loss of another man's life. Not this day of this month.

Beth lifted her gaze and scanned the breadth of the sky, sending out a silent plea to whomever, whatever, might be listening, out there, up there ... anywhere. *Please ... just let everyone be okay today.*

White puffs swirled around her face when she finally let out her breath, checked her watch. One hour and forty-nine minutes. In one hour and forty-nine minutes it would no longer be the first anniversary of Andrew's death.

Her right hand drifted to her left, fingers fussing over her naked ring finger, familiar lump filled with grief and guilt clogging her throat. She swiped at her wet cheek and edged backwards until she found the doorway. Slumped against the doorjamb, her shoulder and hip sagging into the solid frame, *s* he embraced the ache radiating through her muscles, the dull pain a welcome distraction from the searing ache pounding her heart. Even if it wasn't today, wasn't the first anniversary, the last nightshift of rotation was always the hardest.

Quickening footsteps behind her hauled her upright and onto her feet. She swivelled to face the woman striding towards her.

'Excuse me, Captain Harper, sorry to interrupt your break, but I thought you'd like to know that our unidentified soldier is conscious. Disoriented, but conscious.'

Cautious relief flooded Beth's system. It'd been just over three hours since she finished his surgery, and even though he wasn't close to out of the woods yet, this was good news, really good news. She flicked a glance out towards the starless night.

Thank you. Thank you. Thank you.

'Thanks, Lieutenant.' Beth dragged her socks and shoes back on and they both hurried along the hospital corridor towards the recovery rooms. 'Anything back from Intel on who he might be? Where he came from?'

'No, ma'am, not yet. Intel said due to the heavy combat in the last forty-eight hours, it might take a bit longer than usual. And there's been nothing on the two kids who brought him in either.'

Beth chewed at her bottom lip. 'Hmmm, the whole situation is concerning.'

'Yeah, it really is. And I still don't understand how those kids could've come so close to our perimeter without detection,' said Lieutenant Saunders.

Beth glanced at her colleague. 'Yes ... but I've no doubt there'll be an explanation, something we're not aware of yet.'

'You know, I've been thinking about it non-stop, and I've got some theories. Are there any other specifics you can share about the breach, Captain?'

Beth sucked in her cheeks, smothered the grin pulling at her lips. She'd often thought Lieutenant Saunders naturally curious nature would have her better suited to a career in Intel. Beth considered the full gamut of the information she had. Major Lawson Black, her direct superior and chief surgeon hadn't updated her on the matter since their initial discussion, immediately post the soldier's surgery. What he'd shared wasn't classified, so there wasn't a reason she couldn't share all the particulars she had with Lieutenant Saunders.

'I really don't know much more than you've mentioned, but I do know that the two civilian boys delivered our patient right to the wire before taking off, and as you know, they did this before anyone got a hold of them. They're barely in their teens and armed, but not at all hostile.'

Both women paced the next few steps in silence.

'Well, I reckon there's definitely more to the story than that. We just haven't heard it yet,' said the Lieutenant.

'Maybe, but they'll let us know what they can, when they can, as is protocol,' Beth said, slowing her stride, shooting more than a glance at her nurse.

Saunder's cheeks flushed pink. 'Oh, yes, yes, of course, ma'am. I didn't mean to be disrespectful. I'm so sorry, Captain ... I just, um ... it's good we were able to narrow the patient down to Special Ops.' Her words tumbled over each other as she hurried to make an appropriate comment.

'That's definitely a plus,' Beth said, pleased she hadn't had to go any further in reminding her favourite nurse about protocol and appropriate behaviour. 'Let's hope we have something that'll shed more light on the whole situation soon. With any luck he'll be able to tell us the details himself.' Beth didn't stifle the sigh that escaped with her thoughts.

Minus dog tags and with only shreds of his uniform intact, the soldier was rushed into her operating room unidentified and alone. His injuries consistent with blast trauma, and his condition critical, her surgery team were on an even higher alert than usual. Thankfully, there'd been one clue they could start with in an effort to narrow down who he may be.

During her initial evaluation, Beth noted two tattoos. The one above his heart she recognised as Australian military. Two black diamonds joined by a sword and finished with the banner: *foras admonitio—without warning.* It identified him as a Second Regiment Commando, Australian Army. A laceration directly below the emblem obliterated any unit details that may have been inked there, so the crest was the only specific they had to go on for now. That, and the knowledge that these men didn't go down without a fight. So whatever it was that happened out there, it had to have been big. A total ambush, or worse.

'Finnegan ... I have to find him ... Out. Let. Me. Out.' A man's raspy shout echoed through the corridor, the increasing agitation with each word, unmistakable.

Still five rooms away from their John Doe, Beth and Lieutenant Saunders broke into a jog, reaching his bedside in moments.

‘Where are we at, Lieutenant Matthews?’ Beth said to the nurse struggling to keep their patient contained to his bed.

‘He’s been conscious about ten minutes, Captain. Just started in with this a couple of minutes ago.’ Lieutenant John Matthews, their nursing unit manager, a six-foot-three bloke who took his weight training seriously, and didn’t usually have a lot of trouble restraining distressed or disoriented patients, spoke in clipped bursts, sweat beading his forehead.

‘Lieutenant Saunders, we may need to help our patient out with some chemical restraint. Prep five milligrams of midazolam please, just in case,’ said Beth, her eyes pinned on the angry and disoriented man in front of her.

‘Yes, ma’am.’

Giving Lieutenant Matthews a nod, one he returned, the unspoken moves between them well practised, he stepped slightly to the side and Beth tried distracting their distressed patient. ‘I’m Captain Harper. Can you tell me your name?’

His attention still dedicated to losing the IV inserted in his arm, he didn’t acknowledge her or react like he’d even heard her, so she tried again. Same reaction. Without hesitation, she squeezed the pressure point between his neck and shoulder. *That* got his attention.

His head twisted towards her awkwardly, but there was nothing awkward about the way his blazing eyes fixed on hers, their slate grey depths filled with fight. His shoulder dipped sideways towards the bed as he tried to shove her hand off his shoulder.

'Who's Finnegan, sir?' she asked ignoring his strong fingers as they wrapped around her own, squeezing, crushing, trying his hardest to make her release her hold on his shoulder.

'Dog. He's my dog,' he said, his words barely coherent. Slowly, his grip on her fingers relaxed, his hand dropped away and fell slack onto the bed. She loosened her hold on his shoulder. For now.

'What kind of dog?' Beth asked, removing her hand from him completely. She kept her gaze glued on his, prompting him when he didn't answer. 'Sir?' She couldn't identify his rank, but given his age—she guessed him to be early thirties—if he'd made a career of the army, he'd possibly be at least her rank or close to it, and respect wasn't something she gambled on.

'BDD,' he said, panting with the effort of speaking. 'Black Lab.'

He shoved his body upright again, one hand thrashing at the air above his IV ports, the other tearing at the bandages on his chest, the thought of his dog the likely reason for the renewed burst of adrenaline.

'Gotta get him ... and the others. Gotta find them,' he said, the power in his voice dropping on the final words.

Lieutenant Matthews' firm grip settled back onto one of the man's shoulders, Beth grabbed the other. 'We'll look for them, we will. Finnegan, your bomb detection dog, and the others,' she said, positioning her face directly in front of his, drawing out her response, buying precious extra seconds of his attention until Lieutenant Saunders arrived back with the sedative. 'We'll work on finding all of them, but right now, I need you to settle down, okay?'

'Will you go today? Find them today?' His enormous pupils were like magnets, even if she wanted to, she couldn't look away from him.

'We'll do our best, we will, but before we can—'

His legs pushed out against the sheets, his arms back to swinging at the equipment and bandages. Clearly her promise to do her best didn't cut it. She motioned for Sergeant Matthews to step back a little. Maybe if he didn't have another bloke restricting him, he'd calm down a bit quicker.

'Hey, hey, look at me,' Beth said gripping both of her patient's shoulders, relieved when Lieutenant Saunders appeared in her periphery. She shot a nod to Saunders, consent for the nurse to go ahead and administer the prepped tranquiliser straight into his IV. 'Listen, we'll get onto it today. I promise,' said

Beth. 'But I need you to talk to me first, calm down, okay?' She circled her fingers rhythmically at the back of his shoulders as she spoke. 'We're giving you something now to help with that.'

He stopped grabbing for the equipment and stared at her, his breathing still choppy, his body still swaying from the effort. He looked like he was considering what she said, would do what she asked, his eyelids closing and opening in a slow blink. She ignored the jolt of fear spearing through her belly. *God I hope I can help him.*

'Can you tell me your name, sir?' She flicked a look at Lieutenant Matthews, his lips set in a thin line. He gave her the 'this could go either way' look. She refocused on their patient, his eyes glassy, and positioned herself to be able to move quickly if needed.

'Sergeant Nate Calloway, ma'am,' he eventually said, his words running together, his eyes slowly losing their fire, their focus. Within seconds, his shoulders curled inward, his head dropped and his eyelids drifted closed.

'Three, two one ... he's out,' said Lieutenant Matthews.

'Thank god we got his name before the midazolam did its job,' said Beth.

They both eased Sergeant Calloway's lax head and shoulders backwards onto his pillow and Lieutenant

Saunders detangled the twisted tubes and lines around their patient's arm and torso.

'I tell you what, I'd hate to come up against this bloke when he's firing on all cylinders,' said Lieutenant Matthews.

'I hear you,' Beth said, appraising the breadth of the man's shoulders, the sharp muscle definition across his chest, the breadth of his upper arms and sculpted forearms. 'He's certainly not lacking in strength.'

'He'd give you a run for your money, Matthews,' said Lieutenant Saunders with a smirk. 'Reckon you'd have to look up to him too.'

Beth smiled, enjoying the warm banter between her colleagues, pleased the tension in the room had evaporated and their patient hadn't done any major harm to himself, or anyone else.

'Thanks. Both of you,' she said, glancing between the two nurses. 'That could've turned ugly quickly. These guys, they're so precise, wired for action, you never know how they're going to react when they come to.'

'You're telling me,' said Lieutenant Matthews. 'My first year deployed, I had a bloke come out of his anaesthetic swinging. Broke my damn jaw.'

'Ouch,' said Beth.

'Mustn't have been too bad, it didn't damage you're ability to talk the leg off a bloody iron pot,' said Saunders.

Their good-natured jibing continued. It helped loosen the knot in Beth's belly. She wasn't a person who made a promise she couldn't keep, and right now, she hoped she'd find something—anything to support her in-the-moment-guaranteeof locating Sergeant Calloway's dog and unit, before he was back to fully lucid.

'We'll be able to start searching for more of his details now that we have his name,' Beth said as she proceeded to check his vitals, keen to focus on what she *could* do.

Lieutenant Saunders followed her process clerically, noting the bandaging for repair, equipment that needed to be resecured.

'He really is lucky he didn't do any major damage to himself,' said Lieutenant Matthews.

'Yes, he's a pretty lucky guy all round,' Beth said, her assessment complete, she was relieved nothing too concerning had presented. She ripped off her gloves, threw them into the bin. 'Alrighty, I'll leave you both to it, and go and get onto Intel. See what we can find out about our Sergeant Calloway, his dog Finnegan and the others, whomever they may be. Call me if anything changes.'

'Yes, ma'am,' the nurses responded in unison.

Beth noted the time on the wall clock as she left the room. Seventeen minutes till midnight. She'd almost made it.

Alone in the corridor, Beth wrapped a hand around the back of her neck and pressed her fingers into the stiff muscles at the base of her skull. She only had to make it through a quarter of an hour and it'd be finished. The day would've passed. *Finally.*

With her heart rate still elevated, the earlier adrenaline hit slow in wearing off, Beth filled her chest with oxygen and exhaled deliberately. Kneading her knuckles deeper into her neck, focusing on her breath, out of the blue, her dad's voice drifted into her thoughts, spouting his favourite mantra: *Every minute is an opportunity to do something worthwhile, honey. Don't waste even one of them—work hard, be good.*

Beth smiled despite herself. Her father always knew when to drop in his two cents worth, invited or not. Why should it be any different when she was a million miles away?

She stretched her neck from side to side, shook out her arms and picked up her pace in the direction of their comms room. Her dad was right. She had seventeen minutes to work as hard as she could to deliver on the promise she'd just given Sergeant Calloway. She'd do what she could to help find Finnegan and the others. And she'd do it today.

Chapter 2

'Morning, Sergeant Calloway,' Beth said, sliding into the plastic outdoor chair alongside her patient. 'You're looking so much better than when I saw you last ... what was it, this time last week?'

She knew exactly when she'd last seen him. She'd kept tabs on her Sergeant during her days off. Pushing Intel, her superiors, all the associated units for the answers she'd promised to find, and wanted to deliver to him today. But there hadn't been much to discover. And now, frustrated that she hadn't made good on her word, she had to see him and admit to as much.

'Six days,' he said eventually, staring straight ahead. 'I've been stuck here for six bloody days.'

There was no missing the ice in his tone. This wasn't going to be easy, but if she could at least illuminate some physical wins he'd had in his short recovery, it'd help before she delivered her nonnews, a blow that could seriously set him back emotionally.

'So how's your hearing today? Lieutenant Matthews said you'd made some good progress over the past forty-eight hours.'

'Yeah?' His lips pressed into a thin line, the muscle in his jaw flexing hard and fast. 'There's still ringing in my left, bit of a buzz in the right, but I can hear you well enough. So if that's worth throwing a party over, go right ahead.'

'Good. That *is* reasonable progression,' Beth said, ignoring his sarcasm. 'You warm enough out here? Can't believe the temp's already starting to drop and it's not even morning tea time. It'll be snowing up in the mountains before we know it.' She wrapped her jacket tighter around her middle, not at all certain it was just the chill in the air making her shiver.

'I'm fine,' he replied. 'Prefer to be outside.'

'Fair enough,' she said, sucking in a breath. Clearly Sergeant Calloway wasn't interested in small talk. She best cut the crap, get on with giving it to him straight and get out of his way. Beth shoved her hands deep in her pants pockets. 'Oh, I nearly forgot,' she said with a little too much enthusiasm, savouring the few moments the distraction offered her confessional reprieve. With an upturned palm, she held out a blue stone with faint black smudges and some barely visible white streaks. 'Thought you might want this back.'

He turned towards her slightly. 'What is it?'

'You don't recognise it?'

'No—' he shook his head, '—I've never seen that before.'

Beth pulled her hand back and had another look at the polished rock, rolling it forward and back in her palm. 'I'm pretty sure it's the gemstone Lapis Lazuli.

It's fairly easy to come by around here.' She looked up at him, and for the first time since she'd sat down, he was staring at her. His irises, the deepest grey she'd ever seen, flashed like lightning-infused storm clouds. Their charcoal depths glinting with annoyance and ... something ... something that made her belly somersault, and a slow burn creep up her neck. *What the hell?*

'Ah, um, it was in the pocket of your fatigues, the side that wasn't shredded when you came into surgery,' she said, annoyed she was suddenly stumbling over her words.

He didn't blink, or look away, his eyes searching her face millimetre by millimetre. She forced herself to hold his gaze, her breath suspended, lungs bursting. It was like he was assessing her, grading her. *But for what?*

Finally, he broke his stare, reached for the stone. His long, strong fingers brushed hers, his touch skimmed her skin like hot wax dripping across her flesh. She jerked her hand away, the somersaults in her belly now trapeze-worthy acrobatics. Her heart rate thumped at double time. *What the hell is wrong with you?* She concentrated on steadying her breathing, totally thrown by her body's foreign behaviour and reaction to this man, *her patient!*

Calloway rolled the oval-shaped rock around his fingers, inspecting each facet. 'I've definitely never seen this before,' he said as he turned his body towards her, grunting with the effort.

'Are you hurting?' Her embarrassment forgotten, Beth's training kicked in and she was out of her seat. 'Let me—'

'Don't.' He jerked his body sideways. 'I'm fine ... it just jabs a bit in my gut when I twist.' He thrust the stone back at her, she took it, and he resumed his forward-facing position. Beth stepped backwards, sat down, fought the urge to press her hands to her cheeks, and hoped like hell her face wasn't as red as it felt. *Seriously, get it together. You're being ridiculous. Focus. Focus. Focus.*

She slipped the rock into her pocket; thankful she could legitimately look down for a moment, and not concentrate on him. Trying to block out the barrage of long dormant emotions now awake and joyriding across every cell of her body, she managed to notice both of them were breathing quickly, heavily. *Why? Did he feel it too?* 'I wonder how on earth this ended up in your pocket then.'

'No idea.'

Realising she'd shared her thought out loud, Beth swallowed hard, wishing she'd stuck with silence. She glanced at Sergeant Calloway, his forehead creased, eyes narrowed, his entire body rigid. Now wasn't the time to remind him he'd suffered some short-term memory loss and this might be something he'd simply forgotten. And given he'd seen the rock, she wasn't behaving negligently if she didn't mention it right this second. In fact, it was very likely that his mind would throw up something later that would jog a memory he could work with. So, best she just stay quiet and keep it safe for him until then.

With her hand still buried in her pocket, Beth rolled the stone over and over between her thumb and forefingers, working up a rhythm with the motion, the repetition helping force her thoughts away from the sensation of what felt like firecrackers exploding in her belly. Silence filled the air for what seemed an age, but determined to get back to her norm, behave like the professional she was, Beth cleared her throat, sat straighter, and launched into some safe, factual observations.

'You've come a long way for someone with the injuries you've had. A partial lung collapse, burns and some pretty decent lacerations, I really can't believe you're out of bed, sitting out here in the sun, so soon.'

'Yeah? Well, I've never been one to follow the rules,' he said, intensity radiating out of him like magnetic lava. Hot, dangerous, irresistible.

I bet you haven't! Beth clenched her fists into balls inside her pockets. *Stop it!* Never ... never in her career had she considered any of her patients with anything other than a professional focus. Never had she blurred any lines, or even wanted to. *And now is definitely not the time to start.*

'Well, I can safely say we're opposites in that respect,' she said, struggling not to roll her eyes at how pathetic she sounded.

With his gaze still pinned on the horizon, Sergeant Calloway ignored her comment, and without moving, asked the question she'd avoided till now. 'So where are we with locating my dog, my unit? The bastards who tried to blow us up?'

One, two, three seconds ticked by, the silence awkward as hell.

'I'm sorry, Sergeant,' she said, 'there's still nothing definitive to give you yet. I know Intel's working on the data they have and—'

'Are you kidding?' The interruption wasn't a question. He swivelled to face her. 'I've had enough of this shit. I want to talk to someone else. Today. I want a face-to-face with whoever's handling the investigation, because it's not you, and clearly, you're only good for actioning annoying fucking small talk.'

No stranger to verbal abuse and men trying to put her in what they considered her place, Beth still stiffened at his remark. At least her heart rate was thumping for an entirely different reason now, one she was way more comfortable with handling. She stood and faced him, square on.

'Major Black's in this afternoon, he'll have any updates that have come through today from the first response search team. Now, if you'll excuse me—'

'This is bullshit.' Sergeant Calloway's knuckles cracked as he gracelessly pushed himself up to stand. His face now inches from hers, she was forced to look up so she could continue to eyeball him. 'I'm not going to just sit here like a fucking useless invalid, waiting on you white coats to deliver your useless fucking updates.' He was staring at her like she was a target at the end of his riflescope.

His anger was understandable, but she was rapidly approaching her limit of emotional temperance. 'Your personal insults and insubordination aside, I get it, I really do, Sergeant, but if you continue to—'

'No, you don't. You don't have a fucking clue how I feel.' His raised voice drew the attention of the smattering of patients around them. 'And don't try any more of your psychobabble-platitudes, it's insulting.'

Limit reached. She was done.

'I won't. And in the future, you'll address me as Captain.' No matter what he was going through, he'd damn well respect her. 'I came out here to inform you that Major Black's arranged for you to be medivaced to Germany the day after tomorrow. Take the rest of your concerns up with him. Good morning, Sergeant Calloway.' She turned and walked towards the hospital entry, her breathing far more laboured than it should be.

'Have you—any of you listened to a single word I've said?' he shouted after her. 'I told you, I told him, I told the goddamn Commander, I won't board any fucking plane until I retrieve my dog.'

She swivelled to face him, blood thundering through her ears. 'I'll remind you that you're addressing—'

'Finn, and every one of those men would lay down their lives for me, so, with all due respect, *Captain,* I'm telling you again, there's no way in hell I'm leaving here without them.' Red-faced, sweat beading at his temples, he sucked in breath after breath. 'And I'm sure as shit done with just sitting here, waiting for answers.'

She ignored the murmurs of the two other patients convalescing closest to her, gripped her stethoscope and dug the heels of her boots into the dirt. She'd never had someone so overtly disrespect rank protocol. With anger driving each step, Beth made short work of the distance between her and Calloway. She stopped directly in front of him, her entire body vibrating, her belly twisted into a sharp knot.

'Do you really think you're the only one who feels like you do? Do you think you're the only person here who's lost someone, who feels useless? Who wishes they could change their past? Take a look around you, Sergeant Calloway.' She swept her arm wide, encompassing the four other patients sitting outside. 'Everyone here has a story every bit as devastating as yours. Everyone.' She leant in closer, her low tone sharper, firm. 'You want to help find your men, your dog? Then accept the treatment you need and do as you're goddamn told. Otherwise you're nothing but a disrespectful pain-in-the-arseliability to everyone.'

She straightened and crossed her arms over her chest, more than ready for whatever he threw back at her. He eyeballed her for one, two, three seconds before he dropped his glare. Stumbling slightly, he collapsed back into his chair, his chest heaving.

'Ah shit.' He clasped his hands together, bent forward, his forearms resting on his thighs; shoulders hunched. He looked up at her. 'Sorry, Captain. That was out of line ... I've been a prick.'

She gave him a nod. 'Yes, you have. And you're pretty close to this going on your record too.'

His head snapped up, his gaze locked with hers. 'Finn's the closest thing I have to family. Finnegan and my men.' His voice cracked on the last word. 'It's been nearly a week, and it's killing me sitting here doing nothing to help find them. I know you're doing what you can, but with respect, it just isn't enough.' He slumped back into the chair and shoved his hands through his dark, copper brown hair, fisting them at the back of his neck.

Her body still humming with annoyance, Beth's heart squeezed, recognising his pain. Her concern for the man won out over her head's argument against it, and after only a moment's hesitation, she slid back into the seat beside him. 'Tell me about Finnegan.'

It took a minute, but eventually, he released his grip on his neck and looked skyward, a smile tugging at the corner of his mouth. 'Best bloody dog I've ever had,' he said. He pinched the bridge of his nose, sniffed. 'He shows up, gets shit done, never falters ... reliable as a sunrise. You know?'

Beth nodded, pleased and relieved he'd seemed to simmer down in his frustration.

'He doesn't give me any grief and is just the happiest little bastard to be around.' Nate dragged a hand down his cheek, rested his chin in his palm.

'He sounds like a one in a million.'

'Yeah, he's definitely a once in a lifetime kinda animal.'

'I'd love a dog.' Beth tried for a slight diversion. 'Pretty hard to have one with this job. Found a cat though. Well, the cat kinda found me.'

'Yeah?'

'Yeah.'

His gaze drifted back towards the horizon, his emotions restrained again, his thoughts clearly still on Finnegan, his comment likely just an effort to be polite.

'So, where you from?' He pulled the collar of his jacket up around his neck and she resisted the urge to ask him if he wanted to move inside. He'd made it clear he didn't do fuss. And maybe she'd made some headway—he'd asked her a question. She tried to ignore the burst of butterflies skittering through her belly.

'Sydney,' she said.

'Yeah? Whereabouts?'

'Clovelly. You know it?'

'Yeah. Been to Bondi a couple of times, drove past Clovelly, I think.'

'Oh right, well, I have a little, well a tiny, terrace there. About a five minute walk from the beach.'

'Oh right.' He raised his eyebrows, nodded a bit.

He probably didn't give a damn about what she had to say, was trying to make up for being an arse. She really should go, get back to her paperwork, check on her other patients, do anything to get her away from this defiant man who made her feel all kinds of flustered. But she didn't want to. Instead, she stared out at the smoky horizon.

'Yeah, it's a great little spot, but it doesn't ever feel quite like home,' she said, fiddling with the seam of her cuff. 'I'm a country girl at heart, really. Grew up on a dairy farm down the South Coast, not far from the beach. My parents still live there.' She drew in a deep breath, imagining the clean air, the sea-salt on her skin. 'We're so lucky to have the best of the country and coast so close together. I always head straight down there when I'm first back home. Clears my mind.' She glanced back at him, pleased to find him looking at her, actually interested. 'What about you? Where do you call home?'

'Ah, I've got a place in the Hunter.'

'Oh, I love it up there. My older sister and I did some horse riding camps near the Molly Morgan Range when we were kids. Such beautiful country. You on property?

'Small vineyard.'

'Ahh, okay.' She so didn't expect that as an answer. Would have picked him for the kind of bloke more at home by the water than nestled in the mountains, and a winery of all places. Nervous flutters quivered in her belly. She suddenly wanted to know more about this angry man who'd rattled her hard-earned, even-as-silk emotions. She wanted to know about his vineyard. What kind of grapes he grew? How the hell he kept it all going when he was deployed? What else he did in his spare time? *Is there anyone waiting for you at home?*

But she couldn't. Couldn't ask anything that personal. It wasn't an appropriate discussion for his superior to be having with him, on duty, *or at all.* Let alone the fact she was his doctor and needed to maintain professional distance. *Distance ... yep, that's a definite priority right now.* She'd already blurred the lines of her professional compass by even having this much of a conversation. But reluctant to stop, Beth forced herself to settle with something basic. 'Did you grow up in the Hunter Valley?'

His shoulders stiffened. 'Nah. Moved around a lot as a kid.' He shoved his hands into his jacket pockets. 'So what happened with the cat?'

'Oh yes, that's where we started, wasn't it?' A nervous laugh bubbled out of her. 'Well, he wandered in my back door with the attitude of forty tanks and plonked himself down on my hall rug. It was the same day my little sister moved in actually. He's owned the place ever since.'

'Really? You let a filthy stray bunk in, just like that? You don't seem the type.'

Type? What the hell did he mean by that? As much as she wanted to ask the question, she didn't want to lose the momentum, the lightness of the conversation, so she filed it to think about later.

'It was weird actually,' she said. 'He was in pretty good condition, didn't look like a stray. We spent a few weeks looking out for lost notices, posting pictures on lost pet communities on Facebook and all that, and, well, no luck. Andrea, that's my sister, she loved him on sight, and I figured he'd keep her company when I'm away. So he sorta just stayed.'

'Got a name?'

'Yep. Wait for it, it's super original. Grey. We called him Grey.'

'Let me guess, grey fur?'

'Yep.' She laughed again.

'You're right, it's genius that one,' he said with a smirk, his face relaxed. His hands lay flat in his lap. It was the first hint of ease she'd seen in him.

'Do you like cats?' Beth said, aware she was dangerously close to the line of a way too Chatty Cathy. She pushed the worry aside.

'Never known anything but mean cats.' He gave her a sideways glance. 'Pretty happy sticking with my dog.'

'Fair enough.'

Tension crept back into the easy silence.

'Listen, Doc, I'm sorry, real sorry about before.'

Despite herself, Beth smiled at him. 'We all say things under pressure. I understand you've been through a lot, you're not yourself.' *Neither am I for that matter.*

'Appreciate it,' he said, scrubbing at the back of his head. 'Listen, I know you and the Major think I need outta here to recover fully, but can you have another look at whatever it is I gotta do to keep my pass to stay on base? I want to be here. Actually—' he pointed to the smoke haze in the distance, '—I want to be out there.' He turned to face her, desperation blazing deep in his eyes. 'Please.'

'There's a few things that need to be considered,' Beth said eventually, her damp palms pressed into the fabric of her pants. 'I can review your progress again in forty-eight hours, maybe delay your transfer, but you have to understand, we'll only do what's best for you, follow the safest course so you have the best chance at a full, uncompromised recovery.'

'I understand,' he said quietly. 'Thing is, I won't recover, won't want to recover, if I'm safe and they're not. These men, I've sworn an oath to protect them, Finn too.' The steel in his tone raised goosebumps over her arms. 'And like I said, I won't get on that plane without them.' He reached for her, wrapped his hand around her forearm, the heat from his fingers burning through her jacket into her skin. 'Please ... you have to give me the chance.'

Every argument she had ready to go evaporated from her mind. She fought the urge to lay her own hand on top of his, and instead, pulled her arm free, and pushed up out of the chair.

'I'll see what I can do,' she said, swallowing hard. 'But I'm not making any promises, okay?'

'Okay,' he said, still leaning forward, 'then neither am I.'

Chapter 3

Cold sweat covered Nate's body, and relentless pounding hammered against his eardrums. He pushed up onto one elbow, his hand pressed against his chest, and noisily sucked in air. Edging up from the hard hospital bed and into a seated position, Nate grabbed the plastic water cup he'd left on the bedside table and drained it in a single gulp, filled it, drained it again. He wiped the back of his hand across his wet forehead and swung his legs over the side of the bed, gripping the edge of it with two hands, unsure he'd be able to stop his churning gut from spewing its contents all over the goddamn floor.

Slivers of the dream, part-memory, part-nightmare flashed in and out of his mind, nothing staying long enough to make any real sense. Except one crystal-clear show-reel that had hauled him from his sleep almost every night for the last week, the images now swarming through his thoughts again.

'Hey,' said Johnno, 'that cardboard box don't blend with the rest of the shit on the roadside.'

From inside the six-wheeler they all eyeballed the wriggling square object that lay five hundred metres ahead of them on the left-hand side of the road.

'I'll be damned.' Johnno's voice filled the cabin again, his eyes glued to his binoculars. 'There's two, wait, three pups in that bloody box.'

They cleared the perimeter and disembarked from the truck. Johnno hit the dirt first, Fish second. Longy next, then him and Finn last.

Nate asked, surveying the landscape surrounding them, assessing the risk. Finnegan stayed calm, and nothing hit Nate's internal radar as outta whack, so he ordered they close in on the box. 'What d'ya see, J?'

Johnno hadn't answered him.

None of them had.

The last bloody thing Nate remembered was staring at Finnegan's glossy black body jammed hard in alert, but it was too late.

'Hey, you alright, man?' Lieutenant Matthew's shadow filled the cubicle's doorway. 'I was way back in the tea room, heard you shout out.' He crossed the room to Nate's bedside.

'Yeah, I'm good. Sorry. Did I wake anyone?'

Matthews shook his head. 'Nah. Not this time.' He pulled his stethoscope from around his neck. 'Let me have a listen to those lungs, you've got that wheeze back. You still have the headache?'

'Yeah.'

'What would you rate it now? I know it was a seven—' Matthews checked his watch, the chart in his hand, '—just over five hours ago. Better? Worse?'

'About the same.'

Nate had hoped it would've eased off a bit more by now, but the bastard of a thing was hanging on. The meds didn't do a hell of a lot, and the news he'd had from the head doc, Major Black, before lights out hadn't helped either.

The Major had delivered the brief in person, had come in especially. He'd said there was info suggesting Nate's unit had been captured and were being held somewhere in the mountains, but still no word on Finnegan.

The doc had stayed a while, asked him more questions around his recollections of the incident, but the snatches of memory he had to offer the man were bloody useless.

'So, just to be clear,' said Major Black, 'you have no memory of the explosion, and no memory of who delivered you to the hospital?'

'None, sir. On both counts.'

'I see.' The surgeon had gripped his shoulder, looked him dead in the eyes. 'The recovery of your men and Finnegan is the army's top priority. I want you to know that.'

'Thank you, sir.'

'The second search team will be mobilised in two days and we've every confidence they'll find success. Best thing you can do now is rest up, recover. And let's see if that memory throws anything up that'll help out.'

'Yes, sir.' Nate's gut had twisted like a cut snake.

Lieutenant Matthews interrupted his thoughts. 'I can give you something stronger if you'd like?'

Nate huffed out a deep breath. 'Nah, thanks, but I'll see if another few hours of shut-eye helps.' Truth was, he couldn't take anything heavier. Stronger meds might affect his review in the morning—shit, in a few hours now, and he needed to be part of that search crew ... had to be.

'Suit yourself. But I gotta tell you, not many patients fight this hard to avoid medication.'

'Yeah, well, I've been doing okay without it,' Nate said, letting his head fall back against the wall. 'I need to be on my game, and I can't do that if there's too much shit clogging up my system.'

Lieutenant Matthews didn't look up from the notes he was charting. 'Like I said, suit yourself. Let me know if you change your mind.'

Nate waited until the Lieutenant replaced the binder at the end of the bed before he spoke again. 'Can I ask you something?'

'Sure, shoot.'

'What are my chances of being cleared to stay on base, accompany the search team? Just give it to me straight.'

Lieutenant Matthews rested his hands on his hips and faced Nate square on. 'Truthfully? I really don't think it's going to swing your way, no matter how much you want it otherwise. I'm surprised you've got these extra few days here to be honest.' Matthews raised his eyebrows and smiled a little before his face turned serious again. 'I'm sorry, man, I know you want back out there, doing what you do, but the only way I can see that happening is if you find a goddamn fairy godmother that'll dress your burns, monitor your head, your lungs and every other bloody thing you need sorted on your way to the goddamn battlefield ball.'

Nate forced his mouth into a tense smile despite the knot tightening in his gut. 'You're not a funny man, Matthews.'

'So I've been told. Now get some shut-eye, I'll be back to check in before I finish my shift.'

Nate's blood felt like ice sliding through his veins. His options were rapidly disappearing and he was running out of time. There had to be something he could do. There was no way they'd get him on that plane in anything other than a damn body bag.

Chapter 4

'And you're gone. That's your black sunk good and proper.' Beth circled the pool table. 'Who you gonna lose to when I'm back home?' she asked Lawson, laughing.

Major Black held up three swaying fingers. 'Three weeks, isn't it?'

'Yep. Can't wait,' she yelled above the music and chatter, the rec bar crowd extra festive because it was Halloween—any excuse for a party. Truth be told, she'd give anything to be heading home tomorrow. Aside from being desperate to hug her family, especially her brand new twin nieces, she also wanted out of here to stop the crazy behaviour, the crazy thoughts she'd had about the very unpredictable, very off-limits Sergeant Calloway.

Never in her life had she had such a visceral reaction to a man, any man, like she'd had with him when they'd been outside the hospital. The couple of guys she'd hooked up with at university had generated a few sparks, and Andrew, he'd been a nice, warm burn, but if she was honest, hadn't really flamed out above cosy. But Sergeant Calloway, his hand on her that once ... the way he'd looked at her, his voice, even just the thought of him ignited a scorching blue flame through her entire body, one that after thirty-six hours she still hadn't been able to tamp down. She'd resisted the impulse to call by the hospital when she was off shift, see how he was doing, actively reminding herself that he was a stranger, a difficult one at that, and she had no business being anything other than his *off-limits* superior and doctor. And even then, only when she was assigned to be. It'd been hard to stay away. Much harder than it should've been.

'Well, I better quit playing this game while I'm ahead.' Lawson's gravelly slur pierced her thoughts, reminding her she wasn't anywhere near Calloway right now.

Her boss gulped down the straight scotch in his hand, and picked up another already waiting on the bar—the fifth one she'd counted in the past hour, and he'd arrived well before her. *Strange?* She'd never seen him drink more than three or four drinks in a sitting, ever. And he'd been totally stonkered then. She hadn't noticed just how drunk he was until right this moment.

'Why don't you sit?' he said, and patted the chair beside him. 'You know—' he turned and ordered another drink before finishing his sentence, '—one of the first things Andrew told me about you was that you're a bona fide pool shark.'

'Really?' Beth smiled and dropped onto the stool debating whether to suggest to her boss that he'd probably had enough. 'He never told me that,' she said, Andrew's smile drifting into her thoughts stopped her worrying for a moment. She imagined her fiancé warning his academy mates about her, secretly loving that he knew she'd whip their chauvinistic arses. It was one of the things she'd admired most about Andrew. He held his own, but he'd never really fit their boys' club mould.

The jittery hot feeling she'd had thinking about Calloway evaporated, and in its place, a cold stone settled deep in her belly. She sipped her sparkling mineral water, swirling the straw around the glass, swallowing down the grief threatening to make her gag.

'My brothers taught me to play when I was twelve,' she said. 'I bet them both a month's stable duties I could beat them after an hour of playing.'

'Hell-bent on beating the men even then, were you?' Lawson said, as he tried to tuck the heel of his shoe on the lower rung of the stool, but missed.

Confused by his out of character comment, Beth sucked the glass dry before answering, stabbing the straw into the empty base. 'Nah, just hell-bent at being the best at everything I could.'

'Ahhhh, of course.' He swayed a little. 'Well, don't keep me waiting in suspense. Did you end up free of stable duty?'

'From my older brother I did, still can't roll my younger brother.' She twisted the straw around her finger then tossed it back into the empty glass. Unsure of where Lawson was going with this, the implication of his question annoyed her.

'Really?' he snorted. 'Did your sisters share your passion for bettering the males, or is that just specifically in your DNA?'

Wow. Now he was really pissing her off. 'No, not really, but we're all competitive in our own way.' She looked over his shoulder towards the exit, her mood well and truly soured, her dilemma over whether to tell Lawson he'd had enough no longer of consequence. Now, she just wanted to leave, let him shake off whatever it was that had crept under his skin. 'Actually, our parents are pretty big on pushing limits for yourself where you can, no matter your gender,' she snapped.

Beth had spent her entire adult career proving her achievements weren't better or worse than her male colleagues. And that she wasn't either special or inferior because she was a woman. Of all people, she'd never have expected quasi-chauvinistic comments like this from Lawson. Not just a colleague, not quite a friend, he and Andrew had been mates. They were a couple of years ahead of her at the academy, and she and a few of her classmates first met them out at the local pub. Lawson had been a rock when Andrew died. He'd been here for her too, supported her during the hard months of this, her first deployment back. So, what on earth was he getting at? Maybe the alcohol brought out an arsehole gene she hadn't really noticed before? Or maybe she was just being ridiculously sensitive?

If he picked up on her irritation, he showed no sign of it.

'All I know is, Andrew loved it when you two played doubles,' he slurred. 'You always beat the rest of us hands down.' Lawson's chin dropped to his chest, his head shaking slowly from side to side.

Tears stung the backs of Beth's eyes, and she suddenly felt mean for being angry with Lawson. Clearly he was only trying to remember happy times with Andrew. The anniversary had to be hard on him too.

Lawson looked up at her with blown pupils, slung his arm around her shoulders, and dipped his head towards her ear. 'It's been a tough week, hasn't it?'

Beth shrugged, turned her head to face him. 'For you as well.'

'Yeah. I miss him.'

She reached up and squeezed his hand, still wrapped around her shoulder. 'I know he really valued your friendship, Lawson,' she said.

His eyes reflected her pain. He was still hurting too. She swivelled to face him.

'Listen, I'm not sure I've really ever thanked you properly for your support, both then and now. I'm not sure I would've made it back here without your encouragement.'

'You would have.' He swallowed a mouthful of his fresh drink. 'Besides, it was my duty—' his gazed darkened, he leant forward, '—and my pleasure.' Before she realised what was happening, he pulled her head towards him and kissed her. Hard, wet, urgent.

Shoving at his chest, she leapt to her feet, backed away. 'What the hell are you doing?' She pressed her fingers to her lips.

'Sorry. I'm sorry.' He dragged the back of his hand across his mouth. 'I don't know what ... I, ah, I just thought...' She squirmed as his red-rimmed eyes searched her face.

'I think you've had enough of that.' Beth snatched the half-full glass from his hand and dumped it on the bar, her anger overriding her shock.

'I'm so sorry, so sorry, Beth.'

Goosebumps pricked up over her arms, her fury turning fearful. Who could hear them? See them? He was her boss, dammit, her superior and direct report. And he'd just kissed her. In the middle of the rec bar.

She swiped the back of her hand across her mouth. She didn't dare glance around, and hoped that with all the noise and activity, no-one had noticed.

'It's okay. Really,' she said, her legs starting to shake. Nothing about this was remotely okay. Her belly clenched in random, painful spasms. 'I'm going to go now. I think that's best. Will you be alright to get to your room?'

He nodded. 'Sorry, Beth. I-I just thought you might, ah, it'd been long enough, and—'

She cut him off, didn't want to hear any more. 'Forget it, it's nothing.' She tried for a laugh, but didn't pull it off. 'See you at the hospital when you're back on.' She waved and headed for the door, didn't look back. Every muscle in her legs wanted to run. She'd barely rounded the first corner before dry reaching. If anyone saw, if anyone reported this ... It would *not* be *nothing.*

Beth sank into a final agonising squat before dropping onto her butt and flopping onto her back, muscles burning. Usually, a two-hour cross-fit session at the gym drained her mind from anything other than gasping for her next breath. But not today. Last night's unwanted kiss and the possible consequences were still circling her every thought. Lawson, her boss, her friendly but never too friendly direct report had kissed her. What the hell happened now? Maybe he wouldn't remember. And even if he did, should she just have a frank discussion with him about it, sort it out? Put it down to an emotional, drunken moment ... a misunderstanding?

'You're looking very serious, Captain,' Lieutenant Matthews said, peering down at her.

'Hey, Matthews,' she replied, grateful for the distraction his arrival offered. Ignoring Matthews' raised eyebrows, Beth hauled herself up to sitting. 'How's things?'

'Sweet. It's my first of three days off.' He swung his leg over the weight bench beside them.

'Well, don't let me interrupt you then.' Grabbing her towel and drink bottle from the floor, Beth stood up, wiped the sweat from her face, swigged a couple of mouthfuls of water.

'Good luck with Calloway this afternoon,' Lieutenant Matthews grunted as he lowered a ridiculously loaded barbell. 'I feel for the bloke. Anything new back from Intel today?'

'No, nothing other than what Major Black's already shared with Calloway. And I feel for the guy too.' *Understatement.* 'But, unless he's magically recovered and grown some new skin, maybe a new lung in the past twelve hours, I can't see any way of him staying, let alone heading out there.' Beth jerked her chin towards the window, bit down on her lower lip. She wasn't looking forward to having *that* conversation.

'Poor bastard. I told him he'd have better hope of finding a bloody fairy godmother than being cleared for duty.'

'Fairy godmother?'

'Yeah, you know, someone to tend his every need while he's off doing what his heart desires and all that?' Matthews' smirk didn't hide the seriousness in his eyes.

'Oh, right, I get it.' Beth smiled, pulled her hair back into a tight ponytail and shoved on her baseball cap. 'It'd be nice if we all had a fairy godmother right about now.'

'Don't worry too much, Captain,' said Lieutenant Matthews. 'Saunders is on shift this afternoon, she's got your back.' He winked and returned to grunting over his metal and steel.

'I'm all good, don't you worry about me. Have fun, I'll catch you later.'

'Adios.'

Beth dug around her sports bag for her sunnies, squinting as she left the gym. Her belly flip-flopped at the thought of having to face Lawson as well as Sergeant Calloway in a few hours. She sighed. Lieutenant Matthews clearly thought she was in for a tough time handling Calloway's reaction, but his concern was wasted. It wasn't her patient's reaction she was worried about managing. She had no idea how the hell she was going to manage her own.

Chapter 5

Lawson hurled the brush and tin of boot polish at the wall. The thud of the wood, the rattle of the metal cylinder as it rolled in diminishing circles before settling back at his feet riled him further. He kicked the tin across the room.

Never before in his life had he made such a damn fool of himself.

He'd waited so long for his turn, for his time to have her, to take action on the feelings he knew they both had, and had totally messed it up.

The chair clattered backwards as he stood up and strode across the room to his bed. Dropping down on his haunches, he reached underneath and dragged out his metal trunk, the well-oiled hinges silent as he pushed open the lid. Careful not to tear the loose interior canvas, he slid his fingers into the lid's lining and extracted her leather-bound dossier, his fingers gliding slowly over the letters he'd painstakingly embossed in gold along the side—*Beth Adelaide Harper.*

His hand slid over the well-thumbed, meticulously referenced contents. Clippings from her parent's local paper citing her award winning academic achievements, articles she'd written at university, mostly about the rights of various minority groups and published in assorted journals, blogs and such. A portrait of her at the academy graduation, vibrant, smiling and staring straight into his lens. She'd been so proud. He flicked over some reference documents she'd submitted to a medical journal, detailing natural Afghani remedies she'd found helped in treating several ailments—*that ridiculous line of thought will stop when we're married*—until he found more photos. Beth running on the beach, coffee with her friend at their favourite café. At her terrace, sharing a red wine on the balcony with her sister. He drew out the last picture slowly, his favourite. Taken last year, not long after Andrew died.

She'd spent months at her parent's farm, a place she spoke of so often, described the surrounds, the community so fully, he'd had almost no trouble identifying its exact location.

There was an upstairs art studio in the Hampton-esque style farmhouse. She'd been the only one who used it. With enormous glass windows—to let in the natural light and maximise the view of the ocean, he supposed—it showed Beth off to perfection too, especially in the early evening, the time of day she painted most.

He took his time scouring the farm's surrounds until he'd found an ancient white-cedar tree in the neighbouring property's unused upper paddock. It gave him the perfect vantage point to view her, hidden, for hours on end. He'd needed binoculars, had used them often during the week he'd watched her, noting her every move, her routine, until he knew it like clockwork. It'd been worth the discomfort, the waiting.

She'd seemed so sad, so lost inside herself that he'd almost wanted to feel guilty for what he'd done. It wasn't like he'd planned for Andrew to die. The explosion was meant to maim, disfigure at best. Not kill. That wasn't ever his intention, not really. Intention counted for something, didn't it?

Lawson snorted out a huff, the sliver of concern that'd been twisting in his belly quickly evaporating. Beth needed a man, an intellectual equivalent. A worthy partner. One who challenged her, satisfied her at *every* level. Not a goddamn doormat who'd cut off his damn testicles if she asked him to. He'd needed to show her, wanted her to see that Andrew had faults, failings, which he, the right man for her, didn't. Lawson pressed his fingers into his temples, the pressure relieving the tension. He hated thinking about her with Andrew, hated thinking about Andrew. Period. Pretending to be the man's friend 24/7 for all those years, just so he could see Beth, had been its own special kind of torture.

He turned his focus back to the photograph in his hand, tracing her face with his thumb. He'd captured her image mid-brush stroke. The way her surgeon's hand stroked and brushed watercolour over the taut canvas took his breath away. His mouth watered now as he imagined her hands, her slender fingers wrapped around him, stroking his cock, slowly, rhythmically ... 'No!'

Shoving the photo back into the folder, he snapped it shut and swallowed hard, a growl pushing up from his throat. He paced the length of his room and back again, grounding his back teeth together, ignoring the heat pulsing in his groin. *You acted too soon, that's all.*

'Damn it all to hell.'

Lawson circled the room, collected the discarded brush, the tin, ordered his belongings and packed everything back into the trunk, the routine of it helping to settle his thoughts, diminish his erection. It'd be okay. He'd go to Beth again before she left for her stint home. Help her see how suited they were, how he should've been her choice all along. She'd get over the guilt, give in to her feelings for him eventually, he knew it. She just needed more time, more encouragement.

And then another thought struck him, the tension suddenly lifting from his chest.

Could it be that she liked the thrill of the chase? She was so damn competitive—maybe that was it? Maybe he needed to be less accessible to her?

He manoeuvred Beth's file back into the lining then reached into the furthest corner of the trunk, searching for the small black box wedged beneath his standard issue belongings. His fingers curled around the smooth leather and he drew it out. He snapped open the miniature hexagonal case, her 1.5carat square cut diamond glittering in the mid-morning light. The box, the ring, it soothed him, reminded him of his plans, the life he'd mapped out for he and Beth.

The buzz of the burner phone vibrating on the desk interrupted his thoughts. He clenched his teeth, glanced at the time. Her calls were never early or late, they were always exactly on time, as planned.

'This is Black.'

'Major Lawson Black, the shipment, it is ready?'

'It is, ma'am.'

'Good. We make exchange day after tomorrow. All same same as last month.'

'As you wish, Zoreed.'

'And, Major Lawson Black, you did good. You give me big bang to show media. Whole world will sit up and listen when I make spectacle of what you have given me.'

'I am pleased you approve, Zoreed. I'll look forward to your—'

She disconnected the call before he finished.

His fingernails dug into his palm as his hand curled into a fist. *Bitch.*

The infamous Zoreed Zadran, the most feared, and only female warlord in Afghanistan knew his secret, kept it out of the hands of his superiors—*the non-corrupt superiors*—for a price, a price that was becoming increasingly harder to pay. And right now, she didn't know it, but he'd short-changed her on her latest request. Hadn't meant to, but the idiots on the ground made a mistake, left one behind, the one damn link that could undo his entire plan.

Calloway.

Why couldn't the fools have captured him with the others? They'd taken the rest of the unit, the damn dog, how hard was it to get the last man? Interrupted by those bloody kids, his men had detained who they could, and disappeared. They didn't think to come back, just kill Calloway on the spot. Didn't think about the fact that dead men don't talk. And now, as a consequence, he had to clean up the mess before Zoreed got wind of it, or worse, Calloway remembered something that'd sink them all.

Chapter 6

A ferocious rap at her door sent Beth's sketchbook skittering sideways off her lap.

'May we speak, Doctor Harper?' Lawson's booming voice filled the silence.

Beth picked up the sketchpad, her graphite pencil, and set them on her bed. She hurriedly gathered up the array of calming herbs she'd picked up from the market. 'Ah, sure, just a sec,' she said, stashing the herbs under her pillow. Rubbing her sweaty palms down her pants, she made her legs move towards the door, a mix of annoyance and a little fear bubbling in her belly.

It'd been two days since the bar, and thankfully she'd been on days off, so had easily avoided him. There'd been no repercussions from the situation that she knew of. Seemed no-one had taken any notice, or if they had, hadn't bothered to make an issue of it. *Yet.* But she still felt on edge, and a little hurt that he hadn't sought her out to apologise ... explain. Not to mention, she wasn't remotely in the right frame of mind to have it out with him right now.

Beth opened the door and stood awkwardly opposite his six foot four inches. He seemed even taller somehow as he looked at his shoes before catching her gaze with eyes she'd only ever noticed as brown, but today seemed closer to black.

'Hey,' she said a little too brightly. 'Come in.'

He moved inside the door and closed it behind him. Beth resisted the urge to launch forward and open it again, the unknown status quo between them uncomfortable. They both stood on the spot.

'I want to talk to you about—'

'Lawson, I really need to discuss—'

They both offered each other a strained smile.

'Why don't you go first?' Beth said. She really wanted to hear what he had to say before she shared her own thoughts, suddenly feeling like maybe she'd overreacted.

He cleared his throat. 'I just wanted to let you know that Sergeant Calloway has been granted provisional permission to accompany the second search team assigned to find his unit.'

Dammit. He wasn't here to sort out the kiss issue. *Hang on! Sergeant Calloway leaving?* Her heart lurched in her chest. 'What? When? But his assessment's scheduled for this afternoon.'

'We brought his review forward,' Lawson said. 'There's been more intel, some pressing information. We wanted to know ASAP if he was fit to go, for his sake as well as ours. As you know, the man is desperate.'

'Why didn't you consult with me on this, Lawson? He is my patient, and he's—'

'I knew you'd be onboard with a decision that's in the best interest of the patient and well, truthfully, we didn't want to worry you on your days off.'

Her tongue felt thick, her mouth dry. She shifted her weight from one foot to the other. *We? Who the hell is we?* 'How did he pass the assessment?' she asked. 'I know he's been progressing quicker than expected, but how on earth has the Surgeon General approved this? And who the hell conducted the evaluation?'

'I did,' Lawson said. 'Myself and Lieutenant Colonel Fraser.' He cleared his throat. 'As I said, Fraser and I didn't want to call you in during your time off. You've been working long hours, and with the additional pressure of it being Andrew's anniversary, well...' He let his voice trail off. 'We had Sergeant Calloway's charts, the data, and quite simply, thought it best we take immediate action.'

How dare they! HOW. DARE. THEY. The play on Andrew's anniversary felt like a deliberate punishment from Lawson, or worse, a cowardly attempt to explain away his recent behaviour. And why the hell was Lieutenant Colonel Fraser involved in Sergeant Calloway's assessment instead of her, the next most senior medical person responsible, let alone Calloway's doctor?

She forced herself to think logically, work to understand their actions. Responsible for field operations, Fraser had protocol to manage, decisions to make regarding the search teams. But she'd never previously seen him involved in a patient review. No, she couldn't understand it, and now, had so many questions firing around her brain.

'I see,' she said after a moment, not quite able to decide which concern she wanted addressed first. 'I still don't understand why I wasn't included in this decision.' Fuming, she crossed her arms over her chest, hoped the extra support might steady her heart from smashing back and forth into her ribs. This whole situation was totally foreign territory for her.

Break it down. Get the facts.

'You said provisional permission. What does that mean?'

'It means he's permitted to join the team if he can secure a doctor willing to escort him outside the wire.' Lawson rocked back and forth on his heels, sighed loudly. 'But it's very unlikely anyone would voluntarily follow the poor man into danger like that, so perhaps he'll be shipping out for Germany posthaste after all.'

Speechless. She was absolutely speechless. Medical personnel voluntarily accompanying a soldier into combat? Situations like this were rare, so unusual that she'd only ever heard of something similar mentioned in training, once. She'd never seen it actually happen.

And asides from all that, maybe it was her state of frustration, but Lawson seemed almost happy at the prospect of Sergeant Calloway being forced to leave. But that would be ridiculous. Why would he be happy about the fact that their patient, at the eleventh hour being offered what he desperately wants, only to have it almost impossible for him to take it?

Her thoughts scrambling, Beth knew that before she could speculate on Lawson's motives, or the reasons for her own feelings about Calloway leaving, she needed to address Lawson's behaviour from the other night. She needed back on an even playing field, professionally at least, pronto, and then she'd damn well deal with his exclusion of her from this decision, as well as every other issue that this single action from him had brought into question.

'Actually, Lawson, before we discuss Sergeant Calloway any further, I need to clear up a few things about what happened at the rec bar.' With his body barely an arm's length from hers, she suddenly felt like the walls were closing in on her.

'Right,' he said. 'Well, I think it's best—'

'Look, this is feeling awkward as hell,' Beth said, 'and I don't want it to.' She forced a smile. 'I was heading out, so why don't we go grab something to eat, talk on the way?' Without waiting for his response, she edged around him, grabbed her jacket and moved towards the door.

'Sure.' He scrubbed at the back of his head, swung her door open and waited for her to walk past him.

Trying not to let her anger overshadow what needed to be a careful conversation, because at the end of the day, no matter how she felt, he was still her superior, Beth replayed the scenario back in her head, catalogued the events, planned her opening words.

'About the other night,' she started, 'I think you may have had the wrong idea about my feelings towards you, when we were talking about Andrew.'

Lawson stopped walking, turned to face her, his breath frosting in the cool air, his face unreadable.

'Captain Harper.' His entire body straightened, his limbs rigid. 'I thought we'd developed something ... something more, lately.' He widened his stance, shuffling his feet in the dirt. 'Seems I was somewhat hasty, maybe insensitive in my timing.' His tone chilled on the last few words, the hairs on the back of her neck bristled into her collar.

'Lawson, I'm sorry, I had no idea that—'

'So, I think it's best if we keep our distance for a while.' His clipped words held a harsh edge. 'We'll only interact as necessary on shift,' he said, clenching and unclenching his hands into fists. 'And best you revert to calling me Major Black. At all times. It'll help.'

A shade of anger rippled through her at his insistence she only refer to him by rank, but it didn't overshadow the sliver of guilt she felt about the fact she'd hurt his feelings. Perhaps she owed him this one error of judgement after all he'd done for her? Without thinking, she stepped forward, placed her hand on his arm.

'Lawson, I really am sorry. I truly had no idea. I thought we were mates and—' Beth lost her voice as he brushed her hand away and motioned for her to stop talking, his outstretched palm in front of her face signalling her to stop.

'Please.' His breath released on a shudder. 'It's done, and probably for the best. You were always Andrew's first, anyway.' He stared at her for a few long seconds, the corners of his mouth downturned, jaw set, before rotating on his heel and marching away.

Beth closed her mouth. *Andrew's first?* Clearly she'd had no idea of Lawson's true feelings, had in fact, been a complete fool on that front. How the hell had she not realised he had a thing for her, and, it seemed, had done so for a long time? Andrew had once joked that both he and Lawson vied for her attention on that first day at the pub, but she'd never given it a second thought after that. In fact, prior to Andrew's passing, she'd thought Lawson felt mostly indifferent towards her.

She gnawed at her lower lip, pacing back and forth in the dirt. What now? How on earth was this going to play out? She'd never known him to be nasty, or hold a grudge. Would he be relatively okay now he'd said his piece, drawn his line in the sand? A sliver of anxiety shimmied down her spine.

He could make it really difficult for her if he wanted to. He outranked her, and had done more tours. He'd worked with people in almost every unit they came into contact with. He was well connected, and could easily make her name mud. She smoothed her hand over her ponytail. Surely, he wouldn't. Would he? A week ago, she'd have said this man had her back no matter what. Now, she wasn't sure he'd even speak to her again.

Bastard. Guilt gave way to hurt and disappointment, and she kicked the living daylights out of a nearby sandbag. Her entire damn career had incidents where the males at her rank, as well as those above and below, did all they could—*within the law*—to shake her loose from her tree. It'd stopped for a while when she'd been dating Andrew, and hadn't been too bad this deployment, but perhaps her reprieve was over?

Anger pulsed a jagged beat in her temples. *You know what? Screw you, Major Black.* Her hands shook as she stalked back towards her room. She'd done nothing wrong here. Nothing. She'd never been a flirt, or anything like it. Wracking her brain, she was certain she'd never given even the slightest hint she'd been interested in him. Even when she'd been distraught over Andrew and he'd comforted her, held her, it'd always been brief, and now that she thought about it, awkward. She'd worked damn hard and never deviated off track from being whom and what she signed up to be, a brilliant surgeon whose sole focus was on saving lives, and teaching others what she knew.

Bloody men who let their bloody egos run away with them. Well, no more. This little black duck didn't play ball with egos. There was no way Lawson, or any other man or woman, was going to ruin the end of this tour, let alone her career. She had just over two weeks left, and she'd be damned if she'd spend it stepping on eggshells around a man absorbed in licking his wounds.

Changing course, Beth jogged towards the hospital. Glancing at her watch, she upped tempo into a sprint. If she was lucky, she'd catch the Surgeon General before he left for field duty. He was the only one who issued and approved travel orders. If Sergeant Calloway still needed a medical escort, he damn well had one.

Chapter 7

Purposeful pounding at Lawson's door interrupted the glorious crescendo of Tchaikovsky's 'Pathetique', his favourite symphony.

'Yes, what is it?' he said, slamming the Royal Albert teacup into its saucer and striding across the room to open the door.

One of the young nurses who'd been on duty with him earlier stood in his doorway. 'I'm sorry to interrupt you, sir, but Lieutenant Colonel Fraser said you should know that Sergeant Calloway's preparing to join the search team.'

'I see.' Lawson kept his voice low, calm, despite the adrenaline rocketing around his body. 'He's secured a medical escort?'

'Yes, sir, Captain Harper's going with him, sir. Captain Stokes has agreed to take over her roster.'

It took every ounce of Lawson's self-control to convey an appropriate response. 'Oh, good. Well, I best head back over to the hospital, see if they need any extra hands to make it all happen.'

'Yes, sir.'

'Please let Lieutenant Colonel Fraser know that I'll be along shortly to assist with the preparations.'

'Yes, sir.'

He watched the nurse go, waited until she disappeared around the corner before he turned and closed the door, the aching smile sliding from his face. *Bad. This is very, very bad.* The hard-to-get approach was meant to entice Beth closer, not send her running from him, and what's more, straight into harms way.

Think. Think. Think.

With shaking hands, Lawson restarted the music.

He'd just issued Calloway's extraction—*extermination*—team their new orders. But now Beth was in the mix, they'd have to be revised. Along with their disposal of Calloway, Beth had to be removed, returned to him without harm.

His measured footsteps back and forth across the concrete were silently in time with the music's morose melody. The sweat sliding between his shoulder blades and from his temples chilled his flushed skin. When the closing note of the near to fifty-minute symphony sounded and the room was finally silent, Lawson too was finally still. He'd formulated a detailed plan that wouldn't compromise the job at hand, or his own safety. Or Beth's life. He powered up burner phone three and sent a text to Banjo, his Special Ops soldier on the inside.

Your sister's now coming to the picnic too. She'll need to be home before the fireworks.

It wasn't part of the code they'd agreed, but Banjo would figure it out, the guy was smart, and, frankly, couldn't afford to make a mistake.

The text back was swift.

Nice. I'll bring her home. The 2 kids from down the road r still away. Won't b coming.

Another loose end.

How could two civilian children deliver an almost dead man to the perimeter of the hospital, right under the noses of the Australian Army's finest, without detection, and then disappear? Unease churned in his gut. He prided himself on his instinct, and something was off here, he just couldn't pinpoint what it was ... yet.

'Dammit it all to hell.'

He'd have to worry about that particular problem after Beth was back safely. Right now, he had more immediate concerns.

Lawson tapped out another message.

Ok. We'll see them when they're home. He hated the lazy, ill-educated abbreviations people insisted on using while texting.

Powering off the phone, he pulled out burner phone two, and briefed the extraction team to stand down, await further instruction. He'd wait for his second inside man to give him Calloway's search team's timetable, then re-schedule the elimination, and add in the rescue.

Lawson stowed the phones, filled the kettle and set it to boil. He spooned fresh Earl Grey leaves in the infuser, and when the water had boiled, poured himself a new cup, treating himself to a second slice of lemon. His heart rate near to normal again, he sipped at the steaming amber liquid. For the first time in days he smiled, felt hope bloom in his chest again. There was actually a silver lining to the Calloway mess he couldn't have engineered better himself.

Now, he would be integral in saving Beth's life, in a practical way. Knowing her heart, her benevolent ways like he did, he knew she'd feel indebted to him for such an act. And then it would happen. She'd see him, truly see him, and finally recognise that he was all she'd need or want in a man, a lover, a husband. Surely, there'd be no way she'd want to deny her feelings for him after that?

Lawson pressed start on his MP3 player again. The jaunty opening of Mozart's *The Marriage of Figaro* filled the room. He closed his eyes. Exhaled.

Soon ... soon everything will be as it should, as he'd planned.

Lawson made his way to the hospital just over an hour after the nurses' visit to his room, his confidence in his actions, his strategy, restored. He just needed to farewell Beth, and let her know he bore her no ill will, that he harboured no bad feelings towards her, before she departed. Then the foundation would be set for the remainder of his plans.

'Are these the most current patient charts for review, Lieutenant Saunders?' said Lawson, pointing as he approached the nurses' station.

'Yes, sir, I've just collected them for your handover with Doctor Stokes.'

'Thank you.' He scooped up the files and rounded the corner of the admin block, where he immediately pulled up short. Standing directly in front of him, with his significant bulk blocking the busy corridor, was Lieutenant Colonel Fraser, the man who'd helped him sell his soul to the devil.

Lawson swiped at the sweat beading his upper lip, and not for the first time wondered how the hell he'd allowed himself to stumble onto this path. An excellent surgeon, he'd received commendations for his fieldwork in Timor and Iraq, and had been deployed to the Middle East more times than most at his rank. He was smarter than almost everyone he met, had the intellect to outwit most too. That particular skill helped him out of some pretty intense situations. Except for one.

He allowed the detail of the events, from the lead up to Andrew's death, until now, to filter into his skull moment by moment. Ordinarily, he'd never entertain the frustrating memories, but given today had already taken an ugly path, he let them come. *Penance for your errors.*

He'd spent months gathering information before finally driving four hours to meet the civilian explosives *expert* he'd sought out—a known local criminal, whose entire fetid, drug-fuelled person, made Lawson's flesh crawl. Holed up in a tin-walled, putrid hovel, shunted in amongst many just the same, and intent on finalising the deal to arrange an *accident* that'd damage Andrew and strip him of any ability to be the man Beth deserved, Lawson reviewed the specifics of the plan, paid the first instalment to the shifty-eyed, weed of a man and departed. In his haste, he didn't see Fraser concluding his own business further down the row. But he learned later, Fraser didn't miss seeing him.

Explosions expert he wasn't. The imbecile had botched the job, killed not only Andrew, but three others too. Lawson swiped at the sweat drenching his upper lip, frustrated the memory could still illicit such a visceral response.

Within hours of Lawson learning the job had gone to hell, Fraser came to him, revealed evidence that left no question of Lawson's involvement. Detail that would at best see Lawson court marshalled and incarcerated for life, and at worst ... well, Beth wouldn't ever feel his beating heart next to hers, which had been the whole damn point of it all.

He'd been waiting for the military police to show up, but Fraser had offered him a choice, if that's what you could call it. Said he'd make all the evidence disappear if Lawson used his networks and influence to *assist* with Fraser's side business—a business that supplied drugs, hidden in medical supplies, to an influential Afghani warlord.

He wasn't sure he'd even paused before agreeing to Fraser's offer, not really his proudest moment. The joke, of course, was he was anything but free. Fraser and Zoreed, the mastermind of their operation, alternately, frequently and mercilessly, pulled the strings controlling his world.

He ground his back teeth together.

Not for the first time, he thought about where he'd be if someone on the straight and narrow had seen him, pieced the puzzle together like Fraser did. *Living out the consequences of a disastrous mistake, that's where.* Consequences that would have stripped him of his career, of everything he'd worked for, and would've lost him Beth forever. It wasn't an option then, and definitely wasn't going to be one now, not after everything he'd suffered through.

The painstaking foundations he'd been laying to extricate himself from the situation, the building of evidence that made him invisible in the play and only implicated Fraser, hadn't been down long and weren't complete. But he prayed they'd be sturdy enough for him to take action soon, because his time to extract himself from it all before it blew up in his face, was fast running out.

'Ah, Major Black, you're here to celebrate the good news?' said the Lieutenant Colonel, his eyes narrowing.

'Yes, I am, sir. Sergeant Calloway must be very relieved he's secured a doctor?'

'Indeed.' Fraser clasped his fleshy hands behind his back. 'Satisfactory outcome for all, wouldn't you agree?'

'It seems so, yes,' said Lawson, well aware of Fraser's double meaning. 'As to the safety and security of Captain Harper, I take it you've ensured everything is well in hand?' He volleyed the steely tone back at Fraser.

'Of course, Major. All necessary precautions have been taken, I've seen to it personally.'

'Thank you, sir,' said Lawson. 'We're all very grateful for your personal attention I'm sure. She's one of the army's best surgeons.'

The murmurs and nods of the hospital team surrounding them echoed the sentiments of Lawson's less than hushed tones.

'We are well aware of her credentials, Major, and appreciate her willingness to help in this matter. No need for your concern though, Captain Harper and Sergeant Calloway have made a safe and successful departure.'

Lawson's lungs deflated like a three-day-old balloon. 'I see.' He struggled to swallow. *Why had their departure been so swift?* He shuffled his weight from one foot to the other. 'Ah, I'll be on my way then, cover off some of Captain Stokes rounds before our formal handover.'

'Yes, let's hope there's nothing out of the ordinary for the team here today, hey, Major?'

There was no mistaking the warning in the Lieutenant Colonel's tone, or the intention that accompanied his slap on Lawson's shoulder, one that was a little too hard, his hand lingering a little too long: steer clear of Beth and Calloway, and go about business as normally as possible today.

'Always an out of the ordinary day around here, you know that,' said Lawson, the lightness he forced into his words pricking into his throat like shards of broken glass.

'Indeed, indeed,' said Fraser with an almost inaudible chuckle.

There was no doubt Fraser would be watching his every move from here on in like a hawk.

Neither of them could afford another mistake.

Lawson waited as his superior moved slowly past him in the direction of the hospital's exit. Not wanting to give the pig any level of satisfaction or appear to be in any way rattled, Lawson pretended to survey the charts still in his hands.

'Oh, Major Black,' Fraser said, turning to face Lawson again, his jowls swaying with the sudden movement. 'I do hope to see you at my farewell tomorrow. I'd hate for you to miss my retirement celebrations.'

'Of course. Wouldn't miss it, Lieutenant Colonel.'

The smile playing across both their mouths didn't reach either of their eyes.

Sweat snaked the length of Lawson's spine.

Fraser well knew he'd liaised with the extraction team earlier, but was unlikely to know the newer plans he'd just issued. Lawson prayed it stayed that way. He'd delivered an unmistakable warning to the men, specifics of what would happen to their cosy little worlds should the detail of his new orders be leaked to anyone else further up the food chain. These men didn't respect a chain of command, only a chain of payments and volleyed threats. Confident his threats were enough to buy adequate time to secure Beth, he'd be a fool to believe it'd be long before one of them dared to trade up for a better offer.

Lawson sucked in a deep breath. Fraser would also be aware that the scheduled meet with Zoreed's courier in two hours couldn't possibly go ahead. Lawson had no way to fabricate a legitimate need to remove himself from Captain Stokes' unexpected shift handover, and Fraser hadn't offered any influence or options, so there was no way he could slip away without provoking questions. Another cause for concern as to what Fraser was playing at.

He had to call Zoreed, offer her a persuasive reason for the delay. While it wasn't in the other man's best interests to give Zoreed a heads-up on the colossal mistake of Calloway being left behind, Lawson didn't trust Fraser to have his back either, not this close to his retirement. The snake was just as likely to serve up his head on a platter, ensure his own safe passage out of this mess before he was out of the army for good.

Glancing out the window, Lawson scanned the grounds, pleased to see Fraser was still here, talking to Brigadier James, his direct superior, just outside the hospital entry. *Good.*

Striding the length of the corridor, Lawson checked his surrounds then slipped into a vacant stores cupboard. With his back to the door, he typed a text to Zoreed, instructed her to call him, gave her a time that was directly after lunch. He hated that his fingers shook, hated that he was forced to cow-tow to a damn woman, but mostly he hated Fraser, his golden ticket into this whole goddamn mess.

'I'll have the cargo ready in two days.' Lawson tried not to shout down the static-filled line. He'd explain away the call to anyone who heard as a medical related one, but he didn't need some fool hearing him offthe-cuff, and blathering on to the wrong people.

He'd checked the chow hall before coming out, and knew he was all clear for now, but the kitchen crew would be back for dinner prep shortly, and he'd already taken on way more risk than he'd originally planned. He'd almost missed the call window, and couldn't afford to lose the line now.

'Major Black, your delivery, it will be late to me? I tell you, you make it come now.' She hacked out a spasming cough, hawking up phlegm and spitting loudly. His stomach clenched and he held the phone away from his ear. 'You listen, Major Lawson Black, you don't deliver my money and the sugar, two days, they dead.'

Click.

Her heavily-accented voice gone, the silence in his ear warred with the pounding beat of frustration.

He hadn't really believed Lieutenant Colonel Fraser when he'd revealed Zoreed to be a f*emale w*arlord. How in God's name could that be? Women were barely allowed to breathe in most places here, so how could one be reigning, and from a mountain bluff no less? But reign she did, Zoreed Zadran. On their first meeting, she'd taken great delight in explaining the meaning of her name to him—*one who meets with strong intentions and decisiveness*—she'd certainly lived up to that, and more.

The legend surrounding Zoreed's power had grown a life of its own over the past twenty something years, and the fear surrounding her supremacy seemed to hold more weight than any military prowess she came up against. Of course, she'd had some near misses, she said, but always managed to come out breathing, and from what he'd seen, ruling with an iron fist. Not to mention two dead husbands in her wake, certainly sent a strong message to anyone questioning her level of control.

Highly religious, these were also a superstitious people. Believing ghosts and evil walked the earth alongside their beloved religious leader, he knew many of them considered Zoreed part both. Maybe she was? If he hadn't seen her in action himself, he'd never have believed all that she was personally capable of.

It'd been almost eighteen months since he'd met Zoreed, presenting himself to her, disarmed and disguised in tattered civilian clothes, he'd journeyed for just over nine hours to meet her in her fortified mountainside compound. He'd barely stepped off the putrid, smoking motorbike when she'd welcomed him by calmly smoothing her hijab, her skirts, then made him stand to attention, rifle at his temple.

'You look right here, Major Lawson Black,' she'd said, and pointed to a patch of muddied snow about five metres in front of him. Three gagged and hog-tied people, her people—a woman and two men—from the local village he learned later, were writhing on the ground, clearly terrified and in agony. Broken fibula on one, patella smashed on the others he suspected, given the localised swelling. He'd watched, partly concerned he'd be next, and partly fighting back his excitement. Imagine wielding this level of open power without a scalpel.

'Shirzad, kill them now.'

A man who strongly resembled Zoreed, maybe in his mid-twenties, shot the thrashing humans. Shot them point blank in front of the children milling around with the handful of other spectators. No-one even flinched, well, except him, despite his best efforts. He'd glanced at Zoreed the moment after it was done—her beady black eyes staring at him, her wide jaw set, chin up, daring him to ask the question. He stayed silent, recognising it for the test it was.

'They didn't do what I asked.' She spat on the ground as a full stop, and stared at him again. Lawson nodded, hoped his face conveyed his wholehearted endorsement for her actions. He didn't abide insubordination either. With no idea if he was allowed to speak, he decided there was only one way to find out.

'What didn't they do?'

'They work with enemy, didn't report to me fast.'

He'd nodded. 'So, because they were slow, they were bad?'

She'd responded with a broad, gapped tooth grin, and didn't say a word, just walked and stood directly in front of him. Since that day, he'd witnessed many of her justice system practices, and the presence of that smile worried him far more than any other weapon in her arsenal.

'I turn bad man good, Major Lawson Black. That is why you are here,' she'd said, his question to her ignored, dismissed.

'Sorry? I'm not sure what you mean?' He knew this visit to her was a non-negotiable part of Fraser's deal, the initiation component of his acceptance to act as the primary conduit for her couriers, but what else was he dealing with here?

'Lieutenant Colonel Fraser, he tell me he see you hurt a man, kill him. He say you are sorry. He tell me you want in, take his place when he go home for good. Is he wrong, Major Lawson Black?'

'No, no of course he's not wrong.' *Bastard.* Fraser had swapped out, traded his place on her run and dropped him in it. He felt like a noose had been looped around his neck. Despite his attempt to control it, Lawson's insides quaked.

Zoreed clapped her large hands towards a posse of women. An attractive teenage girl emerged, brought forth a bowie knife, the pristine silver blade glinting in the fading sunlight.

What he didn't know then, but had witnessed with interest since, is that Zoreed kept a handful of women close to her who behaved and responded to her demands as if they served a male. Cooking, cleaning. Shooting on request. Oh yes, heaven help him, they were all well-schooled in the use of an AK-47 rifle, the women along with all the males in Zoreed's circle. No matter their age, Zoreed required everyone in her *family* to be excellent marksmen. He'd seen five-year-old kids shoot targets, then run off to fly a kite when practice was over.

Crazy world here. Totally crazy, but thankfully, one that wouldn't be his problem for much longer.

The girl stretched out her arms, presented the knife to him, and Zoreed spoke.

'You shed blood. You shed blood at my feet, feed my earth.' She grabbed his wrist, forced open his palm.

'No, no. NO. Not my hand.' There was no way he could hide the tremor ricocheting through his arm into his hand. 'I'm a surgeon. I-I can't help you if I can't work.'

'Do arm then.' She hauled up his sleeve, dug her nail into the tender flesh at the underside of his forearm. 'Here. Now.'

Every fibre of his being screamed resistance, his hands curled into fists. Infection happened quickly out here, and god knew what else the damn knife'd been used for. But what other choice did he have? So he did it and prayed like hell that by the time he could get antibiotics, it'd be soon enough.

'Good. Good, Major Lawson Black. You bonded to my people, my land now,' said Zoreed, as the steady ooze of his blood dripped and pooled at her feet. 'Your journey, it begins.'

In the months that had passed since then, he'd outwardly agreed with her rules, nodded and promised atonement for his mistakes as required. When necessary, he'd murmured the right, but not too right platitudes, and had participated in her self-indulgent rituals whenever he was in her company. She'd seemed relatively satisfied with his efforts, his progress towards 'good man' as she liked to call it, whatever the hell that meant. She'd never explained further. He'd never asked again.

And it had worked, he'd stayed off her radar, until now.

This was the first time he'd not delivered, not played by her rules to the letter. Hopefully he'd earned enough goodwill, deserved some leniency if it did in fact all come out. Because god help him, he needed her onside, not gunning for his head on a stick. He needed her to trust him, at least until he had Beth, and then, maybe, he'd have a decent chance of getting them both the hell out of this cesspit.

Chapter 8

'Thanks again, Captain Harper, for agreeing to escort me.'

Nate forced the words past the golf ball-sized lump jammed in his throat. He couldn't say anything more to her—all five foot, nine inches of honey-haired, smart, gorgeous woman of her. A woman who embodied every last piece of hope he had. So he just jammed his gob shut instead, suddenly felt like some bastard had punched him square in the chest.

It'd come down to the wire. If Doc Harper had offered to escort him twenty-eight minutes later, he'd have had no chance at dodging the medical transfer bullet. Because of her, he was on his way to Finn and the boys. She'd saved his arse. Again. 'You're welcome, Sergeant,' she said. Her faltering smile dragged at something deep in his gut. 'You've done me a favour actually,' she continued. 'I've trained for this kind of work, just never been in a situation to utilise it.' She cocked an eyebrow. 'And anyway, you know what they say about change and a holiday and all that?' She waved a hand in the air as if she'd just offered to bring him an orange juice, not risk her life chaperoning his sorry arse outside the wire.

His head swam with images of what might cover her type of holiday. By the look of her, he reckoned she spent most of her down time enjoying physical pursuits. She had the shape of an athlete, held her body upright and stood strong. Unlikely she was the kinda chick who preferred the indoors. Or maybe she did? Maybe she was the kind who preferred wine and books inside, worked out at home? A flicker of more than a passing interest sparked out of the blue. *Get your priorities right, man.* Christ, he didn't need any distractions.

'Well, Captain,' he said, 'I'm not sure what kinda holiday floats your boat, but this one isn't gonna be too postcard worthy.' He willed the rippling frustration he had towards his own useless reaction to kick in and override his increasing interest in her.

'I know what I'm headed into, Sergeant.' The lightness in her tone evaporated, her face dialling back to super serious. 'And I wouldn't be here if I didn't want to be. So, let's focus on the job at hand, shall we? I'll grab your treatment plan and review the contingencies with you, make sure there's nothing we haven't considered.'

He nodded. 'Okay. Sure.' *Shit.* He felt like he should apologise. He'd clearly offended her. Nate's thoughts ping-ponged around his head as he chewed on his lower lip. Nah, probably best to leave it for now. Fact of the matter was, the situation here's dire, the risk to all of them, extreme. He had to make sure she truly recognised that before she hit the track for real, she was his responsibility out here. He flicked a glance towards her, she had what looked like his paperwork tucked under her arm and was scouting her pack for something.

With the past few weeks of him doing jack shit, it'd at least been good for observation of the people around him, and when he wasn't bullshitting himself, he'd have to admit he'd spent a good amount of the time observing just her. He pegged her as a no-fuss-no-musskinda woman, and a bit of a soft touch despite that all-too-tense back and forth outside the hospital. But maybe there was plenty more to see under that good girl skin. *Not that you're ever gonna be anywhere near her skin.* Her abrupt change in manner just now made him wonder what he hadn't seen. Maybe underneath it all, she was actually more hard-arse than honey?

She looked up at him, stared at him actually, and headed over to stand face-to-face.

He pulled his thoughts back to her statement about focusing on the job, his heart thudding in his chest at the thought of getting back out there, finding Finnegan and the guys. 'Listen, like I said, I appreciate you, ah, making it possible—' he cleared his throat, '—for me to be able to join the search, find my men.' He clamped his mouth shut, shoved his hands deep in his pockets for focus. Didn't need her to hear anything desperate push through his lips. 'I just want to know that you're up for whatever happens out there.'

She shrugged slightly and took a deep breath. 'I am, Sergeant. I wouldn't dare do anything to risk lives, I can promise you that. And you know what? I'm glad I can be here, gives me a chance to do something different, help on a bigger scale.' She fiddled with her hair, the second hint of self-consciousness she'd shown in as many minutes.

Man, if an aged French oak merlot had a voice, hers was it—smooth, full-bodied and sexy. And those eyes, the colour of a perfect Courvoisier cognac. A man could drown in eyes like those. *Back away. She's not someone you won't see tomorrow.*

'Anyway,' she said, moving closer to him, her all female scent sling-shotting his thoughts from dangerous to delinquent. 'I reckon there's no way we'd have got you on that plane without you creating some hell-fire drama, right?'

'I told you I wouldn't go,' he said without hesitation, holding her gaze, watching her pupils blow out as he spoke. 'Can't say I'm happy I caused you some grief, but I'd do the same thing tomorrow, the next day. Every day. Finding my unit is my end game, period. The idea that Finnegan's alone and trapped, hurt or—'

'Yes, you certainly told me,' she interrupted. 'And I get it. From what I've seen, I've no doubt you're a man of your word. So now, this way, I get to make sure all my hard work in theatre doesn't go to waste. I'd say that means we have a win-win all round. Right?'

Despite himself he grinned. She'd lightened the all too serious tone the conversation had taken, and hadn't made him feel a dick over it either.

'Yeah, well—' he sighed, '—s'pose that wouldn't have been fair if I'd messed up all your handy work, would it?'

'It did take me the better part of a day to save your arse, so, it'd be nice to have it last longer than a couple of weeks.' She mirrored his grin. 'Listen,' she said, a frown wrinkling her forehead then disappearing. 'While it's just us, you don't need to address me so formally. It's going to be intense enough, so it's Beth, just call me Beth, okay?' She sucked her lower lip under her teeth, shot a look at her shoes before eyeballing him again.

'Alright,' he said, fiery tension spreading though his gut, the silence surrounding them circling the edges of awkward again.

Leaning into the wall at his back, Nate tugged at his collar. *Jesus.* This too good, too nice, too tolerant woman was suddenly taking up all his damn air, making him feel hot and, and ... he didn't know what. Fuck it. He needed space. He motioned towards the doorway out of their bunker. 'On second thought, how 'bout you take five, Doc. Once we get moving, you won't have much time to yourself, so you might as well grab it while you can. We've nailed the plans, don't reckon we need to revisit them right now.'

She nodded. 'Alright, as long as you're sure?

'I am. We've already reviewed the details, they're solid. Good to go.'

'Okay then.' She returned the paperwork to her bag, straightened the hem of her jacket and moved past him towards the door, that all woman scent trailing in her wake. 'See you in a bit then,' she said.

*S*oon as he was sure Beth was out of range, he let the air escape from his burning lungs. He just couldn't be thinking about all this random shit to do with her.

When he'd first come to in the hospital with her leaning over him, grabbing him by the shoulders, he'd copped an eyeful of her perfect breasts, her pristine white shiny bra moulded around flawless curves. For a few moments, he'd had no idea she was real, thought she was just the figment of a kick-arse beautiful dream. Then the pain hit. He was definitely awake. And there she was, a gorgeous woman ... and as real as it gets.

Nate snorted at the memory. It had to have been the meds or his semi-comatose state at the time ... something. He had never gone for white wearing, straight laced A-types. *And she's definitely one of those.* Doc Harper was not remotely like the women he hung out with once in a while. *And it'd been a long damn while.* Women who enjoyed his preference for a no strings attached fuck, who were happy when he made sure everyone got what they came for, and split. No pressure, nothing cosy, nothing complex. He didn't do sunrises and breakfast. Ever. And Captain Doctor Beth Harper was definitely a league above all of that. In fact, he'd wager his vineyard that despite every other reason she was a no-go zone, the top one was that she'd definitely want more than what someone like him had to offer. More than to relieve a bit of tension in some dark corner, with her back against the wall and her shoes still on. And anyway, there's no way a woman like her wouldn't already be hooked up.

He'd never apologised for who he was, who he'd never be, but right now, the idea of her thinking badly of him worked on his inappropriate arousal as swiftly as if he'd doused himself with a frigging bucket of ice. *Why the hell do you care if she thinks you're an arse?*

'Get the fuck over yourself, man.' The rumble of his mutter absorbed into the stone walls. Even though she'd been nothing but a damn near superwoman to him, and he owed her big time for the fact he was standing right where he needed to be, the fact still remained that despite her being his superior officer and totally off limits, he'd never met a woman, not one in his whole damn life, that hadn't caused him trouble. And definitely never one he could trust.

Nate pulled over a wooden crate that'd seen better days, and lowered himself down, pain rocketing up his spine. He drummed his fingers against his leg, breathing through the ache. Maybe he did have a goddamn brain injury. He'd never thought this much about a woman, ever. Well, not since Amy Bentley promised she'd be there when he got home, then screwed his mate the next day, the day before Nate first deployed out. And that'd been ten lifetimes ago, so didn't bloody count.

Jesus. His gut was churning like a frigging washing machine, and his usually unshakable focus was anything but centred.

'Shit.' Nate rubbed his hands up and down the sides of his legs. 'C'mon, Finn, don't take too long to show your furry black butt ... we really need to get outta here. Fast.'

Chapter 9

She came back into the bunker laughing, the husky happiness rolling out of her throat the best sound he'd heard in days.

'Got a great team out there,' said Beth. 'Pack of jokesters.'

'Yeah, they are.' Nate focused on the now blurred topical map in front of him, didn't dare let himself clap eyes on her. She'd been gone a while, long enough that he could get himself and his damn testosterone back in check. He couldn't risk revving it all back up again, no matter how much he wanted to look at her. She was off limits. Off. Limits.

'It's time to get your dressings sorted. You ready?'

'Ah, sure.' Bloody hell, he'd forgotten about that, and wasn't ready to have her that close to him again. He didn't want to have to look at her, watch her lips while she talked, or focus on any part of her until he had something else to keep his brain fully engaged. 'Do you mind if I keep working on this while you do what you have to?'

'Of course, no problem.'

Thank Christ.

As she moved through her process, the silence between them started as an easy one. She finished with dressing his leg wound, and by the time she stopped, he was well and truly pissed off, with himself. He'd had to work way too hard to focus on something other than her. It was bullshit.

'That'll be right now till we make our first stop,' she said. 'Just your antibiotics to go, and you're done for at least the next few hours.'

He stretched the limb out slowly, his sutures pulled at the healing skin like stabbing needles. She prompted him to roll back his shirtsleeve for the injection.

'You really are lucky the swelling's completely gone, and the burns are in such good shape,' she said. 'You're one of the fastest healers I've ever seen. It's just your lung that could be our biggest concern.'

He didn't comment as she infused the liquid into his arm then rubbed over the injection site with alcohol and a cotton pad. He nearly jumped through the roof when her fingernail scratched his skin.

'Oh sorry, Sergeant, did I hurt you?'

'Nah, just a bit tender there. I'll be right,' he said. Now he'd just become a bloody liar on top of everything else. 'You just about done, Captain?' His words came out harsher than intended.

Concern etched across her face. 'Nearly, just let me check your arm again. There's a chance your sensitivity is latent tissue trauma, which could mean other issues.'

She assessed the flinch site again, pressing gently around the area she'd scratched. Her fingers felt like warm rays of sun sliding over his skin, her breath on his neck soft, sexy. *Christ.* He somehow stayed mute and resisted shoving her hand off his arm.

After what seemed like two lifetimes, she looked convinced his arm wasn't about to drop off, and stood, faced him. 'Okay. Well, let me know if it gets worse, or the sensitivity flares again,' she said, searching his face, rolling down his sleeve.

'Thanks, but you're done here.' He snatched his arm from her hand and shoved the remaining shirt fabric down to his wrist. 'I mean, I'm done. Listen, Doc, I like my space, and you're in it. Can you just move over there a bit?' He pointed to the furthest corner from him.

He'd just been a total prick, but it had to be done, for both their sakes. Truth of the matter was, when any part of her came into contact with any part of him, he felt like he'd been hammered with an electric rod. And if the heat in her face while she inspected his arm was anything to go by, she felt it too. *Not good. Not good at all.*

Her expression changed from concern to caustic in a heartbeat.

She stayed exactly where she was and sucked in a chest full of breath. The intensity in her glare enough to shatter a frigging missile.

'Unfortunately for you, Sergeant, *your space* is what I'm responsible for, so no, I can't move. You'll have to get used to me being here.' She waved her arms around them in a circle. 'Just think of me as your new damn shadow.' She snapped the lid back on the syringe before taking a step closer to him. 'Is that going to be a problem for you?'

Well shit, she was definitely more hard-arse than honey. He could tick that question off the list.

His knee-jerk reaction was to spar with her, hold his ground. But given what she'd risked just being here, not to mention the fact she outranked him, it probably wasn't the wisest choice right now. Regardless of anything else he might feel, or want to say on the matter, he needed her like he needed oxygen, and pissing her off through disrespect just wasn't a good idea. And, despite the necessity of it, he felt a bastard for pressing her buttons like that.

Nate exhaled slowly. 'No, ma'am, it isn't going to be a problem.' He dragged his hand over his mouth. She crossed her arms over her chest, said nothing, waited. 'Ah shit. I'm sorry for being a rude arse just now. I appreciate you being here, helping me out, I really do. I just want to get moving, get the fuck out of here, you know?' *And to stop thinking about you.*

She shifted her weight, wedged her hands on her hips. Silent seconds inched by.

'Thanks. For the apology,' she said finally. Her hands dropped to her sides, she exhaled. 'You know what, I get it, Calloway, I really do. But just so we're clear, here's how it goes from now on. Out there, you're in charge, no question. I'm not stupid enough to pull rank in a situation I know little about, so I'll follow your lead without issue. But when we're covered, and I'm doing my job, we operate under my authority. That means you'll do exactly what I say, when I say it. Or all bets are off, and you're on a plane home.'

It wasn't a discussion. She didn't wait for any reaction from him before she turned and went back to sorting her medical supplies, all calm, like shit hadn't just gone down. Mind you, he didn't miss the red stain spreading across her neck. *Maybe not so hard-arse?*

She slid a marker pen into her right chest pocket, and two sheathed scalpels into the left. Mildly intrigued at her random selection of what to store close to her body, and needing a distraction, he decided to work on learning a bit about her, her methods, facts that'd help him work with her in the field.

'What are those for, specifically?' he said.

'What these?' She patted her breast pockets.

Jesus. Don't do that.

'Standard items I might need in the field,' she said.

Was she provoking him now? Trying to make him feel a dickhead? Man, he so didn't have a bead on her yet.

'But basically, I guess you could say they're to note shit and slice shit.'

Her out of character smart-arse retort came at him low and fast. She didn't look up as she spoke, but the indent in her cheek wouldn't be there if she wasn't smirking. She was totally fucking with him! His annoyance evaporated and a different kind of frustration filled the gaps. Seemed like she didn't hold a grudge, and had a pretty good sense of humour. Maybe this'd work out okay after all.

'C'mon, Doc, quit bullshitting me.' He smiled at her despite himself. 'You know, the devil's in the detail out here. Means the difference between life and death sometimes. So, if I don't know your detail, I'm telling you now, you're gonna know my devil.'

'Your devil?' she said, crossing her arms, sliding them slowly beneath her breasts. 'Thought I'd already met that guy good and proper?' The shine in her eyes, the honey in her voice speared heat straight to his groin. *You better shut this down now, man.*

'Captain, you ain't seen nothin' yet,' he replied.

He was way outta line, but screw protocol. Screw working inside the square. If they were anywhere else, sparking like a bloody lightning storm across a cane field, he'd already have her halfway to naked by now. He watched her pupils expand, her cheeks redden, her gaze drop to the floor. *God she was hot.*

He took a step towards her, the muscles in his legs twitching, the irony of the moment not lost on him. He so wanted her *back* in his space, now. But she took a step, actually a leap, away from him. Waved her hand in front of her face, her arm pushed straight out from her body.

'And I hope I don't see anything, Sergeant.' Her raised voice wavered. She cleared her throat, avoided his gaze, kept backing up. 'I don't want to see anything other than professional, focused work from you.'

What the fuck? He didn't move.

'As you said,' she continued, 'it's life and death we're dealing with out here.' She looked straight at him now, her breathing choppy, indecision stamped all over her flushed face. 'And you're right, I should tell you exactly what I'm doing, no matter how minor the detail.'

And just like that, she'd shut him down. The sassy woman from a minute ago evaporated in front of him, and in her place stood the stranger she was.

She returned to her preparation, angling her body side on to him, the stain at her neck darker, her chest pumping fast.

'No problem,' he finally managed to say.

Nate pulled the map from his pack, pretended to be engrossed in it again, but kept her square in his periphery. *What the hell just happened?* He should probably say something else, deflate the elephant in the room. Did he need to bloody apologise again? He replayed the last few minutes in his head. There was only one conclusion to reach. She'd pulled the brakes. Made sure nothing stupid went down. *Lucky one of them had.* Jesus, he couldn't think about doing that shit again. He'd been reckless, wrong. Better get back to his head making the frigging decisions, stop behaving like a goddamn horny teenager.

A few strained minutes rolled by until she pulled each of the zippers closed on her pack and turned towards him, her stance all serious and no-nonsense. It felt like she'd raised up a double-glazed sheet of glass between them as her full focus speared into him.

He had no frigging idea how to play this out. Silence was probably the best bet for now, take a minute to gauge his next response on what she did next.

'So what do you think happened to you between the explosion and the operating table? Got any theories?'

Nope. Didn't expect that. Not. At. All. Why the hell would she pull that question out of the blue like that? *Jesus.* He'd never had so many conflicting thoughts smashing through his skull at once. Felt like he was suffering goddamn emotional whiplash.

'Pardon?' He needed a minute; her change of tack hitting a raw nerve. He couldn't ignore that her question poked at thoughts already stuck on repeat in his head.

Hellish dreams had plagued him nightly since he'd woken from the surgery. Flashes of images that might've been related to the incident, that might help tell him something, but made no real sense, hovered in his subconscious, just out of reach. He reasoned it could just as easily be his mind playing tricks *but not likely.* The sweat inducing, all too real wake up calls straight after the nightmares told him otherwise.

'Calloway? I asked about the attack,' she said. 'Your transport to the hospital? Do you have any theories? Intel said it's a good eighty kilometres from the explosion site to our hospital. That's a helluva distance for two kids to carry you, on foot.'

'I've got no idea, Captain,' he said eventually, not ready to give voice to the broken pieces of information he'd been trying to mould together.

'Really?' Her eyes narrowed. 'Well, I thought we could consider the options, discuss them, while we have a bit of time. Might help later.'

'Listen, Doc, I appreciate your concern, but I really don't have any solid ideas.' Best he make sure she stayed on a strictly need to know basis for the duration of her time out here. Even if he wanted to discuss something, give her a small piece of the puzzle, he just couldn't. It was too dangerous for her. And given her tone, he was pretty keen to do what he could to keep her escalating agro to a minimum.

She looked about to say something in response, and thought better of it. Then changed her mind again. 'Okay then,' she said, 'let's try this one. How much more do you think those guys out there know than what they've told us?' She jerked her head out towards where their superiors were finalising the plans. 'Because I get the feeling I haven't heard even half the story, and I'd really like to know if it's just me in the dark?'

Obviously her frustration over this one had been biting at her since this morning when they'd had their initial briefing. Why'd she wait so long to say something? She was so bloody forthcoming with everything else. Talk about hot and cold. There'd been way too much temperature change in the last five minutes, and he'd just about had enough of trying to bloody figure it all out.

Nate slowly bent forward, picked up a decent-sized stone and rolled it between his fingers, spinning potential answers around in his head. Regardless of how he felt, it was right to give her something. She deserved at least that. But he couldn't risk jamming her thinking, have her worry about shit she didn't need to know.

'I've toured with Patto before, Sergeant Dean Patterson, the first guy who addressed us when we arrived. He'll fill in the gaps after the final briefing if he can, but I reckon we've got the basic nuts and bolts of the intel so far.' It was kind of the truth.

She crossed one ankle over the other and leant into the wall, her face intense, focused on him. 'Really?'

She didn't believe him.

'Look, the only other detail I can offer you is from what I know, the IED was unusual, really sophisticated, and it only blew up the front half of the truck. Only me and Finn were near there. Longy was further up the road, the other two between me and him, so the spooks are pretty sure the rest of my unit's been captured, and Finn's either with them, run off or...' Nate flexed the muscle in his jaw, his heart rate hammering at the thought of his furry little mate. He couldn't say it, wouldn't accept Finn could be anything but alive.

'But isn't Finnegan trained to deal with explosions?' She stood straight again, pushed off the wall. 'Why would he have run off, especially since you weren't running with him? Aren't the dogs trained to stay with their handler no matter what?

'Of course he's bloody trained.' Nate pegged the stone in his hand at the wall. 'But he's still an animal who gets scared, disoriented. Stressed. They're not robots for fuck's sake.' He shoved up off the crate, stifling the grunt that came with the pain. He didn't care what hurt, he needed as much distraction, as much distance as possible between him and her. She asked way too many questions, and made him feel, and want, and think, about shit he shouldn't.

She closed the gap between them in less than a second. Got up in his face before he made it to the door.

'Unless we're under threat, *Sergeant—'* her hot breath hit his lips, '—don't you ever shout at me.' She squared up to him, her heat mingling with his. 'You got that?' She continued eyeballing him, grabbed his wrist. He thought about resisting her for about a millisecond till she shoved his palm skyward and thrust pain meds from her hand to his, all without those burnt-tea coloured eyes even blinking.

'Take these with water. I'm sure you'll find some out there.' She flicked her wrist and pointed towards the door, the *'get out'* message loud and clear. Suited him, he needed to be anywhere but here. Beth turned and moved towards the opposite end of the bunker.

Before Nate could do or say anything, a bloke's frame filled their doorway. Not sure if he was actually thankful for the timing of his mate's arrival, Nate welcomed his friend inside.

'Hey, Patto.'

'G'day, Wolfman.' He pulled Nate in close for a slap on the back and cleared his throat. 'Can't say I'm glad to see you here, mate.'

'Can't say I'm glad to be here under these bloody circumstances.'

'Captain.' Patto nodded in Beth's direction. Nate sensed he was uneasy about talking to him in Captain Harper's company. He knew his mate couldn't share much, if anything with him, the need to know basis is what kept them all alive out here. But Nate hoped maybe there was a chance that what Patto could or would share, might shed a bit more light on the sketchy details they'd been given. It'd be good to have a heads-up before the final briefing.

'So what's news then, Patto?'

'Not a lot.' His friend shot an uneasy glance in Beth's direction. 'Not. A. Lot.'

'She's cool.' He mouthed the words to Pat, unshakeably sure of his gut instinct about Beth.

The other man leant in close, wasted no time getting to the point. 'Intel suggests fucking turncoats gotcha, mate. Looks like we've got a couple of our own working with the insurgents.'

'You're kidding me. Confirmed?'

'Yeah.'

'Ah shit, man.' It took all of Nate's willpower not to punch the wall beside him, his lunch threatening to hurtle back up his throat. He'd never understand how a man, fighting for the safety and freedom of innocent people, kids, women, the blokes, caught in the middle of this hell, could goddamn turn against his own. No amount of money or power, or any damn thing would ever tempt him to betray his side. Ever. And he'd bloody well end anyone he found who did.

'It's bad. Word is, it goes pretty high up.'

Patto's urgent whispers sent chills skidding down Nate's spine. For Patto to risk sharing this with him, it had to be worse than he'd imagined. Tension dug into Nate's shoulders, spasming up his neck. He raked his fingers through the muscles at the base of his skull. *Jesus.* They were dealing with something way bigger than finding Finnegan and the rest of his unit.

'Any idea who?'

'Ah, no.' Pat's blink-and-you'll-miss-it downward glance spoke volumes. 'Wish there was.'

'No worries. Thanks, mate.' Nate grasped Patto's hand in a firm shake. 'Appreciate you stopping by.' No doubt Pat would share the names when he could.

'You take care then,' said Patto. Nate's eyes stayed trained on Patto's lips, the words he mouthed making him sick to his gut. 'Get her back to base. She's not safe here.'

Nate nodded.

'Briefing's in ten minutes, then you head out at seventeen hundred. I'm gone straight after the Commander's done, so I'll see you down the track.' All business again, Patto turned towards Beth, who was making an impressive show of reorganising her already perfectly packed kit and shuffling her body armour around her on the floor. 'Captain Harper.'

'Sergeant Patterson.' She acknowledged Patto and watched him leave. Her attention turned to Nate the second they were alone.

'Well?' She stood from where she'd been crouching, her arms folded across her chest, eyebrows raised. 'What did he tell you? And don't give me any bullshit about it being nothing, *Wolfman.'*

Chapter 10

Beth didn't know whether to be totally pissed off or terrified by the way Calloway reacted to Patterson's visit. His face had morphed from streaked with angry red smears to white as a sheet within seconds, and cycled like that for the duration of their conversation.

'Well?' What did he say?' she repeated, letting the Wolfman thing go. As much as she wanted to know the reason for the moniker, and why it was important enough for him to have a wolf tattooed on his chest, it didn't matter right now. But the men's discussion did. 'I can order you to tell me, Sergeant.'

As soon as the words left her mouth she regretted it. *You fool.* She'd asked him to call her by her name for god's sake, and now she sounded like one of those rank-pulling self-serving wankers she hated. The look on his face told her he thought much the same.

'He said it'd be better if you went back to the hospital, Captain. As soon as possible.' His voice was toneless, cold, but his eyes blazed like he was looking through the windows of hell.

'What?' Every muscle in her body tensed, her worries about what Calloway thought of what she'd just said all but disappearing. 'Why?'

'Intel from the last few hours indicates the mission's more complicated than we realised, and the threat to you greater than anticipated.' His words still clipped, were warmer than his last. *Thank God.* 'He recommended we don't expose you any further. And I agree.' She felt her cheeks flush again, her heart rate ratchet up triple time.

In the last hour, she'd experienced so many emotions she'd struggled to control, something that never happened to her. She felt like she'd ridden a damn roller-coaster ten times in a row. Thank god she'd reigned in that ridiculous flirt-fest before she'd done something rash and ruined her entire career. And his. Time to accept this for what it was, a pressure cooker of extreme stress, emotions and unusual circumstances. People weren't themselves. *You're definitely not.* She had to keep her head, not overreact to something like stupid physical attraction. She needed to be professional, stay focused every minute. Without fail. *Like always.*

'So, I'll arrange for you to return to base today, Captain,' he finished.

It took a minute for everything he'd just said to sink in. Used to the possibility of threats, bouts of heightened danger, and all the other risks associated with the job, she'd never really had much cause for serious concern. Medical personnel were relatively protected, so she didn't ever really have to make many decisions that directly affected her own mortality. But now that she did have to, she knew her answer straight up.

'Sergeant Calloway, the risks for this mission were assessed and outlined for me, in detail, before we left. Like you, I was briefed on the potential outcomes I might face, and I accepted them, am prepared for them, even if they've changed. The one constant here, is nothing stays the same, I know that.' She exhaled loudly. 'I finish what I start, Sergeant Calloway. I told you I'd escort you, and I will. So please, if you will, tell me what I need to know so I'm prepared. And I'd really appreciate the full story this time, Sergeant.'

The thin line of his lips, his eyes searching the ground, avoiding her face, set her nerves further on edge. He looked like he was working out a calculated response, deciding what to tell her. *Better be the damn truth.*

'Looks like there's a fucking turncoat in our camp,' he spat out.

'Oh god,' she said, sucking back the gasp in her throat. She'd asked for the facts, and he'd delivered them. Plain. Simple. Shocking.

Beth sunk down on her haunches, used the wall for support. 'How long have they known?'

'Not long.'

'Do they have an idea on who?'

'Not that Patto said.'

She felt sick. She'd heard whispers round camp that there were insiders who made crimes as old as the dark ages possible. Theft, drugs, weapons, prostitution

... anything that fed greed and power, and prayed on the vulnerable, but she hadn't ever seen evidence of it herself, and had really hoped a lot of the speculation wasn't true, well at least not true of anyone she knew.

'So you can understand why we don't think it's a good idea you keep going. I'll arrange for someone to come and get you, take you back. I—'

'Just hold on a minute.' She was on her feet. 'You can't go anywhere without me. The army won't let you, it's the condition that must be met for you to stay here. So, does that mean you'll be heading back with me too then?'

'No.' His answer firm, held no hesitation. He'd insisted all along that he wouldn't go back in anything but a body bag, and right now, the rigidity in his body, the clench of his jaw; she didn't doubt his commitment to that promise. Likewise, he shouldn't doubt hers.

'I didn't join the Australian Army because the job assured my absolute safety, Sergeant Calloway. This, what I do, protecting, serving and saving lives, it's what I took an oath to do, one that I believe in. Just like you. So I'm sorry, regardless of what you say, I will continue on unless ordered otherwise by our superiors.'

A war of emotion raged across his face. She forced herself to stand still, not move, not speak. Seconds inched by. Finally, he sucked in a deep breath, his head dipping in a slight nod.

'Well then, Captain,' he said, 'I suggest you slip into your full battle rattle before debrief, because if you're coming, you're no damn good to me dead.'

'You ever been outside the wire, Doctor Harper?' said the Commander.

'No, sir, but I'm—'

'You ever fired a weapon outside of training?'

'No, sir.' She so wanted to mention she had a near perfect shooting score for every single one of her yearly assessments.

'Know anything about the terrain, the conditions we're about to enter? The protocols that keep us alive out here?'

'Actually, I do, sir,' she said.

Well aware she hadn't won any gold stars with Commander Angelis yet, she rattled off sound answers to the barrage of questions he continued to fire at her, quoting verbatim the strategy and theory behind each of the safety protocols the unit regularly used. The Commander didn't hide his surprise at her indepth knowledge and understanding of their practices.

'Well, you're a surprise package aren't you, Doctor?'

'I like to be prepared, sir.'

Beth silently sent out a thank you to her father for instilling the Boy Scout mentality in her at a young age. Hours of study and self-testing during down time on nightshift assured she hadn't failed her first real field test.

The Commander and others in authority outlined the mission in overview. Sergeant Patterson and one other had already gone, tasked with scoping out the track ahead. The other specifics pertaining to the next three hours were mapped out, discussed, collaborated over and the final detail agreed on.

'Well, we're as good as we're going to get on this, Doc. Hope you know your shit from clay when it matters,' said the Commander dismissing her then barking out the final orders to the team.

Nate hadn't said a word to her during the entire briefing, and he was still silent while they made their final preparations.

'I didn't know you could be so quiet,' she said, shoving her hand in her pocket, her fingers closing around Nate's small blue stone. She'd run back to grab it when she'd left base, but hadn't yet found the right moment to return it to him.

'A lot to think about. Told you I like my space.'

'Fair enough,' she said, dropping the stone in her pocket, now wasn't the time to give it back either, and she liked the little piece of support its properties offered, and if she was honest, something about the fact it'd been close to his body too made it even more important. Grunting as she wriggled her shoulders under the twenty-five kilos of Kevlar body armour, Beth returned her focus to her task, away from thoughts about his body.

The full *battle rattle* as Nate had called it, was definitely giving her muscles a run for their money. 'You know,' she said, 'I have to say, I've never seen or heard of this situation before, have you?' Beth didn't look at Sergeant Calloway until the last word left her mouth.

'Which part of the situation are you referring to?' he said, continuing to clip and zip his protection gear in rhythmic movements.

'This.' She waved her hand back and forth between them. 'The you and me, patient-doctor-outside-the-wirething.'

He pulled off his hat, shoved a hand through his hair. 'Nope, I haven't. It's why I want you to go back.' He stepped in closer to her. 'I was selfish. I reckon they gave me this—you—as an option because they never believed it'd come off. And now it's all gone too far. Please, Doc, I really want you to reconsider this.'

She fought against reaching out to him. It seemed as natural as breathing right now. Instead, she forced out words. 'Nate,' she whispered, swallowing hard, 'can I call you that?'

He shrugged, holding her gaze long enough to make her hold her breath. 'Suit yourself,' he answered her with words barely louder than her own.

She exhaled on a shudder. 'Regardless of those in authority who okayed this, and regardless of whatever else does or doesn't happen, I made the decision to do this, Nate, to be here with you, all the way. And I'm good with that. Okay?'

He moved even closer to her. So close, that with barely a movement, her body would be up against his. The hammer in her chest, the burn in her belly, was back. His body heat, his woodsy scent completely filled her senses.

'Whatever happens—' he brushed his thumb the length of her cheek, '—I won't let anything happen to you.'

'I know.' She grasped his arm, his hand still on her face. 'I trust you. Or I wouldn't stay here.'

The crunch of gravel behind them broke the connection, both of them jumping back a step.

'Eight minutes. Moving out in eight minutes.' The soldier continued past them, shouting his count down to the unit.

Nate stepped even further away from her, the moment lost. She pushed down the wave of disappointment, instead watching silently while he finished checking the appointments on his uniform until finally he hoisted his pack onto his back. Prepped. Done. His gaze travelled over her face, lingered on her lips, his body as still as hers. 'You ready?'

'Yes.' She nodded once.

Was she?

The tremor in her legs had more to do with the tide of emotion ripping through her than the fact she was about to head out into god knew what.

'It's gonna get cold quick out there. Keep your gloves on, your feet dry.'

She nodded. 'Okay.' Survival 101 out here.

He closed the distance between them. 'Here.' He hauled her pack from the ground, helped her into it. He fine-tuned her straps, checked the rest of her clothes, his breath a whisper on her cheek, his fingers brushing the sensitive skin at the back of her neck. His hand grazed her shoulder, her ribs, as he adjusted her appointments, her remaining equipment, and surveyed her from head to foot, scanning through a visual tick list. One that missed looking into her eyes until the last moment.

'Alright,' he said, 'you're good to go. Let's do this.' His gaze locked with hers.

She desperately wanted to say something, do something, but what?

'Nate...'

'Move out. We're moving out.' It was the solider who'd walked past them.

The moment shattered, Nate snapped to attention, serious. Focused.

'Stay close,' he said, his lips brushing her ear as he passed her.

Adrenaline surged through Beth's body. 'I will.'

Nate walked ahead of her along the narrow track, determined and sure, even though his limp seemed more pronounced than when they'd left, his breath sharper. Twenty minutes in, he'd tripped. Only stumbled, but wasn't quick enough to hide his pain from the Commander who'd been behind them, and moved up the track to meet him immediately.

'Calloway, are you a liability, Sergeant? We've got three hours until our first rest point, you going to make that, son?'

'Yes, sir, I'm good to go. Just a stumble, sir.'

The Commander turned to her.

'Doctor Harper, what's your professional opinion? Is this man well enough to continue? Sure as shit doesn't look like it to me.'

She glanced at Nate's face, his desperation palpable.

'Sergeant Calloway's the best judge of his ability, Commander. He knows his limitations, his capabilities, and wouldn't compromise the rest of us. From my observations, I'm happy to support his decision. If he says he can go on, he can go on.'

It was closer to a lie than the truth.

Nate's shoulders sagged, he nodded his thanks to her. It was the smallest of movements, but she caught it.

She was concerned. They'd only been moving for just over an hour and already he showed signs of fatigue. He'd refused the extra pain meds she recommended. She wondered how much longer his stamina would hold out. His symptoms weren't enough to call it quits yet, but by the way he looked, the colour dropping from his face by the minute, she doubted it'd be long.

She felt like her insides were wrapped around a corkscrew, and hoped to hell she hadn't just risked all their lives by telling the first and last *almost* lie of her career.

Chapter 11

He might as well have a vice clamped around his chest, they'd only been at it for two hours and Nate could hardly breathe. Thank Christ they'd stopped for water and to take a piss. And thank Christ she'd backed him with the Commander.

Beth had disappeared behind a rock shelf to take care of business, and was now seated beside him, her face strained, forming a frown.

'How're you doing?'

'I'm fine,' he said, glancing over her shoulder into the distance, trying for casual. The Commander was an astute bastard, he was already onto Nate's situation, but right now, he didn't want to give the bloke anything extra to sure up that opinion.

'Take these,' she said.

'What is it?'

'Pain relief. I can see you need it.'

No point being a fool. He swallowed the pills, gulped some water and dragged in some deeper breaths to check out what his lung did. Seemed okay, but he had to admit he was struggling. The increasing altitude, although slight, wasn't bloody helping.

'You're far from fine.' She leant in close to him, her sugar and spice scent invading his nostrils. *God she smelt good.* 'Don't you dare lie to me, Calloway.' Her voice was low but fierce. 'I won't be proved the fool who risked five lives, six including yours, because I stupidly agreed to let you play the hero.'

His breath whooshed out of his lips loudly. 'I know, and I appreciate what you did, Doc, and you weren't wrong in what you said.' She did have a point though. The fact that everyone's safety was affected by the status of his health mattered, and he hated the idea that he'd soon be the person stunting their progress. He'd never been that guy, and wasn't going to start now.

His hands curled into fists, his words short and sharp. 'The bigger burn on my leg hurts, breathing's a bit shallow, and there's some pressure behind my eyes, but nothing I can't handle at the moment.' He flexed his hands open, perched them on his hips and looked at her. 'Can't you just sort it out? Can't I just take something?'

'When did the pressure behind your eyes start?' She ignored his other questions, her eyes assessing his body, his face.

'About ten minutes ago. When we hit the incline. Buzz started up in my bloody ear again too.'

She pulled off her glove, slid her warm fingers inside his, and along his wrist, stopping at his pulse point.

'Should I be worried?' he said. There wasn't time for this shit, but passing out on a mountainside wasn't an option, and it wouldn't get Beth back to base safely either. Didn't matter what she said, he'd already decided to get her back as soon as he could. He needed her safe. He couldn't forgive himself if she was hurt because he'd been a stubborn arse.

'I don't know yet,' she said, still concentrating on his pulse. She signalled the Commander to come over to them.

'What the hell are you doing? Don't—'

She ignored his words, his warning glare. 'Remember, my job is to keep you alive,' she hissed.

Their senior officer approached.

'Sir, how far until the incline of this path peaks?' Beth asked. She hadn't moved her fingers, and it felt like they were burning holes into his skin. He edged his arm towards his torso, and she dropped her hand lower, her palm now resting over the back of his hand. She held on, tight.

'It's about another four kilometres or so, and then we start on the second incline.' The Commander frowned, gave Nate the once over. 'Is there a problem, Sergeant?'

'No, sir.' He ripped his arm out of Beth's grip. 'No, sir, there isn't.'

The older man stared at him, tapping his fingers on the rock ledge. Nate's gut told him he wasn't going to like whatever he said next.

'I'm sorry, son, I've gotta call it. You're just not fit enough to be here. I know this is gonna be hard to accept, but I'm ordering you back to base, Sergeant.'

'But, sir—' Nate was on his feet and so was Beth, '—I have to do this, be here. I—'

'I've given my orders, Sergeant.' With the muscle in his jaw working overtime, the Commander turned and walked three paces away from them.

'Take her,' Nate shouted, pointing at Beth, his urgent direction stopping the Commander in his tracks. 'Send Doctor Harper back to base. It's not right she's here, amongst all this. But I belong here. I'll sign whatever you want absolving anyone, the army, whoever, of responsibility. Whatever it takes.' He saluted the Commander. 'With respect, sir, I'm not leaving. If I drop, just leave me, but please don't tell me I can't find my dog, my men. Sir.'

Nate knew that what he was asking was impossible, broke every rule, crossed every line. But there was no other road for him. The buzzing in his ear sounded like a hive of drone bees had set up camp. His gut had seized and his legs were shaking, he felt like he was suffocating. He recruited every tactic he'd ever learned on how to show nothing. Stay upright. Stay strong.

The Commander scrubbed his hand down his face, his eyes reflecting his deep concern. Commander Angelis was a good man. Nate had never served alongside him, but everyone knew his name. The bloke was well respected, and now he'd put this good man in a position no soldier ever should.

If the shoe were on the other foot, he'd be torn up about making the call too. Orders, protocol, they saved lives, made sure chaos didn't reign. But there were the unspoken rules, the code of brotherhood they all laid down their lives for. One that was ingrained in every cell of his body, Angelis' too, he was sure of it.

We carry our wounded, bury our dead.

The Commander flickered his index finger at Nate, tilted his chin upward. Nate moved towards him. The two other soldiers at the Commander's side dropped back, the third, a Lieutenant Banders, didn't move. Nate eyeballed the bloke. Didn't like him. He had the look of a guy on the edge.

'Give us a minute, Lieutenant.' Angelis made it clear what happened next wasn't anyone else's business until he said it was. Banders repositioned slowly, clearly pissed at being ordered to move aside.

Nate willed his legs to walk, made out that he was in no hurry, when really, he was shit-scared he'd face plant into the dirt any second. He flicked a look at Beth, her expression a mix of anger and concern. He doubted she'd ever thank him for insisting a decision be made about her without her say-so, but he couldn't be worried about her feelings. She'd just announced her job was to keep him alive. Well, her safety was his responsibility, not her hurt feelings. It was likely he'd never see her again after this anyway, whether he survived out here or not. He pressed a fist into his stomach. Why the hell did it feel like a frigging rock crusher had taken up residence in his gut?

'Thanks for your help, Captain Harper,' he said, 'and I—'

The zing barely registered as the bullet grazed his cheek. 'Get down, get down.' Nate's shouts echoed with simultaneous orders from the Commander.

Nate launched his body at Beth, dragging them both to the ground; he hauled her up beside him, sliding them both behind the closest boulder.

'What the hell—?' Her voice was strong, but only loud enough for his ears, and she was pale as a goddamn ghost.

'Keep down. Don't talk.' Shoving her hard up against the rock face, he shielded her with his legs, positioned his weapon. He eyed what he could see in the scope, all senses alert, ready. Something to be said for endless hours of repetitious training.

Listening for orders, and struggling to hear through the buzz in his ear, he focused on searching for movement. It'd gone quiet. Neither side willing to give up their position. The initial jolt of adrenaline was fast wearing off, and he was losing his edge, the pain in his ribs strangling his gut, his vision blurring.

Not now. Don't let me drop now. Please, just give me five.

He didn't know who he was begging to silently, but he hoped to fuck they were listening.

The warmth of her curled in a ball against him, made his heart smack against his ribs, the pain in the rest of his body all but gone for a moment. He couldn't let her get hurt. *Christ, she should never have been here.* If it killed him, he'd get her out of here.

A shadow invaded his periphery, he swung around, but it was too late. He followed her scream into unconsciousness.

Chapter 12

'Yes, sir, we have her.'

Nate listened to the male speaking, kept his eyes closed, wasn't sure he could actually open them anyway. Every muscle in his body felt like a fifty kilo weight was attached to it. He kept his breath regulated, worked at appearing like he was still out cold.

'No, not yet, sir. We'll deal with him soon, it's still too light.'

What the hell? Was that Banders' voice? He'd only heard the jerk speak twice, but he was almost certain it was the oversized bastard he was hearing. Patto's words echoed through his mind. ' ...One of our own.' *Jesus.*

'And, sir, there's been a complication.' There was a hitch in Banders' throat before more words piled rapid fire out of the bastard's lips. 'It's Doctor Harper, she's sustained an injury during the extraction, sir.'

Fuck. Where the hell's Beth? Extraction? And who the fuck is Banders talking to?

Nate fought against every muscle in his body, his overwhelming instinct to launch up and make the prick talk. But he had no idea where he was, more importantly, where Beth was, and how many others he'd be up against the minute there was sound of a ruckus. What he did know is if he made one mistake they'd be dead, and he sure as hell didn't want Beth as collateral damage.

He ignored the pulsing pain in every part of his damn body, and took inventory from head to toe. *Shit.* Hands and feet tied, and he was gagged. Aside from that, he felt pretty intact.

Focused, he ignored his twitching muscles and tuned back in to Banders' phone conversation, trying to make sense of the sounds from the male at the other end. He needed to know what they were planning next.

'It's her ankle, sir, she says it's broken,' said Banders.

Nate's gut clenched. Beth was somewhere, hurt and in pain, because of him.

There was more agro from the male shouting down the phone at Banders. Something in the bastard's tone was familiar, but he couldn't place it.

'Yes, sir. Consider it taken care of, sir.'

Nate heard movement, fabric rustling. Banders must have disconnected the call, pocketed the phone.

'And you can suck my cock, you prick.' Banders' words dripping with hatred filled the silence.

Nate tried to place the voice he'd heard snatches of, his concentration interrupted by Banders' next comment.

'As for you, Captain Harper, seems I've scored myself a wanted woman.' He sniggered, his words full of menace. 'If I'd known you were this pretty, I woulda asked for more cash for my trouble.' Banders' footsteps moved away from Nate, crunching through what sounded like rubble. 'Think I'll take my bonus *before* I deliver you to him.'

A woman's whimper—*Beth*—made Nate's eyes snap open.

Banders, on the opposite side of the room was bent over her, wiping his slimy fat finger down her cheek. She was gagged too, her hands behind her back. She leant against the wall, one leg tucked beneath her, the other stretched out, her ankle the size of a grenade on steroids.

'I'm going out to take a leak, check that no smart-arse has followed us,' said Banders. 'When I'm back, how 'bout you and I have a bit of fun, hey?'

Nate bit back the roar burning his throat as Banders gripped Beth's hair and wrenched her head backwards, forcing her to look at him. He licked her face from chin to temple.

She didn't make a sound, just stared into the fucker's eyes, her nostrils flaring in and out.

'Tough girl, hey? I reckon you'll like it a bit rough then, hey, darlin'? Well, I can help you with that.' He slapped her face.

Nate wanted to smash the man's skull through the wall.

Banders straightened, flexed his knuckles like he was lining up to punch Beth, at the last second punched his fist into his opposite palm instead. Nate forced his eyes back to almost closed. If the bastard moved to punch her, it'd be the last fucking thing he ever did. But he couldn't help her dead, and he had no doubt Banders would check if he was conscious before he left them alone. No matter what Nate wanted to do, he had to play this smart.

As expected, the bastard left Beth and walked over to him, landed his boot into one shin then the other with equal intensity. And waited, rubble moving as he shuffled his feet. Nate forced every cell in his body to focus on living, staying immobile, alive and to block the rage eating him inside out, the pain receptors screaming their abuse through his system. Worried he'd pass out, he recruited every ounce of mind control he had. It'd worked as a kid, taken him places he needed to go when shit got bad. It'd work now. Had to.

Banders sniffed loudly before moving away. Nate panicked, worried he'd not be able to swallow the roar of pain clawing at his throat. Thank Christ the stupid bastard didn't get down and feel his heart rate, or he'd be a dead man right now.

'Don't try anything cute, sweetie, or your boyfriend over there'll get a bullet. And you can be the one to give it to him. Got it?'

Nate didn't hear any noise from Beth, but she must have nodded, because Banders's footsteps faded out.

Drenched in sweat, the agony radiating from his shins was almost unbearable, but Nate knew he had less than a few minutes to get her out of here. Then somehow, he'd get back and drop the fucker.

He snapped his eyes open and looked straight at Beth, her gaze meeting his in an instant. She looked scared, but not terrified. Good. He could work with that.

She'd already started bunny hopping her backside towards him. *Smart girl.* He clenched his gut and rocked forward. The whole room spun on its axis once he was upright. Shaking his head, trying to focus, Nate realised she was already in front of him frantically trying to shake something loose from the breast pocket of her jacket. Angling closer to him, she thrust her chest upward to him, glancing at his mouth and then over her shoulder to the door, before doing the same action again.

His pulse was thundering hard through his ears, he couldn't make out what she was trying to say behind her gag. And then he saw it, a sliver of metal poking out of the corner of her pocket. The scalpel. He'd razzed her on it before, but Jesus, now he could bloody kiss her for it. *God, could he kiss her.*

Angling his head forward, he used his chin to try to jag the flap of her pocket upward, but he moved too fast, a searing spasm in his back jolting him sideways. He righted himself, and tried again. She pressed herself into him, this time he paused, resting his chin on the underside of the flap, sliding it upwards against her breast with his chin.

Sheathed in a sterile plastic cover, the blade glinted in the dying light, tormenting them both. Right there, but useless to them, unless they could somehow shake it free. They both scanned the room frantically, each of them desperate for a miracle.

Her eyes came back to look into his, their amber depths swirling with fear. Then, they widened, sparking with renewed light. She urged him back to her pocket, motioning a circular movement with her head. She repeated it, frantic energy making her bounce up and down on the ground. Trying to read her eyes, decipher her gagged words, anything that told him what she was doing, he watched her, concentrated, but just couldn't get it. She kept repeating the move. *Work it out, Calloway, for fuck's sake.*

He hadn't figured it out, but needed to take action. Any action. Bending forward again, he tried to angle his head so the scalpel would slide between his skin and the fabric of his gag.

It took three attempts, but he did it, the scalpel firmly lodged between the gag and his cheek. The relief in her eyes made him realise that's where she'd been going with her actions too. Luckily, she was a step ahead of him, scooting around, so her back was facing him. She winced twice. Her ankle would be giving her hell, but she just kept moving. She lifted her hands upward, and as far back from her body as she could, palms upturned.

No time to consider what might happen if the blade landed in her palm the wrong way, he jerked his head downwards, and repeated the action—a single, forceful movement, until the scalpel slowly shimmied downward, finally slipping out between the material and his cheek. It dropped, missed her hands, hit the floor.

She scrambled around with her fingers and manoeuvred it into her hands, the binds slowing down her every movement.

He watched her, useless, as she manipulated the instrument, feeling for the refined pointed end and angling it for action. She worked at pulling down the plastic covering one millimetre at a time. He wanted to help her, speed this up, but there was nothing he could do, yet.

She freed the blade and flipped the tip towards her back, methodically using her fingers to angle it into the centre of the cable ties around her wrists.

Her fingers trembled, her entire body was shaking but she kept going. She told him she finished what she started, and watching her now, he didn't doubt it.

Footsteps crunching towards them rendered them both motionless. Her fingers closed around the metal, the grip turning her knuckles white.

This was a woman who wouldn't go down without a fight.

And neither would he.

Chapter 13

Long shadows flickered at the entryway. She glanced back at Nate. His body upright, taut and strong, he faced the door. He didn't look at her, kept his eyes forward. The scalpel wedged in her trembling hand the only thing anchoring her to reality. *I'm not dying here. I'm not.*

A figure loomed large at the entry, the nose of a rifle appeared, entering slow, steady. She held her breath. A man's arm, a uniform she recognised. Australian. *Banders.*

Beth gasped behind the gag, tears streaming freely down her cheeks. 'Oh god.' It wasn't him. It wasn't that monster Banders. Sergeant Patterson and another soldier she'd never seen emerged into the light and strode into the room.

'Jesus, Wolfman, not on your game today are ya, mate?' said Sergeant Patterson as he made quick work of Nate's restraints and hauled him to his feet. The other guy did the same for her, before gently easing her up and onto her good ankle, his hands warm and strong around her shoulders.

'Lieutenant Dale Betts, ma'am. Can you walk?' he asked gently.

'Thank you, Lieutenant. Yes, I think so. It's not broken. Just badly sprained,' she said, her voice sounding like she'd eaten sandpaper. She'd told that hideous Banders it was broken, hoping it would buy them some time. Or something. Anything. 'My boot. It's over there.' She pointed to the furthest wall, swiping at her wet cheeks. 'He threw it when he assessed my ankle.'

Sergeant Betts retrieved the boot, loosened the laces. 'I reckon it'll be a while before you can get it on again,' he said.

'I have to try,' said Beth, hoping like hell she could somehow get her foot back into it. 'There's no way a bare foot's going to cut it out here.'

'Betsy? Jesus, what the hell are you doing here?' said Nate with a wary smile. He gripped Sergeant Betts' hand in a firm shake. The move quickly morphed into an embrace, and mutual slaps on the back. 'Thought you'd gone home for good last time?'

'Nah, still had shit to do. Job's not done till it's done, you know?' said Betsy.

Beth felt an undercurrent shimmer between the two men.

'Yeah, I do know,' said Nate. His eyes flickered between the two men before landing on Beth. 'Captain Harper, can you walk on that ankle at all? Are you hurt anywhere else?' said Nate, bracing himself against Sergeant Patterson for a moment, his face creased with pain, his skin a worrying shade of grey.

She recognised his formality for the gesture it was, and understood the implication in the latter part of his question. 'I'll be able to move, Sergeant. Just need to avoid weight baring wherever I can.' She didn't take her eyes from his face, sucked in a breath. 'And no, nothing else is damaged.'

Nate's shoulders sagged. It was slight but she saw it. His hands clenched into fists, his eyes burning into hers, flickered with rage. 'Fucking Banders.' The pulse in his temple pounded against his skin. She resisted reaching out to him, pulling him to her, sagging into his chest, the only place she might feel remotely safe.

'Let's get moving.' She broke their connection. A part of her wanted to drop to the ground and curl into a ball, even with Sergeants Patterson and Betts here she was scared. More than scared. But there wasn't time to give into that rubbish, and it didn't get them any closer to a safe place, or locating Finnegan and the men. But more than that, she needed Nate focused on moving, on breathing, on living. Not concentrating on her, or seeking revenge on her behalf. So right this second, even remotely showing just how close to the edge she was, wasn't an option.

Sergeant Betts made his way back to her, wrapped his arm around her waist so she could lean into him and hop.

'I'll help her,' growled Nate.

No-one moved.

'Save your energy, you'll need it,' said Beth, breaking the silence. 'Sergeant Betts, let's go.'

At the risk of humiliating the proud soldier in front of her by clearly issuing him an order to leave her alone, she had to do it. She just couldn't have him touch her, be any closer to her. She'd lose it right here in front of all of them. He was the only piece of hope she had right now, and needed him at arm's length, for all their sakes. So, before Nate could respond, and without looking at him again, she moved towards the exit. 'How far is it to where we're going?' she asked Sergeant Betts, hoping no-one heard the quiver in her voice.

'Ah, it's about 3k's off track,' Sergeant Betts replied, his hesitation in following her only a fraction of a second. 'We're at the base of the mountain, so we have a few options. Patto and I did a bit of recon earlier,' he said, helping her shuffle towards the bunker's exit. 'Got a couple of places we can hole up till we know what's what and get you where you need to be. Both of you.'

'How'd you find us?' Nate asked, leaning heavily on Sergeant Patterson who was all but dragging him towards the door. 'Where's Angelis? The rest of the unit?'

'No time to tell you that shit now,' said Patto. 'That bastard Banders will have people waiting for him to report in. Won't be long before they realise he's a no show.'

Sergeant Patterson's tone made it clear to Beth that Lieutenant Banders was unlikely to show up near them any time soon, and possibly, not ever again. She shivered despite the warmth of Sergeant Betts body beside her. She glanced across at Nate, but he was focused on the road ahead of them, its outline barely visible in the fading dusk light. She wondered what he made of Sergeant Patterson's comment, or whether none of this was news to him. Beth felt like she was an extra in someone else's nightmare. All she could do now was wait to see how the next scene played out, and hope Nate would guide her through it.

The four of them advanced out, pressed their bodies against the stony rock face directly adjacent to the tomb they'd just left. The melodious invitation for the final *azan,* the evening call to prayer, drifted towards them on the sharpening breeze, the peaceful sound mingling with the twitters and brays of the local cattle, the birds, settling in for the evening. Incongruous with the crushing fear pounding against her ribs, the normalcy of the everyday sounds meant that they couldn't be far from a village. But which one, and were they hostile, or peaceful?

Her questions had to wait.

She didn't move a muscle, just focused on Sergeant Betts, who was forward of her, as he scoped the landscape ahead of them. Nate was behind her, the length of his body pressed into her side, and Sergeant Patterson behind Nate.

Nate turned his head, his lips millimetres from her ear. The heat of his breath made the chilled skin on the side of her face tingle. 'I will get you out,' he whispered. 'I promise.' The urgency in his voice made the ache in Beth's belly tighten. She swallowed the sob crowding her throat. He slid his arm sideways, the movement slight, but enough that he could extend his hand, touch hers. She immediately entwined her fingers with his, didn't care who saw her. He squeezed her hand. And through their gloves, she felt him. Felt his strength, his promise.

'Time to go,' Betsy whispered. He silently motioned the actions indicating the next movements to the group. They'd cross the width of the road just ahead, and take cover amongst the cluster of foliage and trees just beyond the roadside. 'Okay, on my signal, climb aboard,' Sergeant Betts said quietly to her, thumbing over his shoulder towards his back. 'Best I carry you, speed's the top priority here.'

Nate grabbed Beth's arm. 'I'll take you. I'll get you over the road, into the scrub.' His harsh whisper crackled with tension. 'Betsy can help you on from there.'

'I think it's best I take her, mate,' said Sergeant Betts. 'It'll give us the best shot, Wolfman. You gotta get yourself across, Patto's got our backs. I've got your doc.'

Nate's hand stayed wrapped around her forearm.

'I've got her covered, man, we gotta move,' said Sergeant Betts.

Nate's eyes didn't waver from hers.

'He's right,' whispered Beth. 'And I've got nothing to work with if you tear open any of your wounds. You'll slow us all down.' Again, she had to force him to concentrate on the bigger picture, and if she needed to puncture his pride to make it happen, then so be it.

Precious fractions of seconds dragged by until Nate finally dropped his grip on her, and stepped back. 'You get her there, Betsy,' he said. He tapped two fingers over his heart, and in a loud whisper said, 'Alright, let's do this.'

Beth launched up off her feet and onto Betsy's back. She bit her lip to stop from crying out, the sharp, stabbing pain in her ankle sucking the breath out of her. Gasping, she held on for her life as Sergeant Betts sprinted forward into the darkness ahead.

Waking with a start, the dimness disorienting, Beth relaxed slightly when her eyes focused on Nate across from her in a makeshift bed, then Sergeant Patterson just beyond them, standing sentry at the door. It'd taken them more than an hour to reach the remnants of what was once a farmhouse, and now might be better described as a hastily constructed shed. Inside, there were a couple of stools, three pallets covered in hay, a wooden bucket and a kerosene lamp, which

Sergeant Betts had lit as soon as they'd all made it inside. The men had previously stashed a hemp bag filled with water canteens, some apples and a blanket.

Beth had been awake for almost thirty hours by the time she'd thoroughly checked Nate, doing what she could for his damaged wounds without her supplies. He'd eventually agreed to take the pain meds that were somehow still in her pocket, and after a decent fight, his mind and body finally giving in to his fatigue, he'd dropped asleep.

She'd immersed her ankle on and off in the icy water Sergeant Betts brought to her from the property's well, and then strapped it as best she could before squeezing it back into her boot. It took every ounce of strength she had not to scream as she pulled the unforgiving leather over her swollen flesh.

'I didn't think you'd get that on,' Sergeant Betts said, watching her from the adjacent corner, his face grim in the flickering lamplight.

'You and me both,' said Beth, her breath shooting out in white puffs through gritted teeth. It'd taken at least five minutes to get her panting under control as she tried to ignore the pulsing agony radiating from her ankle. All she needed to do now was focus, work her mind around the expected ache, compartmentalise it, and deal with it like any other problem to solve.

'What do you need to sort him out for the next forty-eight hours?' said Sergeant Betts, jabbing his thumb towards Nate, cutting through her concentration.

It'd taken her a second to cotton on to what he was referencing. 'Do you mean medical supplies?' she asked.

'Yeah. I have some contacts. Might be able to arrange something.'

'One of the reasons I brought him along for the ride,' Sergeant Patterson had said, his up until now silent, serious form stepping out of his post at the only doorway.

'Any limits on what you can access?' she'd asked.

'Maybe. Just tell me what your wish list is, I'll see if Santa's in.' Sergeant Betts had grinned, but the tension around his eyes hadn't eased. He pulled out a tiny pencil used near to the nub, and a small notebook.

Beth hesitated, glancing between the men. But in less than a minute, she'd run through what she needed, Sergeant Betts systematically writing it all down. She hadn't asked any more questions, because right then, she'd wanted solutions, needed action, not more damn questions. Every protocol, every rule she'd ever abided on the job, didn't apply here. Best she get onboard with what did, and do whatever she could to get Nate the help he needed. Deal with the consequences later. If they made it to later.

'Let me check over what you've written,' she'd said, holding out her hand to Sergeant Betts. 'I want to make sure I haven't forgotten anything if you're going to all this trouble.'

Glancing over the paper, she said, 'You've got pretty nice writing for a fella.' Sergeant Betts' penmanship was even, neat and an ornate kind of cursive. Unusual for a bloke.

'One of my many talents, Captain,' he replied with a smirk, a dancing dimple in his right cheek making him seem younger than his years.

She'd grinned despite herself, despite the tension surrounding all of them, and handed the list back to him. 'Well, man of many talents, this will see us through the next day or so. But, I'd really like to get him somewhere sterile and better equipped as soon as we can.' She'd directed her comment at Sergeant Patterson too. He hadn't said anything, but Sergeant Betts had nodded. She slid backwards across the straw covered crate, the lightness of the moment before gone, her belly back to clenched tight. 'Can you give me anything at all about what happens next?'

'No, not really, not yet. I'm sorry. I really am,' said Sergeant Betts. 'Why don't you try and sleep? We'll watch him for a bit.'

Dale Betts, Betsy to his mates, didn't say much. But she'd immediately liked him. His green eyes, kind, warm, didn't set off any internal alarm bells. And even though she'd needed more info from them, she was utterly exhausted. So, feeling as safe is it got, and close to delirious, Beth had let it go, pulled the scratchy horse blanket over her shoulder, and couldn't remember another thing until now.

'How long have I been out?' she said, sitting up, clenching her teeth. It was so damn cold here.

Sergeant Patterson turned to face her. 'Just over five hours,' he said. 'It's 0130 hours.' He nodded towards Nate. 'Reckon he'll need a couple more though.'

She glanced across at Nate again. 'Yes, he needs so much more than sleep,' she said, more to herself than Sergeant Patterson.

'Where's Sergeant Betts?'

'Bit of recon down the hill,' Patterson replied. 'Some chitchat with the villagers, see if anyone's willing to talk while he sorts the medical gear you requested.' He glanced sideways at her, then back at the door, the muscle in his cheek flexing as if he was chewing gum. He obviously had something more to say. And given how much sweat was dripping from his face, and the fact that he stood with a hunch, his fist pressed into his belly, he obviously wasn't well.

'Are you feeling alright?' she said, stifling the urge to ask how long it'd be before Sergeant Betts returned, and where on earth was he garnering medical supplies from *down the hill* in the middle of the night?

'I'm fine. It's him I'm worried about,' he said, pacing in the doorway. 'Is he cactus?' he blurted out, staring straight ahead, his hands fidgeting with his weapon. 'I mean, if we don't get him to a hospital soon, is he screwed?'

Her heart squeezed for the man in front of her. Clearly the three of them had some decent history together. 'He'll be okay for a bit longer,' she said with such force, she had to clear her throat to continue. 'He needs medical attention as soon as we can get it, but I can deal with whatever happens during the next twelve hours, if Sergeant Betts can get what I asked for, or something close to it.'

The intensity of her answer was just as much for her benefit as his. She was worried, really worried. If Nate suffered another lung collapse or infection took hold in the burns still healing, he'd be in serious strife. He'd done pretty well till now given the circumstances, but she really didn't want to find out what his limits were.

Sergeant Patterson's gaze bored into her. 'Well, you go your hardest, Doc, he'll do the rest. He's a tough bastard.' He swallowed loudly. 'He saved my life, Betsy's too. We owe him.'

'I will,' she said. Her heart ached even more. It'd be nice to have that. People—a person—who had your back here, no matter what, and not just because they had to. She thought she'd had that in Lawson, but now she wasn't so sure.

Beth blinked back the tears burning the backs of her eyes, and bit back the questions about Nate burning her tongue. How long ago did he save these two men? Where? What happened? But it didn't really matter what she wanted to know, it was actually none of her business, and at the end of the day, she was nothing more to Nate, to any of them, than a means to an end, no matter what chemistry she felt with him. She shouldn't kid herself she was part of any inner circle just because they'd shared one horrifying event. She wasn't a part of this, a member of their team. She simply had a job to do.

The swelling ache in her chest escaped on a shudder.

More than she ever had, Beth longed for her family. Her brothers, sisters ... her parents. They all had their quirks, could drive her up the wall, but she'd never doubted how much they loved her. And she really needed some of that right now ... their love, their belief in her. *Stop it!* Clearing her throat, she forced her thoughts back to now. Pining for her family in this situation was disastrous, and in no way helped her maintain a focused, useful state of mind.

'So, how'd you know where to find us?' she asked Sergeant Patterson after a few moments. Now that she could think straight, and given Sergeant Betts wasn't around, she didn't feel as comfortable as she had when he was with them too. More than ever, she wanted answers.

'Basically, Banders gave himself away,' said Sergeant Patterson. 'Had way too much ego that bloke. He'd pissed off some of the locals so it didn't take much for us to ferret him out. He squealed like a little girl when the pressure got a bit hot.'

'Did you kill him?' She had to know.

'We do what we have to, you know that.'

It wasn't an answer, but he made it clear the discussion was over.

'How's Sergeant Betts involved? He wasn't part of our initial search crew.'

'He was available to help. That's all you need to know.' Sergeant Patterson's snappy response did nothing to make her feel any less ill at ease. But she decided it was probably best not to push that envelope just yet.

'Doc?' Nate's slurred voice made them both jump. 'Beth?' he said more urgently.

'Hey, hey, it's okay. We're good,' she said, limping over to him. She grasped his icy hand, rubbed it between her own palms. 'Patto's here, Betsy's gone for supplies.'

He gripped her hand, pushed himself upright, grunting as he tried to get comfortable. Catching her gaze, he stared at her, a question simmering, but he looked away instead of asking it, and dropped his hand from hers before she had a chance to figure out what he might've been going to say.

'Where's Angelis?' Nate directed his attention to Sergeant Patterson, his words sharpening, his body and mind more alert with each passing second.

'Nothin' left but blood when we got there, mate,' said Sergeant Patterson, his face grim.

Beth shuddered. God, she hoped somehow they'd all been rescued, received medical assistance. Something. Somehow.

'Any intel?' said Nate, turning away from her.

'Nothin'. And we're comms down till we know who the hell's in on this,' said Sergeant Patterson, his neck and face turning red. 'Bastards.'

'How'd you find us?' said Nate, the quiet intensity in his words raised the hairs on Beth's neck.

'Banders coughed up his little hidey-hole when I helped him understand the price of silence.'

Nate hadn't blinked since he started questioning Sergeant Patterson. 'Why's Betsy here?' he said.

He was asking the same questions she had, and it surprised her that Sergeant Patterson was no more forthcoming with his mate, the man that saved him, than he had been with her.

'Needed someone with his skills, and I knew he was around. Asked him to help. Not a hell of a lot of blokes here I know I can trust.'

'Yeah, well, looks like that pool's just about run dry for all of us,' said Nate.

Neither man spoke, but the acid tang of male tension permeated the room.

Nate was standing now, but still hadn't looked at her. *What the hell?*

'How long ago did Betsy take off?' he asked Patterson.

'Couple of hours.'

'What comms have you got?'

'Burners.'

It made sense that radios weren't an option while they didn't know who was listening, so why hadn't they used the phones yet to contact a senior officer, someone with some serious authority? Before she could ask, Nate spoke.

'What's he chasing?' asked Nate, his continuous, rapid questions peppering Sergeant Patterson like machine gun fire.

'Medical supplies. Fresh food. Water.'

'Rescue?' Nate was more agitated than she'd seen him in the hospital, and it made her even more tense.

'Yeah, he's scoping out potential assistance options too. Setting a few traps for the snitches while he's at it.'

An idea flared in Beth's thoughts. *Help.* It's what she did, and what she knew. Why she hadn't considered it an option before now she didn't know. 'I can contact the hospital,' she said, glancing between the two men. 'Talk to someone there? Someone I know we can trust.' *Lawson.* Even though she'd disappointed him, surely he'd be able to action something? Generally, medical teams didn't rate too highly on the food chain, but Lawson knew a lot of influential people in the higher ranks, had managed to build strong relationships with a few. From what she'd seen, what she knew of him as a professional, he'd want to do anything he could to help, but her few seconds of hope quickly evaporated. Both the men's faces shouted their thoughts before their lips made a sound.

Nate coughed, grabbing for his side. 'No,' he grunted through clenched teeth. 'No-one will be contacted until we know more about what we're dealing with here.'

Sweat beaded his forehead, and the purple smudges beneath his eyes deepened to black. Clearly, he was in pain and Beth bet his head was pounding. But his guarded focus on her didn't waver, his entire demeanour hostile, angry. Goosebumps covered her body. She suddenly felt like a caged monkey. There was no reason for his change of character towards her. The way he'd spoken to her, touched her when they'd left Banders' hovel ... she hadn't mistaken the bond between them ... had she? Unless it'd all been an act, and he'd been playing her this whole time. Calloway was clearly a man who wouldn't have any trouble in persuading women if he wanted to—bad boy charm oozed out of him. *Please don't let me be that cliché.*

Had she been that desperate, that gullible, she believed they had some sort of connection that they didn't? Was he actually a part of this whole nightmare? Every fibre of her being screamed he wasn't but what if she was wrong?

Trying to think logically, she reviewed the information she had. He'd made it into the hospital undetected, and no matter what she wanted to convince herself of, that screamed of inside help. And at every turn, she'd been left out of the decision making that now saw her here, stuck in this godforsaken freezing shack, with him and the other two. What if he'd pulled the wool over the entire medical team's eyes? What if this had been the outcome he'd planned all along? She could barely swallow.

With her brain buzzing against all the logic, one thing bounced to the front of her thoughts, something that didn't make any sense in that scenario. He couldn't have known she'd volunteer. She bit her lip, flipping her thoughts back and forth. Or was it that anyone would've done, and she was just the lucky batter who'd stepped up to the plate?

Glancing around she sucked in a breath. There was almost nothing she could use to defend herself here if she needed to. She had no weapons, save her nerve, her wit, and the single fact that she made a difference to Sergeant Calloway's chances of staying well enough to continue on. Surely he must know that, and wouldn't want to jeopardise his ability to survive? Well, best she get on with utilising her best chance at building the only armour available to her, while she still could.

'As we're on the topic of trust, how the hell do I know I can trust any of you?' Anger bubbled up alongside her fear. *Enough was enough.* 'How do I know you're not part of whatever Banders is—was into?' She let her glare linger on Nate. 'You're certainly not the same man I arrived here with.' Eventually she alternated her stare between both him and Sergeant Patterson.

Sergeant Patterson snorted. 'With all due respect, Captain, you *don't* know if you can trust us,' he said, his gaze drilling into her face. He leaned into the doorway, his chin tilted upward. 'But the plain and simple fact is, we're all you've got right now.'

Beth felt her face heat. She glanced at Nate desperate to see something that made her question her concerns about him, them ... all of it. But he was staring at Sergeant Patterson. The two men eyeballed each other, something shifting between them, and not for the better. She'd clearly just missed something,

something vital that had altered the stakes. *What the hell is going on?*

Nate dropped his gaze, the unspoken whatever it was with Patterson over. He finally turned to her, his face a colder version of the man she thought she knew. 'I know all of this is difficult for you,' he said, his voice toneless, 'but how 'bout we get a few things straight.' He squared his shoulders, shoved his hands on his hips. 'If I'd wanted to be rid of you, I've had plenty of opportunities. If Patto or Betsy wanted you gone, you wouldn't be here. So how about you just sit down, take a load off and dial down the drama, hey? There's nothing doing, nothing to discuss, until Betsy's back. Okay?'

Furious, confused, and more scared than she cared to admit, Beth focused on keeping her voice strong. 'Wanting the facts isn't creating drama, Calloway. It's protocol and at the very least, basic damn respect.' She hated that her hands were shaking. 'I didn't risk my arse to be here, to make sure you get to where you need to be, to be treated like I'm invisible and a goddamn fool.' She mirrored Calloway, her feet squared, her hands wedged into her hips. 'That goes for you too, Sergeant Patterson.' Her breaths peppered her words in short bursts. 'So as soon as you have something to share, I'd appreciate it if you could both offer me at least that courtesy of sharing it.'

Nate nodded at her, his glance fleeting before he focused on Sergeant Patterson. 'Of course, Captain.'

His eyes didn't waver from Sergeant Patterson, even though he was addressing her. There was no sarcasm in his reply, but there wasn't anything warm to it either. His lips whitened, pressed together in a thin line. 'When there's something to tell, I'll be the first to let you know.'

'Thank you,' she snapped.

Sergeant Patterson had become more fidgety and restless, and was prowling the entryway like an angry panther. 'Why don't you have some water, eat, see if you can rest for a bit? You'll need it,' he said.

She recognised an order when she heard it.

With no energy for any further confrontation and unsure of how far she dare push either of the men, Beth hobbled over to the supplies pack, the sack still sitting upright and leaning on a wall in the far corner of the room. She pulled out a canteen and tipped the cold water in her mouth. The liquid hitting her throat made her realise how hungry and thirsty she actually was. She all but gulped down the remainder of the drink before taking a breath.

She really had no idea what to do, or think. Maybe there really wasn't anything further to know until Sergeant Betts returned? She wanted that to be the case, but with Nate's total change in behaviour, and Sergeant Patterson's clear displeasure, she sure as hell didn't feel like it was remotely likely.

Tension and silence surrounded all of them.

Nate dropped back onto his crate, stayed upright, his legs angled over the edge, his boots pressed into the floor. He motioned for Patterson to move closer to him.

They spoke in quick, coded discussion. Some of it she could hear, some she couldn't. Her adrenaline ignited again, and she wanted to push back, assert her rank, tell them they were obliged to inform her of what they were discussing, that she didn't have to accept this rubbish from any of them.

But then what?

Other than her medical usefulness, was she only as good as an afterthought to these men? Was she just another tool they were using to get their job done? A disposable cog in their wheel? *No matter what Calloway said about keeping you safe.*

Well whatever she was or wasn't, this was insane. Instead of waiting for their scraps, she needed to work on her own contingency plan, figure out how she could go it alone from here.

Beth made her way back to her crate, stifling a grunt when she nudged passed a broken stool and the jutting wood hit her ankle. Her boot was excruciatingly tight around the swelling, but she couldn't risk taking it off to ice it again. With any luck, the inflammation would start subsiding within the next day, and she'd be able to move around a little better.

Oh, for god's sake. Who the hell was she kidding? Going it alone would get her killed. It just wasn't an option, but she did need to sort a plan B, and quickly.

Easing herself further down onto the bed, she caught Nate staring at her, and looked straight at him. Did he nod ever so slightly, or was it just her wishful imagination? Before she caught anything more, he looked away, bent his head and continued his discussion with Sergeant Patterson. The knot in her belly eased ever so slightly. She couldn't believe he'd hurt her. Wouldn't believe it.

Beyond being able to consider the matter any further, regardless of what she decided to do, she needed rest and energy to do it. She curled into a ball and closed her eyes, hoping that the next time she opened them she didn't find monsters in place of the two men beside her.

Beth had no idea how, but she must've drifted off into a dreamless sleep, because she jerked awake with a tap on her shoulder from Sergeant Patterson. 'I'm gonna check further up the track. Betsy should've called by now. You got this?' He jutted his chin towards Nate, who seemed like he'd found sleep too.

She nodded, pushing aside her questions about Sergeant Betts delay, instead focusing on Nate. 'Is he okay? Have you noticed any changes?' she asked. It was on the tip of her tongue to ask Sergeant Patterson what the two of them had discussed, what plans they'd made. But given his less than friendly air, she left it. For now.

'Nah, said he'd take an hour kip, rest up while he could. That was about forty-five minutes ago.'

She glanced at Nate again, could see his chest rising and falling in uneven motion. She needed to check his vitals.

'I'll need a phone, or we won't have any comms when you're gone,' Beth said, moving to stand.

'Sorry, none spare,' said Sergeant Patterson, his body rigid as a stone statue. 'Just keep this close.' He handed her a pistol. 'Remember how to use it?'

'Of course.' She resisted snapping a further retort at his insulting question.

'Good. And you'll need this if ... well, if you need to make a move.' He thrust a map into her hand. 'This place is here.' He pointed to a yellow circle on the map. 'Wolfman will be able to work with it from there.'

Before she could ask another question, Patterson moved away from her and disappeared out the door, his shadow evaporating in seconds.

A shimmer of fear skittered down her spine.

Where was he going? What if neither of them came back? And there should always be some way for a unit, or whatever they were, to stay in contact, but she had nothing. This was all kinds of wrong.

Stop it. Just stop it.

She had to work with what she had, use her instincts, not concentrate on the unknowns. And she had to trust that Nate was who she believed him to be, not the person he'd just shown her. Until she knew for certain that he meant her harm, she had to keep focused on what they were here for. There was no other choice.

Not one that'd keep her sane anyway.

With effort, she hobbled back to Nate's side. His face was coated in sweat, his limbs twitching and jerking. She started her assessment watching him for a moment, unsure if he was unwell or struggling with a nightmare. She removed her gloves and stroked the length of his arm, working her fingers back to his wrist's pulse point. 'Sssshhhh,' she whispered, leaning in close to his ear, inhaling his woodsy scent. Her insides sparked to life against her will, her heart kicking in her chest, despite the situation she was in. Her heart—*was it her heart or just her instincts?*—was certainly barracking for her to believe she could trust him, rely on him. Her head—that needed some more convincing.

'You're okay. You're safe,' she said, continuing to murmur her mantra to him, and maybe just a little to herself, as she checked his vitals and scanned his body for distension, fresh blood or any other sign of something sinister. Other than further discolouration of the whopping haematomas on his shins, she couldn't detect anything new, and thank god, the biggest relief was there weren't any signs of internal bleeding. As far as she could ascertain, he hadn't deteriorated. His intermittent jerks calmed while she worked, and finally she pressed her ear to his chest, listened as best she could, her stethoscope gone with her pack.

His heartbeat, the rush of air in and out of his lungs, his body heat, it all flowed into her, filling the gaping holes of fear stabbing deep in her chest. She let herself stay pressed against him, just for a moment. Exhaling, she slid her hand beneath his glove to rest over the back of his, curling her fingers around the edges of his hand, the reassuring warmth of his skin seeping into her blood. For a few seconds she let go of efficient, steady, problem solving Captain Doctor Harper and was simply Beth—a woman who didn't want to be anything but safe.

His chest shuddered, jolting her back to reality.

She bolted upright, swiped at a tear that had escaped. *Get it together, be a doctor for god's sake, care for your patient—that's your job.* This right here, right now, wasn't and couldn't be about her.

Sucking in deep breaths, she repeated her review process, cataloguing each step in her head, forcing every thought to focus on her patient, not on thinking about what the next hour, minute, second might hold for her outside this moment, this man and her care for him.

Beth dragged over a stool and scooped up the blanket from where she'd slept. She pushed up onto the seat, resting her ankle on the edge of Nate's crate. She needed to be close to him, monitor any changes as they happened and for safety's sake, they needed to be close together. Because that was protocol, the right thing to do. Yes ... it was what she had to do ... not simply what she wanted to do.

Beth kept herself awake and her thoughts captive by counting in blocks of sixty first forward, then backwards, and after forty-five minutes she checked Nate's vitals again. No change. She scanned his body, finishing with his face.

Maybe it was because she was surviving on adrenaline, or maybe because of the soft glow of the kerosene lamp, but something sparked her painter's eye. As ridiculous as it was in the situation, she paused for barely a second before giving in to it. It wouldn't hurt anyone. She was still monitoring him, he was okay for now, and there wasn't a lot more she could do while he was asleep and the other two weren't back. Leaving her mind idle to think about what the next few hours might hold wouldn't help her. So, she let go, let herself imagine his features coming to life beneath her brush, glorious watercolours splayed across a clean, fresh white canvas. His lashes, thick and black, shadowed his cheeks, the tension stretching the skin around his eyes and mouth, disappearing with each brush stroke in her mind. His jawline, strong, square, and darkened with two-day-old stubble offered so much texture, such a brilliant light and shade to his face, one she itched to drag her fingertips through. She fought the urge to trace his full lips with her finger, the middle indent of his upper lip, ever so slightly off centre.

She wasn't sure how long she sat, still, just watching him. Painting him over and over in her mind, whispering her affirmations—to herself as much as to him—stroking his arm, but it'd grown much colder, the single lamp flickering, the flame diminishing.

His twitching had stopped, but the pooling sweat remained. She ran another once over and slid her hand inside his shirt, laid her palm across his chest. Her belly clenched. Burning. His skin was on fire. He had a fever, and likely an infection. There wasn't any external evidence, so that left his internal wounds. It also meant, given his compromised systems, they were very quickly running out of time to wait for proper medical assistance.

She gripped Nate's hand a little harder, tension bunching the muscles in her neck. Ignoring the urge to rub at them, she pulled the fine-tipped permanent marker from her pocket. Although dented and squashed flat, miraculously, it worked. She jotted his stats on his arm.

He was stable enough for now, but if she didn't get an IV and stronger antibiotics into him soon, it'd be a whole different story.

Please hurry, Sergeant Betts.

Chapter 14

Lawson squeezed the bridge of his nose. The whole exercise had been an absolute disaster from start to finish. He couldn't believe the words hitting his ear. Banders missing, Beth hurt and Calloway still alive.

'What do you mean you can't you bring her to me now? Sort it out. You've got two hours. Don't call me until you have her.' He stabbed his finger at the phone screen, ending the call.

The incompetence of these supposed Special Ops geniuses was infuriating. He couldn't abide any more errors. Zoreed was breathing down his neck and wouldn't hesitate to snap it like a twig if she got wind of any of this. And that outcome was a very real possibility if he didn't get this mess resolved today.

He shuffled his patient files into alphabetical order and shoved them into the tray at the nurse's station. There was only one solution. He had to get this cleaned up now, and had to do it himself. He sucked in a deep breath and punched the Brigadier's number into his phone, cleared his throat. It wasn't out of the question for classified intel to reach him, due to his required involvement with the Red Cross, and the National Information Bureau. He'd already devised a scenario to explain this particular situation, had kept the tactic up his sleeve for a rainy day. And well, hell, right now, he was in the middle of a major downpour.

His call was answered in the standard two rings, his superior's voice clipped and efficient. 'Go ahead.'

'Brigadier James, sir. Major Black here.'

'Go ahead, Major.'

'Thank you, sir.' Lawson cleared his throat. 'I've reason to believe Captain Doctor Beth Harper has been captured by insurgents.' He paused for effect. 'Permission requested to report in immediately.'

Sweat beaded on Lawson's forehead, his heart pounding against his breastbone like that of a man facing a firing squad. The clock was ticking, and all he could do was hurry up and wait.

It wouldn't take Zoreed long to realise the bastards and the dog meant nothing to him, but that Beth, well, she was a whole other story. And if one of these imbeciles let that crucial piece of info out amongst her emissaries before he retrieved her, Zoreed would have his woman replacing Calloway's unit for leverage before he had time to blink.

Without Banders keeping them in line, the other addicts would turncoat on him for whoever offered the right coin. He'd seen it before. Tunnelling a hand through his hair, Lawson sucked in a breath and exhaled loudly. What was damn well taking the Brigadier so long? He'd given the man an outline of what had transpired, the pertinent details only, and the Brigadier had dismissed him to the corridor while he made some calls. Lawson had been outside the closed door for nearly an hour. He wasn't accustomed to being kept waiting, and didn't like it.

Fighting the urge to pace the corridor outside the office, Lawson started working on alternatives in case the remainder of the meeting didn't go as planned. Alternatives that wouldn't lose him any freedoms, ergo, lose him Beth. Just as he'd decided the last stage of a workable plan B, the door swung inward.

'Enter, Major.'

Dear Lord, let this be what I need to hear.

Facing Brigadier James and *what in hell? Lieutenant Colonel Fraser?* Lawson cleared his throat, his gut spasming. Fraser was supposed to be on his way home, starting his retirement. Lawson's surprise fast turned to suspicion. Fraser knew Beth was out there. Maybe it was a message. A way to tell Lawson if he screwed up, didn't play nice, then the Lieutenant Colonel would deliver up Beth to Zoreed, his final parting gift, to ensure Lawson toed the line for the remainder of his life? Possible alternate scenarios hurtled rapid fire through his mind, none of them remotely pleasing.

It would be in his best interest to reveal very little right now. The whole landscape here was totally unknown to him, and with Fraser front and centre,

Lawson didn't have the upper hand as he'd planned. He must listen, listen very carefully to what was said, choose his words like they might be his last, because, it was a very real possibility that if he didn't play the next twelve hours right, they may very well be exactly that.

Lawson's phone pulsed, he flinched, the plastic vibrating through his pants against his thigh. He didn't miss the flicker of interest that crossed Fraser's features, his gaze moving from Lawson's leg to his face. He prayed the caller wasn't a newly enlightened Zoreed.

'Sirs.' He saluted them both. 'Lieutenant Colonel Fraser, you've not departed yet?'

'No.'

The Brigadier spoke before Fraser could say more. 'We've been discussing the situation you've outlined, Major, and your desire to partake in what you believe to be a rescue, with the potential for the need of medical assistance—' Brigadier James paused and grey brows that'd been perched high on his forehead came crashing down into a frown, '—but I feel it's time to appraise you of some other facts.'

'Sir?' The flesh on Lawson's scalp tightened as he worked to keep his face neutral. *What had he walked into here?*

The Lieutenant Colonel spoke next, the gluttonous man made Lawson's gut roil. Every fibre of his being wanted to split the bastard's face with an axe. But of course, he turned towards him and offered his full, and calm attention.

'Seems Captain Harper's involved in a covert operation, one we weren't fully aware of until now,' said Lieutenant Colonel Fraser. 'And of course, being medical personnel, there's no way you'd be abreast of these details.'

Filthy condescending liar.

Fraser sniffed and continued. 'We've been instructed not to interfere, and advised updates will be provided when possible.' Fraser clasped his fleshy hands together, steel entering his washed-out pale blue eyes. 'So we must trust that she is safe, Major Black. It is what we're under instruction to do until we hear otherwise.'

Holy hell. Who else was playing games here? Fraser? The Brigadier?

Lawson doubted that Brigadier Charles James was anything but as straight as an arrow, but maybe he too was up to his eyeballs in Fraser's dirt? Or maybe it was someone above the Brigadier who had Fraser in *their* pocket? *Holy Jesus.*

Presenting his best game face, Lawson returned serve, nodded slowly and addressed the Brigadier. 'May I ask, who exactly *they* are, sir?'

'You know we're not at liberty to offer those details to you, Major.' The Brigadier's words were curt, his displeasure with Lawson's insubordination clear.

'Yes, sir. Of course. I appreciate you giving me the courtesy of letting me know all that you have.' He glanced at the Lieutenant Colonel, then back at the Brigadier. 'Captain Harper has been through a lot, I'd hate to see her involved in anything, willingly or not, that might trigger a relapse, sir.'

An icy block settled in his gut. *Had she been on the inside all along?* No! It wasn't possible—he'd have known. With the level of surveillance he had on her, there's no way she could've been involved in a covert operation without him knowing.

'Rest assured the army wouldn't allow a non-combat member of personnel to be subjected to danger unless there wasn't another choice, or unless they have a part to play.' Brigadier James' face remained impassive as he spoke, but Lawson knew he'd just been warned. Or at the very least, strongly reminded of his place in the hierarchy.

'Yes, sir, and thank you,' Lawson said.

'Thank you, Major Black.'

Following protocol and leaving when dismissed by the Brigadier, it took every ounce of his control to not grab Fraser's smirking head by the neck and wring out every last breath. And now, to make it worse, he also had a question mark over Beth's loyalties.

Shaking, Lawson turned the corner, pushed through the exit doors and left the building. With his pulse racing, he checked for anyone loitering before pulling out his phone. One glance at the screen and his shoulders dropped, the fire in his gut over Fraser now simmering with a dose of cool relief. The call was from an unknown number, not Zoreed. She always called from the same line. She was arrogant like that, didn't care it was a known number. Punching the relevant keys, he held it to his ear and waited for the message to play.

'Son of a damn bitch.' The fiery rage thrust upward from his gut again, bile burning the back of his throat. That bastard Banjo was ransoming Beth for Calloway. Threatening that if Lawson screwed up, Beth would eat a bullet. 'Son. Of. A. Bitch.'

Lawson's eye twitched, frustration pounding relentlessly in his skull as he paced the length of the building and back again, options and plans jostling for space. A sliver of relief surfaced when he affirmed for himself that one thing was clear. That stupid fool Banjo seemed to have forgotten a crucial fact. If he held out, or hurt Beth in any way, how on earth would he get his precious heroin, and guarantee Lawson wouldn't expose his filthy little habit to the wrong people?

Lawson swallowed hard. Sucking in deep breaths, huffing them out. That foolish, foolish man. It wouldn't take much of the prompt Lawson had in mind to remind Banjo of who was *always* in charge here.

Chapter 15

He launched up and grabbed her wrist like a man possessed.

'Nate.' She ripped her wrist out of his grip. 'Sergeant Calloway. It's me, Doctor Harper,' she shouted.

It took him a few seconds to register where he was, who she was, and back off. Lucky for her, he was fatigued. If he'd had his full strength up, he'd likely have broken her wrist.

His head dropped back as he came fully awake. 'Shit, sorry. Sorry, Beth.'

'It's okay. I'm okay.' She forced a tight smile across her mouth.

His temperature had escalated significantly over the last hour. If Sergeants Betts or Patterson didn't get back soon with some antibiotics, it was very possible delirium could set in, and then he'd be a potential danger to her, and to himself.

'Where's Betsy? Patto?'

'Sergeant Betts hasn't returned, and Sergeant Patterson has gone to find him. At least that's what he said.' She mumbled the last bit to herself, because actually, she had no idea where the men were, and Sergeant Patterson had now been gone over two hours. She felt a complete fool.

It was clear he wasn't happy they were alone. His eyes narrowed, his focus laser-beam as he glanced around the room.

'Patto left you here, us here, alone?'

'Yes. He gave me this.' She pulled the pistol from her lap, held it up to Nate.

He pushed it back into her lap. 'Fantastic.'

She didn't like the tone of his comment, or the way his eyes flickered from her to the doorway and back again.

'Did he leave a phone?' Nate asked, dragging a hand down his face.

'No. But I asked for one, and he said he didn't have a spare. Is that normal protocol out here? To leave your unit without any comms?' She knew that was never okay, but wanted to hear Nate's response and didn't need him thinking she was clueless as to how things were meant to roll out here.

He turned slowly towards her, his body tense, fatigued. 'Depends.'

'Depends on what? C'mon, Nate, this is bullshit. I'm not afraid to tell you, I'm scared, really scared. This whole situation is so far out of control, I have no idea what to think, or, or to do.'

'Depends on the next move.' His fingers stumbled as he worked at tightening the laces on his boots.

'What are you talking about? Whose next move?'

'I'm not sure,' he said, searching her face, dragging his gaze up and down her body.

'Why are you looking at me like that?' Beth bit the inside of her cheek, willing the tears burning the back of her eyes to stay put.

'Like what?'

'Okay, you know what, I've had enough of this,' she said, moving away from him. 'I accompanied you in good faith, Sergeant Calloway. My brief was to ensure your health remained stable while you searched for your men and Finnegan, and we'd be outside the wire seventy-two hours max. And now, almost thirty-six hours in, I'm stuck in a shack with men whom I have no idea if I can believe, and who may or may not be on the same side as me.' Tears rolled down her cheeks, she swiped at them with the back of her hand. *Dammit.* She never let herself cry in front of men. Using her frustration to spur her on, she continued. 'If I had half an idea on how to get out of here and back to base without getting myself killed, I'd be gone.' She backed into the closest wall and slid down, hugging her knees when she hit the ground, trying not to whimper as her ankle protested at the movement. She couldn't do it. She couldn't pretend she wasn't terrified. 'Nate, please, I really need you to just tell me what the hell is going on, because I'm really struggling here.'

His eyes, the colour of laden storm clouds, blazed into hers, his face hard as stone ... he said nothing. She wanted to scream. She needed him to tell her he had a plan, and it involved her, and that they would be okay. And for him to stop staring at her like he hated her to hell and back. That's what she needed.

'I have an idea of what's going down,' he said finally, with no urgency and less emotion. 'But I don't know anything for sure.' His voice was stronger, clearer. 'And you're not the only one in the room questioning allegiance.'

'What? What the hell does that mean?' She wanted to punch him, shake him. Something to release the fear and frustration that had her feeling as tense as the springs in an overwound clock. Beth lurched up onto her feet and checked the pistol's safety before sliding it into her pocket. Awkward as it was, she needed to stand directly in front of him, hands free and stare him in the face. 'Are you saying you suspect me of being somehow associated with the bastards who tried to shoot us?' Her body vibrated with anger. 'When or how, or—' Beth shook her head. 'Why would I save your life or, or volunteer to risk my own, if I was working for the other side? Why would I sit here, near to freezing, checking you're breathing every goddamn hour, every minute actually, if I wanted to leave, or, or wanted you dead?

'There's always a reason,' he said. 'Especially from those you least expect.' His shoulders slumped a little on the last word. 'It's not the first time I've seen this, doubt it'll be the last.'

The sound of scattering pebbles and footsteps silenced her furious retort. With her back to the entry, she skidded sideways, pushing herself against the far sidewall, engaging her pistol, steadying it, ready to fire.

She watched Nate manoeuvre himself to the same side as her, but the adjacent corner, his rifle cocked and aimed at the door, sweat sliding from his temple to his chin.

Like before, she pressed herself into the wall as the rifle nose entered the room. She glanced at Nate, his gaze flickered to her and back to the door. She held her breath, wondering if this was it, if this is truly how it would end for her. Backed into a wall, on the losing side of a shootout?

As the uniform emerged piece by piece around the wall, Beth cried out when the face that followed the legs and torso belonged to Sergeant Betts. 'Oh god. Thank god it's you.' She disengaged the pistol, and used the wall at her back to steady her trembling body.

'Jesus Christ, man, what the fuck is going on?' The anger in Nate's voice hissed through his teeth. He engaged the safety clip on his gun, exhaling long and loud.

'Dude, settle-the-fuck down,' said Betsy. 'Shit just took a bit longer to sort, that's all. Good to see you're up and around though, mate.' Betsy's face cracked into a grin. 'Thought we'd have to frigging carry your nancy-boy arse down the mountain.'

'Ah Nancy's up and about then?' Patterson's voice joined in the chorus as he entered the room. Beth didn't know whether she wanted to make a run for it or hug them both with relief. What she did know, is right this instant, she was invisible again and she'd had enough. Of all of it. She was done sitting in a corner crying.

She coughed, clearing her tear-clogged voice. 'Is that the supplies?' she asked, eyeing Sergeant Betts and the package he pulled from his pack. 'Because, while you're all standing around making jokes, Sergeant Calloway over there isn't doing so well.'

The room filled with silence, all three men eyeballing her before two of them fixed their attention on Nate.

'I'll be fine,' said Nate.

She ignored him and kept her focus on Sergeant Betts, waiting for his answer.

'Yep, got whatcha ordered, Doc. Wasn't easy, so put it to good use, hey?' Beth met Sergeant Betts' gaze. Something she couldn't identify radiated back at her, made her spine tingle. Was he warning her? Threatening her?

'Thank you, I'll do what I can, Sergeant. You're sure these are safe? Standard?'

'Yes, ma'am. Of course,' he fired back at her, clearly disliking that she'd questioned him. Although, she also got the feeling Betsy respected her clarifying the integrity of the supplies all the same. And that calmed her a bit.

'Just hurry up and do what you have to so we can get on with it,' Nate said, his breath short, his torso leaning into his injured side. 'You're all looking at me like I've severed my arm and you've just used up the last frigging tourniquet. I'll be fine. Jesus. Lighten the fuck up, all of you.'

'You never were a good patient.' Sergeant Betts' swatted Nate's shoulder. 'Okay, let's get this done. We gotta get outta here ASAP, and you're walking, my friend,' he said to Nate. 'I ain't hauling your nancy-boy arse no place.'

Beth noted Sergeant Patterson's silence, and that he had the fidgets again, kept glancing towards the exit. But she didn't have time to think more about that now. Analysis of the nuances and potential causes of his erratic behaviour had to wait.

Reviewing the labels of the provisions, she was relieved to see they were exactly the same as what she used in the hospital. She prepped everything as best she could and forced out the questions pounding her mind around the procurement of the supplies.

'I'll need to insert this IV, Sergeant. It's just saline and I'll inject the antibiotic separately,' she said to Nate. 'Your temperature spike indicates you've likely got an infection somewhere, and it's making things a whole lot worse for you.' Beth motioned for him to sit back on the bed; he did and moved his hand towards her. She pulled on her surgical gloves, prepped his skin, inserted the canula, administered the antibiotic and then added the needle and fluid bag.

'You'll need to lie down, Sergeant, and I'll hold this above you.' She glanced at the other two men. 'And if neither of you have any immediate plans to disappear again, perhaps we could take it in turns, or find some other solution?'

They all exchanged glances, clearly her directives weren't what they'd expected. She had no doubt they had their next moves astutely planned, and had a way to relay the details to Sergeant Calloway that bypassed her, but for now, this was her floor, her time and they'd goddamn do what she asked.

Nate stared through her, looking at her like she was a stranger. Fear crawled up and grabbed at her throat. The only thing she could do right now was stay professional. Do everything to prove her allegiance until he got over his paranoia—or whatever the hell this was. Because, no matter how much she might want it otherwise, it was the only option she had on the table right now.

'Captain.' Sergeant Patterson nodded at her as he motioned for her to pass the saline bag, and stepped up to hold it. 'It's alright. We can wait.'

The two men glanced at Nate, then rested their gaze on Beth. 'How long before he can move?' said Sergeant Betts.

'I'm not a bloody mute for Christ's sake.' Nate looked ready to rip the needle out of his arm. 'Doctor Harper—' Nate's stare was cold as it settled on her, '—how long do we need to be here?'

'Two hours minimum.' Her curt answer sounded harsh even to her, but she couldn't worry about that. 'So would one of you mind telling me what the hell the plan is after that?' Beth stared into Nate's impassive face, then flicked her gaze across to Sergeants Patterson and Betts. Patterson had moved closer to both of them, still holding the fluid bag above Nate's head.

'Well, it's a bit like poker night, Captain Harper.' Patterson smiled at her, but there was no warmth in his eyes, and his entire body was twitching as if he was connected to high volt electricity. 'We play out our hand to whoever offers the highest bid, and hope to hell our bluff works.'

'Bluff? What are we doing that requires bluff and who's bidding, and for what?' she asked. Beth's head was swimming, the panic returning. She bit her lower lip, shoved her shaking hands in her pockets, halting any more of the questions hammering her brain. She glared at Nate, willing him to answer, but his eyes were closed, his breathing shallow. 'Sergeant Calloway, are you with us?' she said.

'Yesh...' His eyes opened slowly, his pupils the size of pinheads. His eyeballs slowly rolled into the back of his head.

Oh god. She whirled around to face Sergeant Betts. 'What the hell was in that IV? Where'd you get it?'

'It's exactly what you asked for. I checked the details myself.' Betsy's face reddened, the tips of his ears scarlet as he flicked his eyes at Patterson and then back at her, air rocketing noisily out of his nose. 'I give you my word on that, Captain.' She didn't miss his coiled fists and clenched jaw.

She was far from an idiot, but this whole ... debacle, was well out of her playing field. And one thing was for certain, who she was, her rank and everything else that should've had her calling the shots right now, didn't matter one iota to the two conscious men in this room, a room now sparking with loaded tension.

A sharp movement over her shoulder jerked her attention to Sergeant Patterson, who in that split second, dropped the saline bag and pulled his weapon, had it aimed at Sergeant Betts.

'What are you doing?' she screamed at Sergeant Patterson.

'Jesus, man, what the hell did you do?' said Sergeant Betts.

She heard Sergeant Betts' words, but could barely see his face through her tears. He was shaking his head, staring at Sergeant Patterson, sadness radiating from his eyes. 'It's you, isn't it, you bastard?'

Gunfire exploded in her ears. Beth dropped to the ground. On the way down, something hard slammed into the side of head and sent her world swiftly fading to black.

Chapter 16

Lawson strode out of the hospital, counting the steps of the short walk to his room. Final handover complete, he was free, and now had forty-eight hours to retrieve Beth, and sort this damn mess out once and for all.

A foreign feeling bubbled under his skin as he changed into his purpose bought non-descript civilian clothes. Unease? He was about to break the one rule he'd employed for as long as he could remember: never do the dirty work yourself. But unfortunately, it was dirty his own hands now, or the whole goddamn house of cards was going to come crashing down, with him at the base of it.

He'd made another call to Zoreed late last night, played the game of what he supposed could be called bargaining. He couldn't risk Zoreed thinking him unworthy of her continued focus on his so-called redemption, and he didn't need anything to make her suspicious of his motives, or of her role as his saviour, given it was the only thing that kept him off her hit list. So, he'd played the call as if he was utterly distraught by the notion that she might consider killing even one of the men from Calloway's unit, in fact, he would of course, do anything to avoid that.

And with some convincing on his part, she'd bought it. For now.

When he'd arranged for Zoreed to *come by* some hostages for her publicity stunt, he'd pretended the bastard's lives mattered. He'd begged her, just use them for her purpose, rough them up a little, but don't kill them. He'd played the same card with Fraser too. Said he couldn't have another man die because of his actions. Made out like he cared, that he'd sworn an oath to save and protect these good soldiers, and wanted them back, be able to deliver them home to their families and so on. But really, he didn't give one damn what happened to them, they were simply another step closer to him having Beth and extracting himself from this mess. He'd thought hard about the tactic, and had played it that way for several reasons, the main one so he could lay the seeds, collate reams of orchestrated communication directly implicating Fraser. Catalogued details so damning, that if it all went south before he got out, Fraser would go down for it too ... lock, stock and blazing barrel.

Zoreed had issued him the task just over six months prior. It'd taken a while for him to achieve a result, and he'd been mildly concerned he wouldn't be able to deliver on her *special publicity* request in time. But he'd chanced on a stroke of luck. He'd come across one of Fraser's pets, a Sergeant Patterson. Patterson had intercepted a recent shipment of the country's preferred, adulterated form of heroin, brown sugar, en route to the hospital, kept a portion for himself, *forgot* to pass it on, so he said. The fool begged Lawson not to give him up to Fraser, said he'd do anything to settle the debt if Lawson maintained his silence. Well, when Calloway landed in the hospital alive, his time to do *anything* had arrived.

Sergeant Patterson insisted Lawson refer to him as Banjo in the field; the play on his name amusing, though the man was no poet. What he was, was a high-functioning, heroin-addicted soldier in a desperate way.

'No, I can't give you any names. I can't,' Sergeant Patterson had said. His body would've been as rigid as his words if not for his writhing on the ground, convulsively wretching, snot streaming from his nose ... withdrawal really was a hard taskmaster.

'Nothing comes for free,' he'd said in Patterson's sweat-soaked ear. 'I told you maintaining secrets requires payment.' He let a boot to the ribs help Paterson understand the concept a little further, whilst all the while keeping the baggie of his precious brown sugar in plain sight, the carrot to go with his stick. 'So can you help me or not, Sergeant Patterson?'

'Please, there's got to be something else you need. Anything.'

Lawson had ignored his pathetic whining. He supposed he should've been impressed the snivelling fool wanted to protect his fellow soldiers, but it was hard to see anything before him but a drugged up wastrel—high-functioning, but a wastrel none-the-less. 'And what about your dear sweet wife at home? Sally, isn't it? And your little one, what's her name?' Lawson had saved the final piece of encouragement for last.

'Don't you dare touch them,' spat Patterson, struggling to sit up.

'Oh, Banjo, my dear fellow, I wouldn't dream of touching your family. But see my friend over there, Lieutenant Banders? Well, I can't speak for what he might do.'

Patterson, the pitiful excuse for a man, was on his knees in minutes with barely an argument. 'Alright, I'll give you some names,' he said. 'They're the next unit that's due in. They'll be suitable. Please, just leave my wife, my daughter out of it.'

'We don't care who they are, Sergeant Patterson—'

'Banjo, please refer to me as Banjo, sir. I know I'm pretty screwed, but in case there's someone outside this, this group, listening—'

'Sorry, *Banjo*.' Lawson rolled his eyes. 'As I was saying, we don't care who the men or women, if you prefer, are that you supply, we just need whomever it is to be worthy of the international media's attention. Decorated, accomplished. The best. Do you understand?'

'Yes, sir. This group will meet that criteria.'

'Please be sure, Banjo, we don't want any mistakes, do we, Sergeant Banders?'

Banders laughed his maniacal laugh, like the lunatic he was.

'They're it, the ones you need,' said Sergeant Patterson. 'They're elite Special Ops.'

'Alright, I'm listening,' said Lawson. 'How do you know them?'

Patterson paused. Had the decency to hang his head. 'I used to be one of them.'

'Well, well, haven't you fallen from grace?'

Patterson didn't answer. If he'd been anything like the commando he once was, Lawson wouldn't be dealing with him without serious backup at hand. But the man before him wasn't anything close to a threat.

'You still in contact with any of these men?' asked Lawson

'No. Haven't spoken to any of them in over ten years. We were recruited into different specialities after our second deployment.'

'Well, just so you know, if you're tempted to give them a heads-up in any way, I'm sure Zoreed will be happy to give your head up. And Lieutenant Banders here, well he'll pay a visit to your beautiful wife and—'

'I understand the situation, sir.'

The snivelling has-been was smoking the narcotic before the last man's name slipped past his lips, his wife and child's welfare soon obliterated from his filthy heroin-imbibed thoughts.

After locating the unit Patterson had delivered up—Calloway's unit—Lawson used his contacts to track their schedule, monitor their movements. And then, when it was time, he stopped for a coffee at the locally run Green Bean Café, all in an effort to follow the carefully orchestrated steps as instructed by Zoreed. She'd ordered he go to the café and gave him the name of a visiting Commander, a man he hadn't met, but who was obviously high up on her payroll. His brief was to casually share his information with the man, like it was an everyday coffee break between colleagues. So, he'd set the scene and delivered an animated conversation about the unit's importance, the immense success of their last mission and so on. He let out some other relevant titbits too, and did so in earshot of some of Zoreed's best emissaries, just to be sure.

He'd worked out pretty early on whom the men were she'd employed to keep watch on him. But in their presence, he picked one or two of them out every so often. She knew he wasn't a stupid man, and would be suspicious if he didn't. He worked on the philosophy of keeping your enemies close, and made sure that when Zoreed's Commander left, he gave the "watchers" a bit more of a show, pretended to take a call, pretended to be secretive while carefully relaying the final pieces of information that would help seal the deal and limit his involvement. And then, he sat back, let them all play their part.

Zoreed's army actioned their steps like clockwork, just as she promised they would. *Pity his damn men weren't like them.* But it didn't matter, he'd fix it. And when he did, that bastard Patterson, he wouldn't be able to find a bullet for himself quick enough.

Chapter 17

You need to move. Now. There's no time. C'mon, Nate, open your eyes. I need you to move.

'Beth?'

Icy air burned through Nate's nostrils and the sour odour of damp, compacted earth settled into the back of his throat. Remnants of the strangest dream laced his thoughts like strands of a sticky spider web. There was a kid, kneeling by his side, pushing a clay cup filled with murky grey liquid at him.

'Drink, you must drink it,' said the kid, his words a weird blend of English and Pashto.

Nate shoved the cup away a few times, but the kid kept returning it to his mouth.

Then Beth's face filled his vision again, frantic. Terrified. *Just drink it, Nate ... please.*

He did. He drank it, for her, even though it tasted like goddamn swamp water. His gut spasmed, made him hurl. But the kid kept at it, with Beth, till he stopped spewing and kept the grey shit down. That bit was clear as a damn bell.

His next memory was the kid hauling him to his feet, he was older than he'd seemed at first. He leant on the kid's shoulder, and the scrawny boy with the strength of Hercules was hauling his arse someplace else.

'You must stay here. I will bring you water. You not move, I come again. Iskander will help. Like before.'

Iskander.

The name clanged through his head, shovelling up flashes of other memories as it went. But he couldn't quite catch the threads to pull them together.

Cracking his eyelids open, Nate surveyed his surrounds. Dark. Cold. Stone. Hauling his torso upright, a surge of fear spiked through his body. *Where's Beth?*

It'd made him sick to his gut upsetting her like he had at the farmhouse. But it couldn't be helped. He'd had to make out he didn't give a damn about her in front of Patto. Didn't want him knowing Beth meant something to him. He'd felt something was off in Patto before they'd left base, thought it was just his mate's concern about the turncoats. But when they reached the farmhouse, Nate wasn't sure that's all it was. This Patto, the angry, edgy bloke he'd seen in the last coupla days, he wasn't the same man he dug out of the frigging rubble in Iraq all those years ago. And until he knew why, he didn't want the potential for Beth to be any more compromised than she already was.

Nate glanced around, his eyes now adjusted to the dim glow he realised was coming from a decrepit oil heater at the centre of the room. There was a tall clay pitcher, like the type the village women usually filled with water, a loaf of what looked like bread resting on some sort of cloth. Two buckets and a pile of leaves far over to the side, and beside him, a single sleeping roll and a hemp blanket. Glancing downward, he noted the same type of bedding beneath himself. A rough hemp blanket lay across his legs. Where the walls met the ceiling, there were a few cracks that let in the moonlight, each of them barely the width of his littlest finger.

No Beth.

Fear crushed his lungs, he struggled to make a sound.

'Beth,' he called, just above a whisper. He waited, straining to hear something. Anything. 'Captain Harper.' He shoved the blanket off his legs, pushed up onto his knees, the wave of dizziness overwhelming.

'I'm here.'

He barely heard her with the blood pounding through his ears. Her voice sounded from the farthest end of the cave. Gagging, he swallowed down the panic burning the back of his throat. A pain like he'd never felt, that had nothing to do with his injuries, radiated across his chest.

She's okay. She's okay. She's okay.

He sucked in and blew out breath after breath after breath.

Beth emerged from a shadowed corner, her appearance shocking. Her face was pale all over with black smudges beneath her eyes, her lips nearly white, and an ugly bruise smeared out across her cheekbone and jaw.

'Beth, *oh Jesus,* Beth? What the hell happened? Are you alright?'

It was such a stupid thing to say. Fucking ridiculous. She was far, far from alright. He steadied himself, he needed a moment before he could stand solidly, go to her.

'No. Actually, I'm not,' she said, her voice trembling. 'But it doesn't matter what I am or what I'm not, does it? We're here, stuck here. And there's nothing I can do about it.'

He glanced around them again. More slowly this time, torn between wanting to comfort her, and needing to know what he was dealing with. 'Where exactly *is here?'* he said, finally on his feet. His wounds still ached, but he felt stronger than he had for days.

'I don't know.' Her voice still quivered. 'About fifteen kilometres further up into the mountain from the farmhouse, I think.' She sniffed loudly and eased herself sideways to lean onto the wall, shifting the weight off her ankle. 'You don't remember getting here?' A shrill note edged her words; he'd never heard that sound from her before. 'You don't recall Iskander and me dragging you when you couldn't move? Or the three of us crawling for hours on our hands and knees so you didn't slide off the goddamn ridge?'

'Iskander? Who—?'

'Because they're clearly the actions of an assassin, aren't they? That's the kind of thing someone does who's going to fucking screw you over, isn't it? That's someone you can't trust?' Sobs echoed in her words, her arms wrapped around her middle, her hands clutched tight at her sides.

'Oh god, Beth.' He closed the distance between them. 'I know you're not with them. I'm so sorry. I'm so sorry, I—'

'Don't you dare touch me.' She pushed him back, squared her shoulders.

He backed off, but god he wanted to hold her. He needed to tell her, explain what happened. 'I wanted it to seem like I didn't give a shit, that you meant nothing to me in case—'

She gasped. 'Why? Why the hell would you put me through that? Why would you tear away every last part of control I had, every last bit of hope that you cared enough about me to do what you promised? *Do I* mean nothing to you?' Her tortured whisper echoed around them.

'No.' He pulled her into his arms, folded her stiff, resistant body into his chest. Threading his hands through her hair, he tipped her head upward, kissed her forehead, the movement as natural as breathing. Her skin beneath his lips warmed him in places he didn't know were cold. 'You don't mean nothing to me, Beth.'

She finally let go, let herself lean on him, her sobs muffled in his chest as she wrapped her arms around him. 'Oh god, Nate, I'm so glad you're awake. I thought you were—'

'Hey, shhhhh,' he whispered into her hair. 'I'm much better. You did good. With everything.' He held her, stroked her back. The toughest woman he'd ever met, broken. Because of him. He didn't have the right words, didn't know what else to say to her. He'd only honed ways to tell people to leave, never how to ask them to stay.

He cleared his throat, her hurt, a jagged lump blocking his words. 'We'll sort this out,' he said when she'd quieted a little. He pulled back so he could look at her, tilted her chin so she could see his face. 'You're right. I promised I'd keep you safe, and I've let you down on that. But I won't again, I'll fix this.' He'd rather chew off his arm than be the cause of this much pain for her ever again. She roused something in him he'd long ago buried, a need to protect her, to shelter her, shield her from anything that would hurt her ... feelings he'd only every partially dug up before a couple of times, for Finnegan, and the men in his unit.

She stared up at him, cheeks wet with tears, her eyes wide, her lips so very close. 'I don't think you can,' she whispered.

'I'll find a way,' he said, his arm still wrapped tight around her.

'Okay,' she said. She pulled his hand from her back, wove her fingers through his, her grip strong, warm. '*We'll* find a way.'

They didn't breathe, didn't move. He badly wanted to kiss her, comfort her the only way he could. But that wasn't what she needed, or deserved, a bloke who could only fuck away her troubles.

'Beth, I—'

'Let's sit down,' she said. Thankful she'd called the shot, he wasn't surprised when she let him keep hold of her hand as they moved to the bedroll, the only comfortable place to sit. He eased them both to the ground, didn't break contact with her the whole time, kept his arm wrapped around her as they both settled up against the wall. 'Nate, I need to tell you what happened,' she said, her face shadowed with concern. 'What's the last thing you remember?'

Still imagining what it would be like to have all of her pressed against all of him, Nate let go of her hand, the connection between them didn't help him concentrate on what she was saying.

'The only thing I remember clearly is you inserting the damn IV.' He tunnelled a hand through his hair. 'That's pretty much the last memory I have. When was that?'

'Three days ago,' she said, nodding slowly, her gorgeous amber eyes filling with tears again, despite the resolve he'd just seen in them. 'And, Nate, I think Betsy's dead.' A single tear slid down her face.

'What? Jesus, Beth, what the hell happened?'

'It was Sergeant Patterson. He shot him. Sergeant Patterson shot Betsy.'

White spots blanketed his vision. He couldn't believe what he was hearing.

'The IV I gave you was laced with something, probably some kind of sedative. It sent you gaga in under a minute. Sergeant Betts accused Patterson of somehow being involved. And Patterson shot him.' She swivelled around on her knees and faced him. 'And then he slammed me in the head with something, knocked me out.'

'Jesus fucking Christ.' Nate struggled to get his mind around it. Had Beth just told him that Patto shot the man who was the closest thing to a brother the bloke had? Dale Betts was one of the most honourable humans Nate knew. He pressed his back into the freezing stone wall, but not even the cold could jolt any semblance of sense into his head. And then Patto followed that up with assaulting Beth? A women there purely to help? He'd picked something was off with the bloke, but this? 'Did Patto say anything else before ... before he shot him? Did Betsy?'

Beth nodded. 'Sergeant Betts asked Patterson what he'd done. But, Nate, oh god, Sergeant Patterson's face, he looked like a crazy man. And Betsy, he didn't. He was ... devastated.' She was crying again. 'I couldn't stop any of it ... I'm so sorry.' Her sobs drove what felt like a hundred nails deep into his chest.

'Hey, shhhhh ... It's not your fault, there's nothing you could've done,' he said, grabbing her hand, his heart hammering so hard against his ribs he could barely breathe. 'Obviously something's seriously up with Patto. I've known that bloke over a decade, and I'd bet my life he's acting under some kind of duress. He'd never willingly shoot a mate, or hurt a woman. Never.'

'He was so angry.'

'I don't get it.'

Silence surrounded them, the room felt another ten degrees colder.

'I've seen that kind of behaviour,' said Beth. 'In people suffering with serious mental health issues, or, or, a drug problem.' She glanced at him. 'Has he ever had any troubles like that?'

'No.' Nate scrubbed a hand down his face. 'Not when I knew him,' he said. 'He was the biggest health nut in our training unit, always so focused on his body being perfect, you know?' Nate shook his head. 'There's no way Patto would ever be into that shit, and other than the normal agro we've all got—need—to survive out here, he's not an angry bastard ... No. Has to be something else.'

Beth nodded slowly, obviously running the events of the past three days through her head.

Nate exhaled loudly. 'What happened next?' he said.

'I came to, my skull thumping and these huge brown eyes, from a kid's face, were staring at me. I'm pretty sure I screamed, but he calmly explained that his name is Iskander and he'd been sent to help, and kept repeating it till I listened. My Pashto's okay, but he was talking so fast. It took me a few moments to understand what he was saying.' She moved slightly, stretched out her legs. Continued. 'He told me that his mother and grandfather owed Sergeant Betts a debt of some kind. And Betsy, he had seen them that day. He told them if he didn't come back, they had to come for us. Gave them the details where to find us. He showed me the note—it looked like Sergeant Betts' handwriting, so I, I just did what Iskander asked.'

He couldn't make sense of what he was hearing, frustration bubbled in his gut—he was drawing more blanks than answers.

'Betsy's done some pretty secret squirrel stuff out here. Maybe these people, the kid and the others, they're part of a cover crew? This Iskander and the other two?'

'I don't know. But, Nate, as well as the note, which was definitely Sergeant Betts' writing, Iskander called you Nancy, he said he'd come for *Betsy's* friend *Nancy* and pointed to you. He'd only have heard that from Sergeant Betts, wouldn't he? It's what made me go with him ... that and the fact I didn't have another option, it all happened so fast.' Her eyes searched his, burning with what he imagined were plenty of questions.

'It's okay, you did the right thing.' Nate's guts were churning, his head spinning. One of these blokes, either Betsy or Patto had to be on the take, or involved in some heavy bloody shit, something pretty bad, to have turned on brothers like this. Why the hell had they involved him? He hadn't worked with either of them for years. But what the hell did he have to do with it all? 'What happened next?' He circled his thumb around the inside of her palm, waited for her to answer.

She straightened up, wiped her face. Focused.

'The woman and the older man helped Iskander carry us out of the farmhouse. Said something about *Pashtunwali.*'

'The code of life,' murmured Nate. 'The code says they must be hospitable and honour anyone who comes to their home, or who does them a good deed.'

'Yes,' said Beth quietly. 'I am familiar with the term.'

Nate nodded for her to continue.

'They loaded us onto a cart and pulled us partway up a track alongside the bushy part of the lower mountain. When we were deeper into the mountain, they left us, just the boy stayed.'

'What? They left the kid, just him with you—us?'

'Yes, left him standing with a backpack almost the size of him filled with our supplies, and a jar of putrid tonic. The woman, I think she must be his mother, she asked me, in perfect English, to keep him safe. The man, maybe his grandfather, definitely an elder of some sort, spoke to the boy. I don't know what he said, sounded something like a prayer.'

'Jesus, Beth, you must've been terrified.'

'Honestly, there wasn't time for that, Nate, I knew this was it. Our only plan B.'

He linked his fingers through hers, tucked his other hand beneath his leg to stop from reaching for her face. *Stay focused dammit.*

'The tonic, is that the shit he made me drink? That you made me drink too?'

'Yeah, that's it. You remember that?'

Nate nodded. 'A bit.'

'You were a total pain in the arse with it,' she said, a strained smile lifting the corners of her mouth. 'I drank it too. Iskander insisted it'd help both of us. I asked him what was in it, he told me in detail, I caught most of it. I've used a few of the natural remedies the villagers use, and this sounded okay, so I just had to trust that it wouldn't kill us. Your fever broke last night, and the swelling in my ankle's dissipated, and I'm pretty certain that's what helped—that grey, murky water.'

Her cheeks looked pinched. Her eyes shadowed. He could only imagine what the last few days had been like for her, and as much as he wanted to stop hammering her for the details, he couldn't let her rest yet.

'So where's the kid now?'

'He left, came back with the heater, then said he'd be back in the morning.' She'd moved away from him, sat hugging her knees. 'If he comes back. He looked scared, less calm than when he brought us here.' He let her have her space, for now.

'Did you ask him who he'd be back with, or where we go from here? What happens next?'

'I tried to but he hushed me, got all frantic, kept insisting I do nothing, think about nothing except drinking the tonic. And it sounds ridiculous, but, Nate,

I did everything he asked because ... well, because ... of Betsy.'

Nate nodded. 'I understand.' Maybe this was foreign to her, but he'd lived this life, in this place, a world that most people couldn't imagine for a long time. Decisions, actions ... everything you did out here tapped into basic survival instincts, 'cause often, at the end of it all, no matter how good your training, that's all you had to use. And sometimes, what you did, what you had to do, it defied logic. It had to.

'He told me to keep giving the tonic to you too. So I have, I dripped it into your damn mouth as often as you'd let me, for the last twelve hours.' Her chin quivered, a sign she was still barely holding her shit together, no matter how much she wanted otherwise. There was absolutely no doubt he'd be dead now if she wasn't here. 'Thank you,' he said. It was so bloody inadequate.

She nodded slowly, inhaled deeply. 'I just did my job.'

Never in his life had a person, any person, offered the hope of better things like she did. What she'd done, the hell she'd been through, that shit, that wasn't *just her job,* it was all her ... pure, selfless, beautiful Beth. And all of this, it was his mistake, his bad decision ... and one he'd bloody make right. Jesus, he needed to show her how much what she'd sacrificed meant to him, know how much he owed her. There'd never been a time he'd wanted to actually *be* with a woman, *make love* to her ... until now.

But then what? An ache burned in his chest. What if he did—they did? What next? He had nothing to offer, nothing worthwhile to give her after that.

Beth pointed behind Nate, breaking his indecision, stunting the questions still hurtling through his head, searing his heart. 'Iskander camouflaged the entrance, locked it down. I got out, once. Tried to remember a landmark or something I might recognise from the map Patto'd given me, something that'd help, but nothing. I had no way to get any bearings, I have no clue where we are, or what I was looking at, so like a goddamn coward I came back.' She pulled her knees harder up into her chest. 'And now, now I'm here with you, just sitting here wondering if we're ever going to make it out.'

Out of nowhere, an image from the night he'd been dumped at the hospital flashed through his thoughts. So vivid he jolted, his mouth suddenly so dry he couldn't swallow.

'Nate?' She pushed out her legs, moved closer to him, grabbing his arm. 'What's wrong?'

'Beth, describe the boy, the kid. In as much detail as you can. Tell me every single thing you can about how he looked, the way he sounded. What he wore.' He felt like there were puzzle pieces floating around him, just out of reach, and this kid was a huge piece, maybe even the key. The one that'd pull everything else into focus, slot all the pieces together, help him get Beth the hell out of here.

She must've picked up on his energy hit because she sat up, looked him up and down. 'Why? What's so important about him?'

'I think I've seen him before.'

'When?'

'The hospital.'

'He's one of the kids that brought you to me?' Beth pressed her fingers to her lips, shook her head.

'Yes, I think he is,' Nate said.

'Then this is no coincidence.'

'No, I don't think it is.'

'Do you know what it all means then?' The desperation creasing Beth's face made him want to assure her he did, and that he'd worked it out. But he didn't, and he hadn't.

'Not yet. But he's back here tomorrow, right?'

Beth nodded. 'That's what he said.'

'Well, tomorrow, we'll be a whole lot closer to knowing a whole lot more.'

'I hope so,' she said.

Hope didn't come into it. Tomorrow was the first step to getting her back to base. He'd make sure of it.

Chapter 18

'I'm sorry.' Nate's gravelly voice startled her.

He'd been quiet so long after she'd given him everything she could think of about Iskander, after they'd hashed out theories and contingencies until they both fell silent, that lost in her own thoughts, fears, she'd almost forgotten he was there.

He edged closer to her, shrinking the distance she'd made between them. 'I'm so sorry for all of it,' he murmured, his stormy gaze fixed on hers, their faces level. 'You didn't sign up for this,' he said, the muscle in his cheek flexing like it was hinged to an eight cylinder piston. He reached forward, traced a line with his forefinger from her temple to her chin. She couldn't breathe, his woodsy scent messing with her self-control.

'Nate, I—'

'Shhhhh.' He pressed his finger to her lips, then slowly slid it away, leaving her skin burning in its wake.

'C'mon,' he said, levering himself to standing, he held out his hand for her to take, 'let's move closer to the heater.' She slid her fingers across his palm, his warm, roughened hand curling around hers. He pulled her upright, wrapped his arm around her waist. Her face, her body, centimetres from his, she'd never felt safer ... or more in danger.

'I promise you'll make it out of here.' His words, barely a whisper held the strength of a gladiator.

'We—' she dragged her eyes from his lips, held his gaze, '—we will make it out of here.'

'Okay, we...' he murmured, his gaze burning into hers, shooting sparks of light into her soul. She swayed towards him, closed her eyes, lips parted.

'Christ,' he said. A gust of cold air rushed between them.

What? Her eyes snapped open.

He moved away from her. Dropped his arm from her waist, dropped his gaze, turned and strode away from her to the end of the cave. 'I'll make you a tea,' he said almost on a growl.

'What?' Desire and anger warred for first place as Beth sucked in steadying breaths.

'What the hell just happened?'

He balled and flexed his fists, turned to face her square on, but didn't move. 'I'll never be able to thank you enough for what you've done for me.' Heat bloomed deep within her as his gaze explored her slowly from head to foot, his voice thick with emotion. 'But I promised to keep you safe—' his throat contracted as he swallowed, '—and right now, Doctor Harper, if I touch you, you're not safe ... from me.'

'Oh.' She frowned and shook her head. 'Oh,' she said again like a fool.

'I can't be distracted by anything, and neither can you,' he said. 'Our lives depend on it.'

Her heart skipped, but this time an icy fear was the trigger. 'Maybe that's true, but, Nate, I—'

'We need to focus on what we're going to do when Iskander returns,' he said without looking at her, 'and go over everything we know again. Search for anything we missed that will help us get out, get me to my unit, and send you home.' He paced back and forth where he was, the narrow width barely accommodating three steps each way.

Maybe it was the not knowing whether she'd see another day, or that her whole world was on its head. Or the simple fact she'd never been with a man who set her insides alight with just a glance like Nate did. Whatever it was, she needed to get a grip, and fast. Her every cell should be focused on escape, on survival, but it wasn't. All she wanted was to feel his warmth, his touch, his strong, gloriously alive body wrapped around hers.

She met his gaze again, the air between them heavy with want.

'Please ... Beth...' His face was stone, but his words vibrated with something between desperation and desire. 'Please ... I have to be ... I have to do, what's right.'

What she wanted of him, what she needed from him, crossed so many lines, for both of them. She shouldn't—couldn't ask it. Regardless of this hell, this impossible situation, she couldn't ask of him more than he could give, on every level, no matter how much she wanted him to.

A weariness started from her feet, dragged at her body like she was being covered head to foot in thick black tar. The heat in her blood, the fire in her bones from moments before, now all but evaporated.

'You're right.' She straightened up, forced herself to concentrate on what she wanted to say. 'But about your insistence on sending me back without you, without Finnegan and the men ... I need you to know something.'

His body tensed, he crossed his arms over his chest. 'What?'

She blew out a breath. 'My job here is to keep you well until we're done. And unless I'm a liability, I'm not going anywhere until I've completed that task. I know I dropped the ball a bit for a moment, let my emotions get the better of me. But I'm done with that, I'm good. And you need me.' Even though her heart was still racing, her thoughts were calmer, more focused. She needed him to know how damn serious she was.

'Beth, I can't ask you to risk anymore.' His voice rasped loudly in the silence. 'I'm really good at what

I do, including my mistakes. And asking you to be here is one of the biggest I've ever made. You need to let me make it right. Please.' Desperation rumbled through his words.

'We've been over this,' she said, walking towards him slowly. 'And you know what, you're not the only one who has trouble looking in the mirror because choices you've made affected someone else in a way you can't fix.'

He stiffened; his twitching muscles seemed to be fighting between moving closer and pushing her further away. 'What do you mean?' he said.

'Can we sit?' she said. 'It's not a short story.'

'Ah, sure.' Nate strode past her, seemingly relieved at the change in the direction of the conversation. He grabbed the bedrolls, the blankets and moved closer to her, still keeping his distance. They sat as near to the heater as they safely could. He wrapped the blankets over their legs, all without touching her once, and with what she imagined were a million questions churning though his mind. Once they were settled, he waited for her to start.

'I was engaged to a man. Andrew, Andrew Noble. We met at the academy. Nicest person you'd ever meet.'

'You don't have to tell me—'

'Yes, I do. It's important.' He needed to know why her staying was critical, why he needed to stop pushing for her to go back.

He nodded, frowning.

'He died last year, died because I was selfish.' Beth pulled her legs up, wrapped her arms around her knees, the pressure on her ankle just bearable. 'He asked me to marry him at breakfast, and by ten pm that night he was gone.' She exhaled on a shudder.

He pivoted, turned towards her, concern etched into every line of his face. She resisted the urge to reach for him.

'What happened?' Nate's voice low, strong, gave her the courage to continue.

'We'd just called our parents, my brothers and sisters, told them the news, and decided to go for a drink, celebrate at the old rec bar.'

'The one that used to be on the south side?'

'Yeah, that's it. They tore what was left of it down straight after the, ah, accident.' She swiped at her nose. 'Anyway, we both had the next day off but just as we were leaving, Lawso—Major Black called, asked me if I wanted to assist on a specialist cranial surgery. It'd originally been scheduled earlier in the day, but had been pushed back. Of course, I jumped at it, was so excited, I didn't even hesitate in saying yes, all before Andrew even hit my thoughts.' She swallowed hard, the shame of that moment hitting her again as if it'd just happened. 'He was upset, of course, but I promised him I'd make it up to him, that we'd celebrate when I'd finished.'

Nate's thigh was now resting against hers, his heat, his nearness, comforting. Maybe the distraction of her talking was enough for him not to worry about being so close to her? She took a deep breath, continued. 'What I didn't know, not until after, was that Andrew had arranged a surprise party, well, a sort of party, at the bar. He'd made a movie of our lives together, had a cake ... people. He'd gone to so much trouble.' She felt the tremor start in her chin and bit down on her lip.

Nate slipped his hand beneath hers, held tight.

'I should've realised he'd arranged something, and maybe deep down, I did, and just didn't want to acknowledge it.' She looked up at Nate, relieved to see concern etched across his face ... not the disgust she deserved. He squeezed her hand and she pressed her other hand to her churning belly. 'Thing is, Andrew never insisted on anything, never really put his foot down, especially when it came to my work. He was my biggest supporter. Always encouraging me to push boundaries, learn more, be who I needed to be. But that day, he'd almost begged me to stay, pleaded with me to come with him to the bar instead of go to the surgery. *Just this once.'*

Beth pulled her hand from Nate's, scrubbed it down her face.

'He was so annoyed. I'd never seen him that upset before. But, honestly, I was so desperate to get to the hospital that I didn't want to deal with feeling guilty, so, selfishly, I just left.' She sucked in a long breath, glanced at the silent man in front of her. 'Knowing I'd hurt him, knowing I was leaving him disappointed, I walked out, left him alone, on the day he'd asked me to be his wife.' She blinked back the tears burning the backs of her eyes. 'And nine hours later, he was dead.'

She swallowed back the sob pushing deep in her throat. His hand found hers again, his thumb pressing calming, rhythmic circles into her palm. He gave her time, waited while she gathered herself.

'He went to the bar anyway with a bunch of mates,' she said.

Nate grinned. 'Reckon I would've too, no point in letting a good party go to waste.' She shrugged her response, tried to summon up a smile, wanted to acknowledge his attempt to lighten things, but just couldn't.

'His dad's an electrician. Andrew had worked with him on weekends since he was a teenager. They'd arrived at the bar, and someone saw a spark shoot out of a power point near the air-conditioning vent. One of the blokes behind the bar asked if anyone was an electrician, and, when there wasn't one, Andrew being Andrew, offered to take a look at it. He opened the casing, and within seconds the whole thing blew up, blew half the wall out. Killed him and three others.'

'Shit, Beth.' Nate's arm curled around her shoulder. 'I'm so sorry.'

'It was ruled faulty wiring.' She didn't let herself lean into his hard, warm chest, she didn't deserve to feel comfort, to feel like it was okay. Not while she spoke about Andrew. 'The worst part,' she finally said, letting the tears fall, 'the worst part was that he was in the operating theatre next to mine and I didn't know. He was dying right beside me, Nate, and I didn't know. I save strangers every single day, but I wasn't there to save the man I loved.'

He didn't comment. Just rubbed strong fingers the length of her spine and back again, his other hand still holding hers tightly.

She glanced up at him. 'So can you understand now? Can you see why I can't walk away? I can't lose another man that I ... that I know, when I can make a difference. When making a difference is my job, a job I've already sacrificed so much for ... too much.'

He pushed her away from him with a gentle intensity, gripped her shoulders. 'Beth, this isn't the same. There's nothing selfish about wanting to be safe. About me wanting you to be safe. And his death, Andrew dying, it was an accident. A terrible accident, and that's not on you.'

He pulled her into his chest, his strong arms enveloping her. 'It could've been you there beside him,' he said, his voice husky, low.

'Maybe it should've been,' she whispered.

He twisted, pulled her out of his arms, grabbed her shoulders again. 'Jesus, Beth, no, it shouldn't.' He stared at her like she was a life raft and he was a drowning man. 'I'm really sorry you lost your man, I truly am. It sucks, but I'm not sorry you're alive.'

'Show me.' She so desperately needed to feel something other than guilt, fear. Grief.

'Beth, we can't, I can't—' He stood up, walked away from her.

She was on her feet just as quick, following him. 'Nate, I want to feel alive. I *need* to feel alive. I have no idea if I'll even be breathing after tomorrow. Please. I want to *live* in this moment, right now. With you.'

She watched his self-control crumble slowly, tumble like the walls of a detonated building.

'I'm not a man who—'

'I don't care.'

'There's no turning back if—'

'I know...'

His hand found the back of her neck, slid beneath her hair and pulled her towards him, possessive, demanding, intense. Crushing his body against hers, his lips sought hers impatiently; equal parts demand and tenderness. Cradling her face, he kissed her with an intensity that robbed her of breath, left her body trembling with raw need.

He drew back, captured her gaze with his own. 'You are like no-one I've ever known, Doctor Harper.'

She'd never imagined he could speak so gently. In that moment, she felt like he'd climbed into her and stolen her soul.

'And I know there is so much more to you than you show, Sergeant Calloway,' she whispered, 'and I want to see you. All of you.'

She could hear the quickening thump thump thump of his heart as he dipped his head, his teeth grazing her jawbone as he moved lower, feathering kisses the length of her neck, before claiming her mouth again, as both their hands worked fast, freeing their bodies from their clothes.

Whatever happened now, whatever happened next, this moment was theirs, and she was taking it, come what may.

His fingers traced a path between her breasts down to her naval, sliding sideways, outlining the ink decorating the hollow inside her hip.

'Is that a cardinal and dove feather bound together?'

'It is,' she said. 'You know your birds.'

'I get around,' he said with the shadow of a grin. 'Interesting choice.' His finger trailed a circle around the images, heat sparking low in her belly again.

'Dad worked in Virginia for a few years. I was born there. There was a cardinal singing her heart out on the windowsill of the hospital room when I was born. Probably drove Mum mental, and ever since I can remember, Dad's said my voice was as pretty as the cardinal that'd serenaded me into the world. He nicknamed me Red to remind me, and it stuck.'

'Your family call you Red? I'd never have picked that,' Nate said with a laugh. His fingers continued trailing across her skin, the distraction so intense she could barely string two thoughts together.

'Yeah, it's mostly just Dad who does now,' she said breathlessly.

'And you sing?'

'Not really. Haven't since primary school choir,' she chuckled.

'Hmmm—' his eyebrows arced and he leant closer to her ear, '—so why the *two* feathers?' His breath, hot, heavy, raised goosebumps all over her body.

'The cardinal also reminds me of my family. They're loyal, territorial birds, devoted to those they love.' She reached up, traced a finger over his full lips, smiled as they quivered beneath her skin. 'It probably sounds stupid, but I feel my family's strength with me when I look at it.'

He kissed her fingertip gently, his hand moving slowly around her body until his arm settled lightly over her hip, his fingertips lazily caressing the small of her back.

'It's not stupid at all. Must be nice, knowing your blood has your back like that?'

'Mmmm, it is.' She slid her fingers along his jaw, down his neck and across his chest, splaying her palm across his heart, the rhythmic beat tapping against her fingertips. 'What about your family?'

His body tensed, his hand suddenly still at her back. He glanced downward. 'Don't really have one.' He sucked in a breath and eventually met her gaze. 'Mum died when I was fourteen, never clapped eyes on the bastard who fathered me. No loss though, apparently he was an arsehole, had a thing for hitting women.' Disgust boiled in his eyes. 'And Mum's father, her brothers, well they weren't too happy with her having a kid at seventeen, so pissed her off before I was born. She never went back. Probably for the best from the bits she let on about them, the life she had.'

Beth wove her hands through his hair, pulled him close and kissed him, deep, slow. 'I can't imagine what it must've been like for you losing your mum so young,' she whispered against his lips.

He moved away from her slightly, but still kept one hand on her as he scrubbed the other down his face. 'Yeah, it was pretty shit. Don't rate foster care, can tell you that.'

Within a heartbeat, he'd turned, rolled her onto her back. He laid above her, resting on his elbows, his fingers twisting through her hair. 'You haven't explained the significance of the dove feather yet.'

Clearly, any more talk about his family was off limits.

'Purity and peace,' she whispered. 'Reminds me what I'm here for, why I do what I do. What *we* do.'

'Nice,' he murmured, his lips gently finding hers, the pressure of him pressed against the length of her, exquisite, as he dragged their clothes, the blankets up around them. Their bodies had cooled, and the cold creeping up to surround them made the small kerosene heater less than adequate.

'Since we're sharing our ink stories...' She traced the grey wolf above his heart. An animal depicted so broadly in myths and fairytales, she wondered if his represented vice or virtue? 'What's that about?' she asked.

He rolled onto his side, tracing circles on her arm, and gave the smallest of nods, sucked in a deep breath. 'Had an old bloke, a widower, live next to us in the building where Mum died. Helped me with my homework, rustled up a hot meal once in a while. Got me hooked on bloody sweet tea.'

'Sweet tea?'

'Yeah, he'd lived in Louisiana for a lot of his life. Told me sweat tea was the best thing he'd ever tasted.'

'Well,' she said, 'I'd never have picked *you* for a sweet tea drinker.' She winked at him.

'There's plenty you don't know about me, Doc.'

I'll bet!

Manoeuvring her so her back was now curled into his warm, hard body, Nate wrapped his arms tight around her middle, feathering delicious kisses down the back of her neck and across her shoulders. What she'd give for this moment to be at another time, in another place.

'We were up to the old bloke, what was his name?' she prompted, as much to stop her thoughts from careening down a dangerous track of hope, as to hear the rest of his story.

He stopped, drew in a deep breath. 'Mr Mac, that's all I knew him as.'

She cushioned her head on his shoulder, kissed the top of his arm.

'We talked a lot, about all sorts of stuff.' He paused, his tone soft ... this man clearly important to Nate. 'One day he told me about an Indian bloke he'd met, a guy who taught him how to see spirit animals.'

'Wow, seems this Mr Mac lived an interesting life.'

'Yeah ... he did. A really decent bloke too.'

Beth snuggled closer into him, couldn't get close enough.

'Anyway, one day, he said he'd been waiting to tell me something important. Made me sit, told me to cut the crap and listen. I reckon I'll remember his exact words till the day I die, he was so bloody serious. It was like he was giving me the combination to a vault of endless cash or something.' Nate gave a soft chuckle. 'He pulled out a book. It was a really small notebook kinda thing, had an old, scratched brown leather cover on the outside. He told me to open it.' Nate's entire body stilled, perhaps he was lost in the memory. But as quick as it'd gone, his focus returned to her. Beth didn't realise she'd held her own breath until she released it after Nate exhaled.

'It was about me, and my spirit animal—the grey wolf. He'd sketched pictures, listed details, crafted stories across pages and pages of this yellowy brown paper, all about me, *for* me.'

Beth nodded against his shoulder, waiting for more, her chest aching for the desperate young boy he must've been, her heart squeezing for the generous man who found him a safe place to land, some purpose to hold onto.

'He'd explained that the wolf spirit symbolised valour and victory, instinct, intelligence and an appetite for freedom.' Nate sighed. 'Looking back, I think it was just that the old bugger probably saw me for what I was, a kid heading down the wrong path, and wanted to get a fire in my belly.'

'Mmmm,' she murmured. 'It worked.'

'Yeah, it did,' he replied.

'Must've been so interesting to learn about it all, how he knew who you were? Bet that sweet tea got drunk by the gallons for a while after your first introduction to the book.'

Nate drew in a deep breath, exhaled. 'Nah, didn't actually. I had to leave, a week later. Kept the book though.'

She wanted to ask why. And why he hadn't kept in touch with Mr Mac. And what else happened. But, instead, followed Nate's lead, and bit her tongue.

'So when'd you get the tattoo?' Safer topic.

'About a year after Mum died.' Or not. *Dammit.* She could feel him withdrawing from her. Clearly any further questions or talk about his family, or people close to him, was off limits.

'Well, for what it's worth, I think Mr Mac was pretty spot on,' she said, lightening the mood, curling her arm around him, she laced her fingers through his. 'Tell me something I don't know about you, something I'd never guess.' Hungry to know him, all of him, before their time ran out, Beth pushed, with no idea whether he'd run from her or open up. As the seconds ticked by, his body taut, she said, 'Let's make it easier ... how 'bout I go first?'

'Okay,' he said, his body relaxing into hers again.

'I was a French exchange student when I was sixteen, lived in Paris for three months.'

'Geez, Red, aren't you full of surprises. So, do you still speak French?'

'Oui oui, monsieur,' she said, laughing. 'Actually, I think it helped me learn Pashto more quickly,' she said barely ignoring his hand as he lightly trailed a path up and down the inside of her thigh. 'Alright, your turn.'

'You need to be closer,' he said, pulling her into him again. 'I'm freezing my arse off here.' He circled his hips rhythmically against her butt, his hard heat nudging against her.

'No distractions, Calloway,' she said breathlessly. 'Just give me something.'

He exhaled hard against her neck. 'Ummm, I spend a lot of my down time fly-fishing.'

She pushed up and turned to face him, loving that his expression was a mix between anxious and shy. 'Really? That's so, so—'

'Boring?'

'No, that's not what I was thinking at all,' she said. 'It's just so solitary. So very quiet. But then, I guess it's just what you need in contrast to all of this,' she finished softly.

'Yeah, kind of.' He nuzzled her neck, shutting her down again. 'You got another one?' he asked, rubbing his hands down the length of her arms, clearly uncomfortable with her attention solely focused on him. She wiggled into the curve of his body, enjoying the heat, the hard and the soft of him moulding around her, and closed her eyes, breathing in the bliss of the moment. 'Well?' he said nipping her ear.

Fighting the urge to turn and take his mouth with hers, have his body deep inside hers again, she drew out the moment, made herself wait. 'Okay, here's one ... I've got a super slow heart rate. Sends medics into a flap every time I have a review.'

'Good party trick for a doctor,' he said between trailing his hot, seeking lips from one shoulder to the other.

'It is,' she murmured, arching her back as his hands traced the length of her thighs. 'So, what else have you got to share?' she asked as he pressed his hard hot length against her backside, nudging her legs apart. His movements were rhythmic, urgent, his hands moving slowly up her ribs, grazing the underside of her breasts. Trailing kisses down the back of her neck to between her shoulder blades, he nipped her skin, stopped, and rolled her onto her back, arranging himself above her.

'I reckon that's enough talking. How 'bout I *show* you something instead.'

With his broad, warm chest pressed against her back, his body curled around hers, she sunk into his protective arms, savouring the heat of his lips pressed into the nape of her neck, that one action telling her more than words ever could.

She turned slightly, leaned in and kissed him. She poured everything she had into him, wanting him to feel what she didn't dare say. Against her mouth, his lips formed her name, the muscles in his arms tightening, cocooning her against him.

'It doesn't matter what happens next,' Beth whispered, kissing him deeply before turning and nestling back into his arms, refusing to let thoughts of tomorrow destroy the utter perfection of right now. After a beat, the vibration of his voice filled the silence.

'No, it doesn't ... not for now,' he whispered against her hair, his arms curling even tighter around her waist.

Fast asleep, Beth was oblivious to the turmoil swirling through the man holding her tighter than he'd ever held anything before. Nate's heart rolled sickeningly in his chest, ice-cold fear creeping into every cell of his body.

For the first time since he found his mother's lifeless body on the floor of their dingy hole of a bathroom, covered in blood, her wrists slit, the empty gin bottle smashed beside her, he was terrified. What happened next did matter. It mattered a whole damn lot. Because, what happened next had the potential to lose him the one and only person he might ever be able to love.

Chapter 19

Lawson paid the first delivery driver and watched as he swiftly loaded the bulk of the supply boxes into the waiting second truck as instructed. After the changeover was complete, Lawson collected the three remaining boxes he'd insisted be left off, and made his way to the window of the second vehicle. He waved a wad of Afghanis in front of the raggedy clothed, opiate smoking driver.

'Any news for me, Aarif?' he asked the man in Pashto, praying the man had come through with what he'd promised.

He nodded, answering in English. 'Your man, he at second bluff.'

'When did you see him?'

'Morning yesterday. My man, Majeed, he say he watch him closely until you there.'

'Thank you.' He passed the money to Aarif. 'You let me know if there's any change to the situation.'

'Yes, Mr Major Black. Majeed, he keep eyes on your Banjo. He won't let him out of sight.'

'Thank you, Aarif.'

The toothless driver turned his ignition key and accelerated away slowly, his sorry excuse for a ute spluttering and smoking on its way to the border.

Aarif, the brother of Zoreed's late husband had his own axe to grind where she was concerned, and was more than happy to play a part in chipping away at her armour. But Lawson had no doubt a man like him could sway in his loyalty for the right price, even when it concerned the honour of his dear dead brother.

Now to tidy up the other mess.

Zoreed's broadcast, boasting her power at having captured such skilled men without detection, and demanding respect and honour for her women, her people's women, had gone viral, plastered across every avenue of international media within hours of its release. He rolled his shoulders. It was done. She'd made her statement bigger and better than she'd intended. *Thank the Lord.* Now he could get on with his agenda.

Lawson punched the familiar numbers into his phone, walked to his car and got in.

'You fix your problem, Major Lawson Black?' She spoke in Pashto just to annoy him.

'Yes, Zoreed, on its way, on time, like I promised.'

'With my double money?' English, clear as a bell filled his ear. 'And the extra sugar delivery? To me. Not border. That's our deal.'

'I have it,' he said. 'I wanted to bring it to you myself though.' He'd never changed plans or defied her orders, so this was a risk, a big one. And, if he got stopped with the cargo on him, he'd have some trouble explaining his way out of it. But there wasn't another choice. He needed at least twenty-four hours to get Beth back, and this was the best way, the only way to make that possible.

'Why you not send me it all with your courier like always, Major Lawson Black? I don't like different. You know this.' Back to Pashto, she sounded like the worst kind of damn fishwife bellowing in his ear.

'I'd like to see the men for myself,' he said. Absolute rubbish, of course. 'You've made your stand, the world is listening to you, sees your power. That's all you wanted, isn't it? You'll be releasing them soon I imagine? You've achieved what you wanted to do, right?'

'What if I want more?'

'More?' His gut clenched.

'Yes, Major Lawson Black, more publicity. I want more people to see a woman can be strong, powerful, clever.' She slipped into Pashto, her words animated, passionate. 'Not just the men.'

He didn't answer her, hadn't planned for this.

'Zoreed, with respect, that was not our agreement. I can't—'

'You don't trust me now, Major Lawson Black?' Anger bristled through her words.

'Of course I do, Zoreed. You've never given me reason to question you, but as you can understand, I didn't expect this change.' He was on extremely thin ice here. 'It's just if we continue on as planned, and I find the men, rescue them and lead them away from you, as we agreed, then you're safe and, well, I'm a hero. It's an outcome that means more security for both of us, moving forward. Once I'm the surgeon who rescued them, no-one will ever suspect me of wrongdoing. And, after that I can continue to protect you, maintain your business, as agreed.'

She clicked her tongue, he heard the phone swivel against her ear.

'But what if I do care that you are hero, and not me?'

Bloody hell. She wasn't letting up. Clearly she'd seen how quickly she'd made waves around the world, and liked it. It seemed that the high from her new level of supremacy was more powerful than the opiates she sold.

'I can find influential people to tell your story, people who understand your fight for your women, their education, and who will support your choices. I can do that much more easily if I can bring these men home first. But, if you kill them, Zoreed, the world won't admire you or fear you. They'll hate you. If you kill them, the media won't want to hear anything else you have to say.'

Her breathing was heavy. In. Out. In. Out.

He had to think quickly, find the sweet spot in her ego, figure out her intentions and work it to his advantage.

'Zoreed, I can do so much more for you if you let me rescue the men,' he repeated.

'What guarantee do you give?' she said finally.

'Whatever you request, is what I'll do, as always, Zoreed. My freedom's in your hands, and that's a lifetime guarantee of my word to you. You know this.'

Squabbling children flared through his earpiece in backdrop to her silence. The momentary pause reminded him it was vital he calculated every single word he said next. He needed her to continue thinking all he cared about were the men, the goddamn dog. And now, he'd added another item that should light up her list, media attention focused on helping her and her women. The fact that he'd come out of it looking a saint was just an added bonus.

'I don't like this,' she snapped. 'I don't like change in plans unless I make change.' She breathed loudly into his ear. He waited, sweat beading his body. 'But you turned good man, Major Lawson Black.' He heard a clap. 'Okay. You not here by sunset tomorrow, two men, they die and I film it. And your big boss, I tell him, I tell him you and Lieutenant Colonel Fraser, you both help me capture men, I show him proof. That's my promise.'

Holy Hell. 'Wait. There'll be no need for that, Zoreed, I'll—'

Click.

He kicked at the dirt, sending stones flying in all directions.

'Crazy goddam bitch.'

He needed her to implicate Fraser, not him. Fraser would hang him out to dry faster than Lawson could blink, find a way to deflect anything Zoreed did so he came out squeaky clean and only Lawson fried. With Fraser's retirement imminent—*he's had the party, why hadn't he left yet?*—Lawson didn't need anything to interfere with his moving out party.

Lawson's phone vibrated.

'I've got what you want. Meet me. 0600 hours. Map attached.'

It was all he could do not to smash the phone into the dash of the claptrap piece of garbage he was driving.

Christ almighty.

He sucked in deep breaths, exhaled loudly before starting the sedan. He allowed the engine to warm while he oriented himself with the map Patterson had sent. He had to let Zoreed's crazy plans go for now, and hope she didn't do anything stupid before he'd secured Beth.

The location Banjo sent was a good four hours from where he was now, and a serious deviation from his original route. Calculating the time difference, all things being equal, and if he pushed it, once he'd extracted Beth, ensured someone had definitely disposed of Banjo and Calloway, he'd make it. Yes, he'd be close to reaching Zoreed by her deadline, had to be. But he'd have to really move it now.

Slamming the car into gear, Lawson enjoyed the pull at the wheel as the backend slipped sideways across the roadside gravel. Fighting to keep the fishtailing at bay, he welcomed the adrenaline pump, the spark in his blood sharpening his focus on the plan, his goals, and the key part of it all, that Beth wouldn't be witness to a single thing. The sedative tucked in his pack would ensure she'd stay unconscious for the duration of what needed to be done. By the time he was finished, all she'd know, everything she'd hear about is what a hero her future husband had been. He'd worked out the dose so she'd come around just as they arrived back at base. And then, the blame would lay solely on whomever had been around at the time she was unconscious. If he were truly lucky, he'd be able to pin Calloway for it. After all, Calloway's

DNA would be all over whatever he needed it to be, and a dead man couldn't say otherwise, could he?

Smiling, Lawson pressed his foot down on the accelerator, already warming to the idea of another honour medal hanging from his parade jacket.

Chapter 20

Beth woke with Nate's arm still firmly wrapped around her belly, her body humming with an exquisite ache. They'd dressed, eaten, loved; his hands on her, her lips on him. She'd never felt more alive.

'So, do you think you'd be up for a tour of your vineyard once we're home?' she asked. He'd left her side, and was lacing his boots with his back to her. It seemed an age before he turned, so long, she regretted pushing the perfection of the last few hours, and her expectations of what might come. But a half-smile shadowed his mouth. He came back to her, leant in for a kiss, one that made her forget anything existed but him and this moment. He pulled back, cupped her face. 'I reckon I could arrange that,' he said, and kissed her forehead. She felt like her heart might explode.

She kept watch while Nate made his way out of the cave, surveyed their surrounds, and took stock. When he returned, he made her a tea while he relayed what he'd seen, and they discussed some suggestions, changes to their plans. The seriousness of their situation had returned to their main focus, and they again discussed what would happen once Iskander arrived, and the alternate plans if he didn't.

Beth was taking inventory of their supplies when Nate grabbed his gun, aimed it at the entry way, rocks and foliage now rustling with the sound of someone working their way in.

She rushed behind him, both of them silent, awaiting whomever it was entering.

'Oh my god, Iskander!' Beth rushed to him, wrapping her hands around his thin shoulders, giddily grateful for the young man's presence in their temporary tomb. She hugged him tight. Nate stayed motionless, dropped the gun to his side.

'Is everything okay?' Beth asked Iskander in Pashto, stepping back, giving him space. There was a part of her that hadn't really believed he'd come back, her belly flip-flopping with hope. 'Are we leaving today?'

He handed her the bulky hessian sack he carried. 'I bring water, some food. You eat,' he said quietly, in his now familiar stilted hybrid of English and Pashto.

Nate approached Iskander, held out his hand to the young man. Iskander clutched Nate's broad hand between his two smaller hands, and bowed his head.

'I am pleased to see you well again, Mr Sergeant Calloway, sir.'

'Thank you for your help, Iskander. I am very grateful.' Nate's Pashto was pretty good, but he stumbled on the last few words. 'It was you who took me to the hospital, wasn't it?'

Beth couldn't hold her gasp.

The boy nodded, his enormous brown eyes suddenly wary.

'How did you find me?' said Nate. 'Where was I? Did you see anyone else?' He must've realised he was speaking *at* Iskander, pelting questions at him like the kid was target practice, and toned it down at the last, but given it was the first real breakthrough they'd had, Beth understood his belligerence.

'Come, let's sit,' said Iskander, the boy's quiet command, confidant and warm. Nate watched the boy as they all moved to sit, his eyes never wavering from the kid, like he was a snake who might turn and strike at any moment.

'Can you start from the beginning ... from before, from when you found me the first time?' said Nate.

'Yes, sir.' The boy nodded. 'Sergeant Betts, he have you, but couldn't take you to hospital. He call me and my cousin, and tell us where to deliver you, told me soldier to see to get you close to doctor.'

'What?' Both her and Nate's voices echoed around the walls.

'How do you know Sergeant Betts?' said Beth.

'He help my family.'

'How did he know where to find me?' Nate said, ignoring everything else Iskander had said, and Beth's question.

'He come to us to help him,' said Iskander.

'But how did he know where I was? How did he know there'd been a blast? Right then?' The desperation laced with fury in Nate's voice made Beth's belly tighten.

'I don't know, sir,' said Iskander.

'When was the last time you spoke with Sergeant Betts?'

'The day he ask me to find you and Miss Doctor Beth if he didn't bring you to us himself.'

Nate's eyes met hers, anger, questions, the entire spectrum of human emotion marched across his face.

'How the hell do we know we can trust him?' Nate lowered his voice, but he needn't have. There was nowhere to hide, nowhere to speak privately here. So, whatever Iskander heard and understood, there was nothing they could do about it.

'We don't,' Beth said. 'But he has saved your arse twice, and mine too. Why would he do that if the end game was to kill us, or, or...' She couldn't actually verbalise any of the other horrifying scenarios that flashed through her mind.

Nate didn't respond, his gaze now fixed firmly on Iskander. His focus clearly on trying to work out whether this kid was likely to lead them in to, or out of, all kinds of hell.

Glancing between Beth and Nate, Iskander reached into his pocket and withdrew his hand. He opened his palm. He retrieved a blue stone, almost identical to the one Beth had found in Nate's pants when he'd arrived in the operating theatre. 'You still have yours?' he asked Nate.

Hope welled in Beth's chest. This kid couldn't be bad. He just couldn't. She dug her hand into her inner pants pocket, edged the stone from the deepest corner. 'It's here. I was looking after it for him.'

Nate flicked a look at the stone, then to Iskander, surprise and suspicion parrying on his face. 'You gave me this, when you dropped me through the fence. I remember. You said something to me too?'

'Zar bar jor shay,' Iskander said.

'Be well soon,' echoed Beth.

Iskander nodded, his brown eyes shimmering. 'You must keep it with you for our journey, Mr Sergeant Calloway, sir,' he said. 'And, Miss Doctor Beth, this one is for you.' Iskander spoke slowly in English and handed her another stone from his adjacent pocket. 'It will keep you safe.'

'Thank you,' she said, unable to make her mouth form any other words.

'It is my honour,' Iskander said, bowing. 'And now we must speak our plans. Our time here, it is running out. I am to take you to Mr Betts' soldier, he will help you find your friends.'

'Really?' said Beth, feeling a little light-headed as relief and adrenaline surged through her, the thought of being so close to rescuing Nate's team and Finnegan, and all of them making it back to base safely, suddenly a lot to take in.

'Wait just a goddamn minute.' Nate's voice speared out at Beth above the boy's head. 'We barely know this kid, and even though he's been solid so far, you're willing to risk our lives, hell, everyone's frigging lives on his word and a bloody blue rock? All we know here is that it looks like Betsy is somehow involved up to his neck in this goddamn nightmare.'

Beth chewed at her lower lip. Nate was right. She had no idea what on earth was going on, or how Dale Betts and Iskander were connected, but for some reason, deep in her belly, she trusted this boy, *and* Betsy's connection to him. And right now, that just had to be enough.

'Iskander, how did Sergeant Betts help your family?' Beth asked in Pashto.

'He save my sister from Zoreed's army.'

'Zoreed? The warlord?' said Nate. 'I thought she was a myth?'

Iskander's lips curled in, his hands clenched into fists. 'She rule the mountain.'

Beth looked from man to boy, waiting for more information, the name Zoreed ringing a bell somewhere deep in her memory, but she just couldn't place the detail.

'What's the story, Nate?' she asked.

'Apparently she's the only female warlord to ever rule, and has the most profitable drug trade in the country.'

Nate clutched at his gut.

'Nate?' Beth rushed to him.

'Fuck. Oh my fucking god.' He sank to the ground, his face draining of all colour as he dropped to one knee. 'He's in it somehow. He's a fucking mule for her, or, or something.' He shook his head. 'What the hell have you done, Betsy?'

'Wait a minute,' said Beth, refusing to believe Dale Betts capable of something sinister or remotely dishonourable. There had to be more to this. 'Iskander, did you say Sergeant Betts helped your sister?'

The boy nodded. 'He take her back when Zoreed's man kidnap her, take her for marriage.' The boy's eyes filled with tears.

'Oh, Iskander.' Beth went to the child, hugged him to her, her heart breaking for the little girl and her rescuer, who was now almost certainly dead.

'What's her name?' said Beth.

'Aqueela.'

'How old is she?'

'Seven.'

'Oh god,' Beth said. 'Is she okay? Did they hurt her?'

'A little, but she will repair.' His voice, no longer small, was full of fight. 'And they will be punished.' The fire in his eyes blazed hot and fierce.

Nate was back on his feet, listening to Iskander, watching the child's reaction.

'I am sorry about your sister,' said Nate, squeezing Iskander's shoulder. 'What exactly did Sergeant Betts do? How did he extract, ah, rescue Aqueela?'

For the next forty minutes, with effort and some frustration for everyone given the language challenges, Iskander shared what he knew of Dale and his team's mission to rescue six young girls stolen from his village as recruits for Zoreed's army, and who were also destined to marry older men.

'She, Zoreed, she control men, give them girls to marry, so they stay,' Iskander whispered finally.

From what Iskander shared, Betsy's was a dangerous and highly covert operation, and thankfully, a success. All the girls were returned, and their families relocated by their own army for protection and safekeeping.

'And so you see, Mother and Grandfather, we want to repay Sergeant Betts. So we help him when he ask us.'

'I understand,' said Nate to Iskander. He glanced at Beth. 'But what the hell has Betsy got do with me? With the explosion?'

'Maybe this operation wasn't finished, Nate. Maybe that's why Dale was still out here, why he found you.'

Nate listened to her, but didn't comment.

'Maybe Zoreed's involved in your unit's disappearance too. If he's watching her, then the intel might've been what led him to you.' It was the only scenario that made any sense to Beth right now. She wrapped her arms around her middle, her belly aching with tension.

'And where does Patto fit in then?' said Nate. 'They were working together when they found us.' He turned back to the boy. 'Iskander, did you see the other men with Sergeant Betts?' asked Nate.

'Yes.'

Nate described Sergeant Patterson, finishing with the scar beneath his eye. The kid shook his head. 'No, sir.'

'Are you sure?'

'Yes, sir.'

Beth sat silently as Nate asked question after question of Iskander, Nate's shoulders dropping slightly as he continued on. It was obvious to Beth, unless a genius at deception, Iskander's intentions were as he stated. That he really was here to take them to Betsy's contact, and that this person, with no name or details, would in fact lead them to Nate's unit, to Finnegan, and then on to some sort of safety, but she couldn't deny there was still unease bubbling in her belly.

'The issue as I see it now is, we don't know for sure that whoever Betsy's lined up for us, is on our side,' said Nate when Iskander was finished. 'What if Betsy's with us, and he's been duped?'

'Well, the way I see it, we don't have much of a choice, do we?' said Beth. Fear had crept back into her body. She shuddered at the thought of what lay beyond the crude doors blocking out the terrifying unknown beyond this room.

'No, not really,' said Nate.

With diminishing supplies, limited ammunition and Nate's health only just stable, they had to be smart about what they did next.

'Iskander, this man, the one you are taking us to, is he with the Australian Army too?'

'I do not know, Miss Doctor Beth.'

She could see Nate's thoughts whirring, his brain processing everything they'd learned.

'If they're covert, they'll have special clearance, contacts that will help. It'll just depend on the timing.

Getting us out at the wrong time could blow the whole mission, so we may have to just sit tight once we get to the bloke. See what's what then.'

Beth nodded. It was something at least.

'Okay, Iskander, what else is in that bag?'

The three of them reviewed the maps Iskander brought with him, examined the route Betsy had instructed Iskander to take should it come to this. They discussed all the relevant contingencies they'd use, worked out their backup options, and further backup plans to those.

'Betsy had known if it'd come to this, we'd need some decent aces up our sleeve,' Nate said to Beth when they were done. He scrubbed his forefinger and thumb across his eyes as they took inventory of Iskander's pack. A grenade, water, apples and bandages. 'It's why he had this prepped up, on standby.'

'Unless it's a trap,' Beth whispered.

'Well if it is,' Nate sighed, 'we're pretty screwed. Our only option will be to hope we can shoot our way out of it. Beth, no matter what he seems right now—' Nate glanced at Iskander and back to her, '—if he missteps or so much as drops an eyelash the wrong way, I won't hesitate to do what I need to.'

She sucked in a shuddering breath. 'I understand.'

'Alright, let's do this,' said Nate. Let's get us the hell out of here and take my boys home.'

Chapter 21

Lawson raced to make the deadline, cursing when another text came through from Banjo just as he arrived at the meeting point. He'd changed the agreement, said he'd only bring both Beth and Calloway with him if Lawson delivered more cash, and of course, more heroin. *Fool.* He got out of the car, slamming the door of the vehicle with so much force, the entire body of the car shook.

Typing out his agreement to Banjo's terms, playing the part of the patsy-over-the-barrel, Lawson kicked hard into the dirt. The only damn thing extra Banjo would actually get from him was a bullet between the eyes.

'Mr Banjo ... he will be here in twenty minutes,' said the older man now hovering to Lawson's right. The male, who seemed to have just appeared where he stood, was Aarif's *trusted eyes, his man,* Majeed, the most pathetic of Lawson's civilian contacts. If he didn't have to preserve his hands, he would've punched the snivelling excuse for a human into the dirt. The imbecile had been instructed to follow Patterson, make sure anyone he had with him made it back to face Lawson too. But he'd lost him, said Banjo disappeared in a crowd. *Garbage!*

'I heard you the first time,' Lawson said, glaring at the emaciated man. 'I still can't understand how the hell you lost him?' Pulling his pistol from his waistband, Lawson resisted the urge to pop the waste of a human right now.

'I don't know, sir. He disappear, like ghost.'

'When you saw him, did he have a girl, an Australian soldier?'

'No, sir.' The man's shoulders rolled further inward, and he stared at his dirty bare feet. Majeed bowed and moved backwards, turning and shuffling towards the perimeter of the clearing. His submissive hesitation set Lawson's internal radar into shrieking alarm. Even though he'd covered all bases, called every person he paid along this route to assure his own safety, something wasn't right here.

'Hey, don't move. You stay with me,' Lawson snapped, waving the pistol at the cringing idiot. 'I pay you to give me information, to deliver results. To follow people when asked,' Lawson bellowed in Pashto. 'And I don't have what I paid for yet, so you don't go until I say you do. Understand?'

'As you wish, sir.' The man's native accent, slightly affected after spending so much time with allied soldiers, grated on Lawson's nerves.

The tinny whir of the motorbike made both their heads shoot up, both of their eyes instantly fixed on the concealed track ahead of them. A dilapidated bike that looked like a dinky toy in comparison to the male rider, drifted into focus. Lawson's relief was fleeting. It was Patterson. But he was alone.

'Where is she?' Roaring abuse at the motorbike approaching them, he aimed the gun at the left side of Sergeant Patterson's chest. 'Where the hell is she?' he bellowed again as Patterson pulled up a metre from him and silenced the bike.

Patterson swung his leg over the seat and pulled off his helmet, a smirk playing about his pallid, sweaty features. 'Nice to see you too, Major Black.'

Lawson closed the distance between them in seconds, pressing the cold metal to the centre of the druggie bastard's forehead.

'Where. Is. She?'

'Shoot me, and you'll never know, will you?'

Lawson cursed the way his hand shook, and at the fact he could barely hear through the blood thundering past his ear drums. With the hair on his body stabbing into his clothes, Lawson realised that despite all his planning, all his checking, he'd walked into a goddamn set-up.

'I will give you this for free though.' Patterson continued. 'You're screwed. Special Ops are already all over you ... all over me...'

'What? What have you done, you worthless piece of shit?' Lawson's panic morphed into rage, and filtered into his hand, the pistol shaking, bumping against

Patterson's head, grazing the thin flesh on the addict's skull as his finger tightened around the trigger.

'What did I do? I repaid a debt, Black. You know all about that, don't you?' said Patterson, his words calm but full of menace. 'But mine was something decent, something good. All the shit I've done, the lying, the stealing. Using my, my friends ... I've tried to make it right.' Banjo's words dropped to a whisper. 'I owed Wolfman at least that for saving my life.'

Lawson's insides quaked. *Did he mean Calloway?* And what had he done with Beth?

An odd calm surrounded Patterson, his eyes fathomless, revealing nothing, staring straight ahead, like a dead man. Lawson swallowed back the bile crowding his throat, realising in that instant that the man at the end of his pistol's barrel wasn't scared, wasn't hesitant, wasn't anything. He'd seen the look before. On men who'd given up, who welcomed death. Lawson clenched the steel weapon in his hand so tight he lost feeling in most of his fingers.

'This isn't going to end well for you, or your fucking wife and child if you—'

The sound of scattering stones silenced Lawson, his head whipping in the direction of the noise before he could stop himself.

'Major Lawson Black, you have lied to me.'

Zoreed's bulk loomed ahead of him, her words stinging his ears like a nest of crazed fire ants. Her fleshy face was framed by a granite-like stare. He'd seen that look on her before, fury embedded in ice-cold black eyes, the glare usually a precursor to the meting out of agonising torture for the receiver.

With no way out, his brain whirred with desperation, grasping at any possible way to extricate himself from the situation. *God help me.*

He dropped his gun, rested it at his side, finger still on the trigger. 'Zoreed, thank goodness you're here.' He clasped the gun between his hands, held them up, prayer like, and walked towards her, forcing his tongue and lips to make steady sounds. 'These men—' he jabbed a finger in Patterson's direction, '—these despicable excuses for men, they've set us up.'

Her misshapen god-awful hairy black eyebrows arced on her forehead, his lungs were screaming for oxygen as she let them slowly descend.

'It is you who have done the setting up, Major Lawson Black.'

He fought the urge to look around, find the emissaries she'd have surrounding him, their rifles trained at every major arterial junction on his body. For the first time in his life, his heart pumped with pure fear.

'Zoreed, you know that I'm right. I am the only one you can trust here.'

Patterson slapped his thigh, laughing, doubling over with the intensity of his amusement. 'You're fucking screwed, you cold-hearted prick.' Patterson straightened to his full height, walked forward, stopped when he was eye to eye with Lawson, and crossed his arms over his chest, his laughter stopping abruptly. The raucous sound replaced by a loaded silence, despair and defeat staining Patterson's face. Banjo tilted his chin towards Zoreed then lifted his eyes skyward. 'She's my gift to you, Wolfman.'

The crack of Lawson's pistol reverberated around all of them, and Sergeant Dean Patterson, the decorated, once honourable commando soldier, dropped to the ground, slumped at Lawson's feet, nothing more than an inert pile of pathetic blood and bones.

Lawson could barely catch his breath, the adrenaline whipping his heart into a double time rush. The surge of orgasmic rush was indescribable; it felt so good to down the man who'd threatened to hold him over a barrel.

'You make big mistake, Major Lawson Black,' bellowed Zoreed.

Fuck. FUCK. He'd forgotten her for a moment.

'No, Zoreed, he was a weak link, he would've taken us all down.' Lawson gripped the metal in his hand, sucking oxygen in through his nose, out through his mouth. There was no way he'd be able to shoot her or any one of her entourage. Before he could even twitch a muscle, one of her goddamn underlings would end him. Why they hadn't already he wasn't sure, but it made him even more nervous.

His options for recovery, for preserving his life here, were seriously compromised.

'I do not misunderstand at all,' she said. 'And now, you see what happens to traitors, Major Lawson Black.'

Waving into the distance, she clicked her fingers; he braced for shots.

They didn't come.

He sought Zoreed's gaze, forced himself to look her in the eye, his body shaking with relief.

'I am sad.' She sighed theatrically, her face showing quite the opposite. 'You become like my favourite son, and I give special treatment to you. But I made big mistake.' Tut tutting, she thread her fingers in and out the base of her tunic and walked towards him, gesturing for him to hand over the pistol. 'Give me your gun, I have something very special for you, to say goodbye.'

Swivelling his head wildly, he stared into the seemingly benign rock crevices and bushes surrounding him. Jesus lord in heaven he was terrified. Paralysingly terrified. For the first time in his life, he couldn't make his brain piece together what to do next, couldn't figure out how he'd get the upper hand, control the situation. And for the first time in his life, the only option he could see was to beg forgiveness ... really ask for it.

Silent, the muscles in his neck and skull pushed and pulled his head into a slow nod, acquiescing to her request. 'Yes, Zoreed.' He delivered the pistol into her hand.

Standing motionless, four men rushed forward, patting him down in a revoltingly intrusive manner, he didn't dare flinch.

'Please, Zoreed, I can make this right. You're still the queen of—'

'You will not talk, Major Lawson Black, or I cut out your tongue.'

Oh god.

What happened now was anyone's guess. He had to control his nerves, be alert, had to keep his wits about him and exploit any weakness he saw, take any opportunity to free himself. Zoreed circled him until she was standing face-to-face with him, mere centimetres separating them. His spine stiffened.

'You will not die, Major Lawson Black.'

Oh, thank you, God. Thank you. His shoulders dropped an inch, the knot in his gut unthreading slightly.

'Not today,' she continued, dusting her palms together, the slap slap slap of her leathery skin filling the silence, 'and maybe not tomorrow either. Djamilia, come.'

The beautiful girl who'd handed him the blade over a year ago stepped forward, closing the distance between them with small, feather-light steps. 'Your hands,' she said to him, 'hold them out.'

Djamila wasted no time, deft in her application of the cable ties to his wrists. She then reached into her pocket and retrieved a fluid filled syringe. His blood turned to ice, shards of fear stabbing into his chest as she raised her arm, her hand to his neck. He heard a man scream as burning pain seared the muscle at the side of his neck, and then, slowly, quietly, everything faded to black.

Chapter 22

Nate rolled the blue stone around his palm before shoving it deep in his pants pocket. They'd been walking just over three hours, and he'd spun the damn thing in his fingers almost the entire way. *Offers protection my arse.* Even so, he still couldn't bring himself to hurl it into the scrub. They needed more protection than what he could provide right now, so no point angering the karma gods. Not that he believed in that shit, not really. But Beth did, so'd the kid. So maybe that meant something.

He glanced down the track at the woman striding with purposeful steps just ahead of him. *So smart, strong. So beautiful.* The sight of her made his heart jam in his chest.

With her, everything was easy, felt right. She made him want to be more. Be better. She made him think that maybe he had a different kind of future, one that included someone else. He'd shown her who he was, revealed the ugliness of his piss-poor excuse for a family, the kind of man he'd come from, and she didn't flinch, didn't turn away. Happy families were obviously a non-negotiable for her, and yet, she still hadn't pushed him away.

Maybe he *could* do this. With her.

'We are nearly there, Mr Nate. We must stop now, wait for Mr Betsy's man to call.' Iskander's hushed voice pulled Nate's attention from Beth.

'I still can't believe we have a goddamn phone, and we can't make any calls,' said Nate. Iskander retrieved the small plastic phone from his pack. Beth tracked back, stood with Nate.

A burner phone. Betsy had programmed it with access to only one number, to keep the line secure. Great tactic, but frigging annoying right now.

Iskander dropped back, walked in step with Nate as they continued forward, the kid's lanky body tense, aware, ready. He'd observed Iskander the whole way. The kid's reflex reactions, his gut level responses were as good as men twice his age, triple his experience. And as scrawny as the dude looked, he had the fight of a tiger in him, a strength Nate couldn't fathom given the kid's size.

'Hey—' Nate jerked his chin towards Iskander, '—let's stop here a minute.'

'Yes, Mr Nate,' Iskander said, moving closer to Nate.

He grabbed the boy's shoulder, squeezed. 'Thanks. Thank you. For everything.' His eyes stung like shit, and he couldn't swallow past the lump clogging his airway. He'd never been able to warm to a person, no less a kid, quickly. But this boy, this mini warrior, he'd crept in, held on somewhere deep, and wasn't budging. 'You saved me, and I'll never forget that.'

Nate's gut twisted, he probably wouldn't ever see the kid again after today.

Deep brown eyes that had seen way more than a boy his age should stared deeply into his. 'You are warrior, Mr Nate, you and Miss Doctor Beth. Like Sergeant Betts, you do right by my people. I will help you be safe, on my life, I swear this.' Iskander hesitated, then stepped forward, pulled Nate close, his head resting on Nate's shoulder. It was only for a nanosecond before his lanky body straightened, and he squared his shoulders, resumed his ready stance like they'd never spoken.

Jesus, he almost needed to bust out a hanky. Nate sniffed hard, squeezed the kid's shoulder again. Beth was an arm's length from them both, her body turned sideways, giving them privacy. Clearing his throat, Nate leant towards her, tapped her shoulder. 'Hey, you, huddle time. Final recap,' he said.

She grabbed his hand, squeezed, the jolt of her warmth reassuring yet strangling his heart at the same time. He didn't want to let her go, and within less than an hour, all going to plan, that's exactly what he had to do. Both Beth and Iskander would be gone, it's what he wanted, what they'd planned for. What *had to* happen.

And then he'd be alone.

He'd never thought about it before, never cared. But now, now there was a gaping hole in him that he'd never realised needed filling until this moment.

Beth squeezed his hand again, held tight, like she could read his thoughts.

'It's not goodbye,' she whispered, those cognac eyes burning fierce, determined. 'It's. Not. Goodbye.'

'I know,' he said, not sure any sound supported his words. *Lie.* He just couldn't think about the fact that it wasn't ever going to be the *see you later* she wanted. Fighting the urge to wrap his arms around her, desperate to keep her close, he cleared his throat, held her hand tighter.

'Let's get this done.'

They all crouched beneath the narrow rock ledge, hidden behind the dense foliage for over an hour.

'The man, he's late,' said Iskander, his eyes darting between Beth and Nate.

'Yes,' said Nate. He didn't like it. 'Let's go over this once more.'

They each repeated their role, what they'd do when their contact arrived. They reviewed the strategy for what happened next, revisited their well-constructed contingencies.

'So, he'll have weapons for each of us. Take them as soon as he arrives. And if you hear me shout *Nancy,* you shoot to kill. No questions. Got it?' said Nate.

They both nodded. Beth's voice was low, strong, committed. 'We know what we have to do.'

'And once we're secure, I'll give him the run down on our new plans,' said Nate, 'and we'll get you both out of here. He'll have access to comms, weapons. Help. And if he doesn't, well, we're ready for that too.'

Another half hour passed, forty minutes, the sun was dropping; they'd be out of light soon.

'That's it. He's not coming,' said Nate. 'We need to make other plans. Pronto.'

'Something is very wrong.' Iskander dug his thumbnail into the skin of his forefinger, the first sign of anxiety Nate had seen in the boy. It made him nervous.

'Let's find a source of shelter, for tonight at least,' said Beth. 'Decide what to do next.'

Nate flicked his flashlight on and pointed to a densely forested area on the second map they had, one they'd not discussed in detail, hadn't planned on using. 'Iskander, what do you know about this space?' It was an area that was about another twenty kilometres from where they were, fortified each side by mountains, and a lake running through the centre.

'It is the—' The kid's words froze on his lips, sharp, angry male voices floated on the wind, none of them English speaking.

The three of them held their breath. Nate strained to make out the conversation, but could only catch the basic words amongst the heavily-accented Pashto.

'What are they saying?' he whispered to Iskander

'They say she doesn't accept mistakes. She doesn't give second chance.' Iskander shuddered, his skin ashen, his hands trembling.

'Iskander?' Beth reached for the boy's wrist, calculating his pulse, wrapping her other arm around his shoulders. 'What is it? Do you know who they're talking about?'

The kid nodded, his eyes fixed onto an invisible target in the distance. 'It is her.'

'Who?' Beth whispered her question again. 'Zoreed?'

'Yes,' the kid stuttered. 'They are going to Zoreed.'

The words of the approaching men though patchy were louder, closer. Nate couldn't understand most of what they said, and obviously, neither could Beth, and they didn't have time to figure it out, especially when Iskander's reaction made it pretty clear these blokes weren't going to be their best friends any time soon.

'Stay down,' Nate said to both of them, and braced himself to launch from their alcove. Securing his gear, he leapt across the two-metre track, and sprang up onto the rock shelf in front of them, swallowing the grunt of pain crowding his throat. He edged forward, straightened, lay flat on his belly and set his rifle scope Iskander had brought with him, pointed it in the direction of the voices. He kept his back to where Beth and Iskander were crouched, and he hoped, well hidden.

Within minutes, three mean looking thugs pounded into focus. The way they tromped into the open space told Nate they weren't military. But the way they carried their weapons, their attitude, left no doubt they could be just as lethal as any one of his best men.

Clearly agitated, clearly looking for something, or someone, they surveyed their immediate perimeter, the meanest looking one stopping, while the other two continued on. The bastard's stare zoned in on Nate's direction. Nate pressed his finger into the warm trigger, closed his left eye, held his breath. The thug surveyed the area, scanning both left and right, then walked directly towards where Nate was hidden.

The crack of a pistol discharging smashed through Nate's concentration, his finger automatically releasing from the trigger, his head whipping behind him in the direction of the sound. The second crack propelled him backwards off the rock, the thug ahead of him, a second thought, as he frantically retraced his path back to Beth and Iskander.

Staring at the space where he'd left them not even a minute ago, he couldn't breathe.

It was empty.

No. No. No. This isn't how this went.

He clamped a hand over his mouth, stifling the roar surging in his chest.

Jerking the rifle back over his shoulder, he pushed up, spun on his heel, surging forward after the voices. Metres up the track, movement above him had Nate jolting backwards, taking aim as Iskander dropped from the branches of the tree beside them. Sobbing, shaking, the boy flung himself into Nate's chest.

'Miss Doctor Beth, she was with me, she was right with me.' He sucked in a strangled breath, frantic, he repeated his whispers. 'She was there, Mr Nate, and we run, we are running, I turn to help her, and she is gone. Gone.' He clutched Nate around the chest, his shudders rippling through Nate's entire body. 'I am sorry. I am so sorry.'

Nate's entire world shattered into a thousand pieces. He felt like someone had reached in and ripped out his heart.

But he didn't have time to think like that.

Beth didn't have time for him to think like it either. She sure as hell wouldn't waste time if it were him missing. She'd kick his arse and tell him to get his hustle on.

'Hey, hey ... it's okay. It's okay.' He pulled the kid back, made him look him in the face. 'We'll find her. We will. They can't be far.'

With panic like he'd never felt pulsing through his body, paralysing every muscle, he tried to think, forced himself to quiet the noise in his head and sort a plan. Iskander followed his lead, stifling the sobs racking his body, his eyes glued on Nate. How'd they get Beth and not the kid? A sliver of unease flickered through Nate's gut but he pushed it away. He'd stake his life that Iskander had nothing to do with it, but however it happened, it'd been swift and silent. Which meant, it could happen again.

'Do you hear that?' Nate said after several moments.

Iskander didn't move. 'Shouting,' he whispered.

'Yes, male voices shouting,' Nate said, straining to hear more. 'Do you think they're the same voices as before?'

Iskander nodded. 'Yes, Mr Nate,' he whispered.

'We have to go. Stay behind me, keep out of sight.'

Jesus, let his gut be right about what they were about to do. Every damn second counted.

Chapter 23

Lawson eyed the rusted, blackened, blunt axe head, and the blood soaked wood of the tree stump supporting it. *Oh God.*

He'd spent the night in a putrid concrete cell, freezing, and working on a plausible, what-the-hell-to-do-nextplan. He still didn't know what that bastard Patterson had done with Beth or Calloway for that matter, and he hoped against all hope he hadn't given either of them up to Zoreed. Particularly Beth, because she alone, as a woman, may just be able to save his skin, be able to do something. Appeal to Zoreed female to female; help him out of this nightmare.

Zoreed stood before him, arms folded across a chest so round, it blended in with her gut. Her eyes fixed on him like a cobra ready to strike.

'Zoreed, you have three other men. The dog. They're worth much more to those people you want to bargain with for the world's media than I alone would be,' he said.

'You mean these men, Major Lawson Black?'

Four men, likely Zoreed's kin by the look of them, paraded three bruised and beaten shells of humans towards him, shoving and kicking them into forward movement, dragging them to stand front and centre, less than five metres from him. One, the smallest one, fell forward, unconscious by the looks of it. The guards left him sprawled where he lay, face down in the clagging mud. The other two dropped to their knees, frantic, but unable to reach the silently drowning man. The other one, the tallest, tried to shout his name, but there was no way to tell what he was saying, his throat so hoarse, he barely made an intelligible sound.

Lawson didn't have to work hard to summon up a look of shock, he even gasped for Zoreed's benefit, wondering if she'd bound him up, and was scaring the living hell out of him just for show in front of the men. The soldier's hands were hog-tied, their necks bound together by something resembling medieval chain mail. He'd seen some pretty off the wall torture during his career, but this, this was quite a sight. A stab of pity pierced Lawson's gut, but it was gone in a heartbeat, replaced by the fear that he'd be next if he didn't find a way out soon.

'Zoreed, you must let them go, you've used them for what you needed.' He did his best to appear to plead to her, but her face told him his game was up. It was clear she knew he didn't care for any of the good-as-dead men in front of him, but he pressed on with the charade anyway. If somehow one of them made it back, somehow stayed alive, they needed to hear him have at least feigned some concern, enough that they could recount something to anyone asking.

'I'm sure they've served their purpose well enough, Zoreed.' They'd sure as hell worn out their use for him. If every one of them had to meet their maker now so that he could earn a pass out of this hole, then so be it. Sacrifice for the greater good and all that.

Sacrifice. It was something these fools did particularly well, were trained for it. In fact, because of this situation, one he'd engineered for them, he'd actually done them and their families a favour. If they died now, they'd go home heroes.

'Major Lawson Black, for a smart man, you so stupid.'

Zoreed's fractured English dragged him back to the moment.

'I have you all.' She swept her arms wide like she was an opera dame, centre stage, taking her encore, her cackling laughter spewing out of her mouth like an erupting volcano. 'I don't need them anymore. I get much more—what did you call it?—*exposure,* if I damage you.'

The skin on his scalp tightened, saliva swirled in his mouth. He forced back the vomit clogging his throat. *Think. Think. Think.*

'How will you run your business if you kill me, Zoreed? These men don't have the contacts, the access I do. Fraser's leaving, and—wait...' His brain caught up with his mouth. 'Damage? Just me?'

Like a piercing air raid siren, the wail of understanding exploded through his brain. Realisation smashed through his bones, leaving them a gelatinous mess. He stumbled backwards from the massive stump.

'No, oh no, no, no.'

'Pick up axe, Major Lawson Black.'

Two men rushed forward, shoved him back towards the stump, thumping a piece of timber to the back of his knees for encouragement. He cried out as his shins smashed into the tree roots that had just been under his feet. One mountainous man pressed his rifle into Lawson's left kidney, the other pierced his skin with the tip of a syringe, the metal tip already submerged into the subcutaneous flesh at the base of his neck.

'Now lay your left hand down, flat on stump,' she crooned, mimicking the action she'd requested like a schoolteacher demonstrating a new concept. He tried to make his hand move as instructed, but the muscles and tendons had taken flight, refusing to cooperate.

'Do it. Now.'

The plank of wood slammed into his lower back.

He screamed as he collapsed face first into the timber, his face smashing into the unforgiving platform, blood streaming from his nose, his mouth, clogging his throat, sent him into a coughing fit.

The bigger torture merchant standing on the other side forced his hand to the stump. 'I break your fingers first if you like,' he said in perfect English.

Lawson managed to raise his head. The maniacal look in the monster's eyes told Lawson the bastard would like nothing more.

'You will not touch him, Amal.' Zoreed's voice broke through Lawson's pain, the finger-breaking-watchman slowly backed away.

'Now pick up axe,' she said again to him, the grin cracking through the centre of her face gaped wide, like the tear in his self-control.

Every muscle in his body cramped with fear.

She wasn't going to kill him.

'Pick up axe now, Major Lawson Black,' she said calmly, the smile gone.

He was going to kill himself. One body part at a time.

'Sweet Jesus, sweet Jesus, sweet Jesus.' Appalled, he watched as tears, his tears, tunnelled into the dried-blood brown-tinged wood of the stump. The bitch was starting with his hands. His surgeon's hands.

'I-I can't. Please...'

'Do you refuse, Major Lawson Black?' Her lilting voice was terrifyingly calm. Terrifyingly controlled.

'I beg you, Zoreed—'

'I ask if you refuse me. Yes or no, Major Lawson Black?'

His thoughts and desperate ideas collided, blurred and sank into a black swamp of terror. If he didn't do it, would she have one of the bastards beside him do it instead? But what did it matter now? If he even flinched the wrong way, ten-to-one the rifle at his kidney would discharge before the syringe in his neck had fully ejected. At least then he wouldn't know. Wouldn't be conscious if one of them chopped off his hand.

Or maybe she'd do it? Keep him conscious? For fun?

His cheeks, lips, his damn eyelids quivered. He couldn't control the muscles anywhere in his body from quaking.

'You take too long, Major Lawson Black.' She clapped her hands. 'So, that is no for me.'

'Wait,' he screamed at her back, her thick legs pounding away from him towards to the heavily guarded shed at the furthest corner of the property's perimeter. Ignoring him, she barked an order to the guards, each one leaning against either side of the entry. One burst into action, unlocked the door and swung it wide. Zoreed disappeared and in moments, emerged with an Australian Army uniform clad body, the head covered, hands bound, she hauled the writhing human towards him.

She dragged the body to the stump, the person's high-pitched screaming muffled by the sack, and probably a gag. Hauling the sack from the person's head, Zoreed wrenched out the arm, and smashed the hand onto the naked stump. 'Then you have made choice to cut off this hand instead.'

Lawson's vision clouded, blurred, blackened.

'*Oh my god.* Beth?'

Chapter 24

His face wet, likely bleeding from powering through the low lying branches, Iskander beside him, light on his feet, ducking and weaving in unison, Nate pushed harder than he'd ever done in his life. It'd taken some time, more time than he'd have liked. But conscious they had to move very carefully, ensure every movement, every action remained undetected, he'd forced himself not to rush, to stay a reasonable distance away, and finally they'd reached the voices. The men had stopped for a smoke.

Nate waited for his eyes to adjust to the darkness, the glow of the cigarettes just enough to make out their faces.

She's gone.

'She's not there.' Iskander's whisper echoed his thoughts.

'No.' The hope that she'd escaped died in his chest when he saw one of the bastards wearing her jacket. *Fucking arsehole.*

He glanced at the kid, he'd seen the jacket too.

'They must've handed her off to someone else.'

Iskander nodded.

'Zoreed's compound mustn't be far then. My bet is she's there. We need to get up high, see what's surrounding us. Come on.' Nate ushered Iskander to the cluster of pine trees just ahead of them. They climbed deep into the heart of the largest tree, Nate's rifle close at hand the whole way.

Hidden for now, Nate surveyed the men more closely. There were four. There were two hulks, the third was a kid who didn't look much older than Iskander, and the last was a skittish wiry bloke, likely the wild card of the group.

Struggling to shut down his instinct to take the bastards out while he had a clear shot, the possibility it would alert Beth's captor was a risk too great, Nate looked beyond the men to the glow of lights less than a kilometre from where the bastards stood smoking. 'That must be it. Zoreed's place,' he said aloud, more to himself than the kid.

'Yes,' said Iskander, crouched a branch lower down, eyes fixed on the concrete structures within the compound. 'My sister spoke of such buildings.'

Poor kid. Reliving this must be eating him alive. 'We'll get them, all of them, okay?'

'Yes, Mr Nate.' The fire returned to the boy's eyes. Good. Nate needed him to feel the fight, not the fear, it'd drive him harder when he needed it.

Nate strained to make out the shapes, decipher the layout of the buildings. He could see what looked to be around a three-metre high fence, and barbed wire gate to match. Scanning the length of the wire, he'd bet his left ball that the perimeter was electrified too.

He glanced back to Iskander, the kid's face almost glowing it was so pale. 'Are you certain this is it?' Nate asked him. Iskander hadn't made a mistake before, but he was more than a little shaken up right now. And although he seemed like he'd pulled himself together, was actually more angry than scared, Nate couldn't be sure, and uncertainty increased risk. He couldn't have any more unknowns to deal with.

'Yes, Mr Nate. I *know* him.' Iskander pointed through the branches as a fifth player joined the mob. They'd all moved, were now closer to what looked like the entry gate, the swagger and weaponry on the newly arrived male screamed head kahuna. 'That man,' he continued, pointing with a steady finger, 'he took my sister.' The steel had returned to the boy's posture, the tremor from seconds ago gone, rage heating the air around them. 'He steal her to marry her.'

Nate reached down, squeezed the kid's shoulder, a fire now rampant in his own gut at the fact that old ugly bastard would wed a child. 'We'll stop them, I promise.'

It'd been almost all over for them a few times on the way here, but, by more arse-than-class, they'd managed to make it this far with little more than their wits and will. Beth was within those walls, Finnegan and the guys too, he could feel it. He sucked in a breath and exhaled long and slow. 'You ready to go?' The pain in his gut felt as if a horse had kicked him.

'Yes, Mr Nate.'

'And you're clear on what to do if I can't send the signal?'

'Yes.'

'You know how long to wait here before you go for help?'

'Yes, Mr Nate. I will not fail you again.'

He shuffled around to face the kid, leaned in close.

'Iskander, you didn't fail me, or Beth, or anyone. You're the warrior here. You.' He continued eyeballing the kid. 'And I need you to be again. Okay?'

The boy's gaze dropped before lifting, lit full of determination. 'Yes. I will, Mr Nate.'

A commotion erupted, dragging their attention back to the gates. Nate couldn't make out what the men were going on about, but from the tense and agitated movements accompanying the conversation, something had them riled. The head kahuna, the boss-man-weapon-wearer stood back, watching from the wings, his right hand in his pants pocket, no doubt resting on a trigger of some sort.

Good. This was all good. He needed them off their game if he had any chance at all of getting close enough to get inside. He'd only have seconds to take them down and infiltrate, or he too would be joining the ranks of one-wrong-decision dead men.

'It's time.' Nate's gut clenched. 'You are brave, Iskander. You've more courage than most men I've seen out here.'

The kid nodded solemnly. 'Yes, Mr Nate.'

'Okay, let's do this.' Nate commenced his descent to the base of the tree.

'Wait, Mr Nate.' The urgency in the kid's whisper made Nate reach for his gun.

'What is it?' he said, looking back up into the fork where Iskander was perched.

'Kha kismet darta ghowaram.' Determination shone from the kid's eyes.

Nate swallowed, but didn't break his line of sight with those huge brown eyes, needed the kid to feel safe, know he was gonna make it, no matter what happened. 'Good luck to you too, my friend.'

Covered head to foot in putrid sludge, Nate hauled himself through the final five metres of the waste culvert, alternately retching and spitting as he went.

He'd worked on the premise that the perimeter had to contain some sort of waste management system, and lucky for him it was of inferior design. He'd seen two exits, and if he'd calculated right, was about three hundred metres from making it inside the front section of the compound.

There'd been four shots fired in the hour it'd taken him to reach this point. Whoever the hell had upset the apple cart during the fracas he'd seen early had done it well and good. But right now, he had no idea if it'd help or hinder his situation.

The flinty glow from the overhead lights surrounding the barbed wire fence sent shadows flickering across the perimeter, and made it hard to scope out the landscape, define what he was looking at. Scanning the fence, his heart stuttered. He pulled his rifle. Bodies. Three of them. One, headless, strung up by the neck, hanging from the gate—a statement. The other two on the ground he recognised from the group he'd seen earlier. Bullet between the eyes, both of them.

Unrest in the camp could be good for him. Hopefully whatever was going down had distracted the security detail Zoreed would likely have in place, at least long enough for him to make his way in.

Wearing a dead man's clothes hadn't topped his list of to do's but thankfully the bloke was on the bigger side of his size. Nate shucked the jacket over his own, wrapped the stinking scarf around his face and crawling on his belly, made his way to the closest building, grateful for his entry into a sort of courtyard, via the rusting, unmanned sewerage grate at the far end of the enclosure. It'd been a lucky break, he doubted there'd be too many more of those.

Two men stood sentry at the furthest end, but they were lazily leaning on their guns, clearly discussing whatever'd just gone down. He came within a metre of them, dropped one and before the other realised Nate wasn't an ally, he was down too. He dragged their bodies into the darkened corner where he'd just come from. It wouldn't be long before they were conscious again, so he had to move quickly.

Surveying the landscape, crouched in the shadows, he calculated his options. From what he could see, there were four men, two women directly ahead of him. All brandishing AKs, and all intently focused on something to their right, something that wholly held their attention. Their level of concentration pricked at Nate's neck. Something was going down. Something big.

The grenade weighed heavy in his pack. The use of it, the timing, determined who lived and died today. There wasn't any room for error.

Edging closer to the nearest building, slowly, silently, he made his way to a large wooden crate. He crouched behind it, now with the same line of site as the distracted spectators, but at least five hundred metres away from them. Hunching down, he crawled towards them, making his way across the dirt. He'd almost reached them, and had a clear vision of whatever the hell they were all looking at, when a cage, swaying above the group caught his attention. His heart thudded, stopped.

Finnegan.

He couldn't swallow down the sobs exploding from his chest. Nausea rocketed up his throat. Finn, a mess of bloodied fur lay sprawled at the base of a goddamn rat cage. Still, soundless, he was suspended from a pole, swaying above the fortified concrete building. Desperate to get to him, Nate surveyed the rest of the landscape, the bloody liquid filling his eyes made it hard to process what he was seeing.

His heart stuttered again. *Johnno? Fish?* The withered, beaten men shackled together by the neck stood slumped against the stone wall of the building beneath Finn. *Jesus.* Nate's eyes moved to the body sprawled in the mud, the unmistakable red hair almost fully submerged beneath the mud. *Longy. Oh god, Longy.*

Shuffling himself sideways, crouching behind a pile of hay, Nate wrapped his arms around his knees, squeezed his eyes closed, and tried to suck in a breath. He'd failed. Failed all of them. The tears soaked his cheeks. 'I'm sorry, so sorry, my furry little mate...' He buried his chin in his chest and sobbed silently, until a rumble of murmurs penetrated his grief, the noise enough to make him look up. His view partially blocked by one of the men, he watched as a woman, only identifiable as one by what she wore, was dragging someone bound and gagged across the dirt. By the way the crowd hushed, and the fact they were glued to her every move, it was very likely the woman in control was Zoreed. No wonder Iskander had been terrified.

The woman and the prisoner disappeared from his view within seconds, he couldn't see any further without exposing himself. Swiping at the tears and shit dripping from his face, Nate tried to focus on what next. On Finnegan, and Beth, she was here somewhere, and Fish and Johnno, they were still alive. He couldn't sit here crying like a frigging baby. He was the last chance they had—last chance he had to make this right.

Before he'd moved a muscle, Beth's scream crashed through his ears. He was on his feet and running towards her voice, the cheers of the surrounding blood-thirsty spectators deafening.

Chapter 25

'Lawson? Oh my god, Lawson?' Beth's terrified whimpers ricocheted off his eardrums, her grotesquely swollen face, her half-closed eye inches from him as she frantically searched his face for answers, a way out of the situation.

Like a flipped switch, disgust quickly swallowed his shock, and he suddenly saw her with fresh eyes. An explosion of anger, frustration ... disappointment wiped out the feelings he had for her, this woman who'd rejected him. As of this moment, he was no longer her way out of anything, but she might as well be his.

'Oh, Beth.' He glared at her as he shook his head. He'd worked so hard to make a life for them both, one where she should've been proud to be his wife, one where she would've been so happy, satisfied. A life she should have been so grateful to be chosen for. But instead she'd humiliated him, rejected him, then chosen instead to accompany Calloway and his cohorts, leaving him, and all he was prepared to offer her. Revulsion whirled in his gut. She'd taken all that he'd given her, his time, his experience, his attention, and thrown it in his face. And now, because of her, he was here on his damn knees, begging for his life.

Well, she'd made her bed, and if it meant he'd get out of here, he'd happily help her lie in it. The best part of it, Zoreed still thought Beth was his Achilles, a way to make him suffer. But oh god, she was so wrong. Zoreed had just handed him a perfect gift, a perfect way of delivering his retribution.

He prayed Beth could read his mind, see the grin sitting just behind his feigned distress. Know that for what she'd put him through, he'd enjoy every second of her pain, her suffering, and ironically, doing it all while playing the part of the grieving lover. Brilliant really. Just such a shame he wasn't in a more *liberal* predicament to enjoy it fully.

'DO IT NOW.' Zoreed's roar was deafening, and her pacing around the two of them quickened. The enormous cretins stepped in closer.

He tuned out Beth's begging, her pleading, her snivelling desperation for him to help her. Raising his arms directly above his head, the axe suspended above them, he savoured the moment, her screams reminding him of Tchaikovsky's desperate crescendo he loved so much.

Chapter 26

The explosion brought the chaos Nate needed.

He'd had a fraction of a second to make his decision. Scrambling backwards, he ran towards the perimeter he'd come through, pulled the pin of the grenade and hurled the explosive towards the far end of the arena. He'd had to make a calculated risk, that every man, woman and child in the place was watching the arena spectacle. He couldn't be sure. But he had to do it, it was the only chance he had to get Beth out.

The screaming women, scared children and shouting men were a faint background to the pounding blood hammering through Nate's ears. Sprinting towards the mêlée, he kept his face down, zigging and zagging through the rush of people, his eye line trained firmly on Beth.

Zoreed grabbed the kid nearest to her, wrapped its face in her flapping hijab, and disappeared around the closest corner. He couldn't worry about Zoreed right now. The thugs next to Major Black hauled his arse off with them, and two others rushed forward, grabbed Beth.

'Beth.' He kept his head down as he shouted her name, hoping to hell she heard him, as she too disappeared around the corner. He passed Longy, had to leave him. Motionless face down in the mud, he was gone. *I'll come back for you* he promised silently. To his right, Johnno and Fish were being dragged by the neck towards another building. Close to dead, both of them, they couldn't help here, and he couldn't help them. Not yet. He was on his own, had to choose. It was them or Beth.

A keening whine, so low, he almost missed it pierced through all the other noise. Looking back towards where he'd come from, Finnegan's bright eyes shone down at him through the bars of the suspended cage. Finn was alive! Nate shuffled into an alcove, gasping for oxygen.

He had to get him down. He had to get Finnegan down now.

Beth.

Johnno. Fish.

He glanced in the direction they'd taken Beth, people still running everywhere. Frantic, he worked all the scenarios in his head, calculating the risk, the threats.

Zoreed's likely MO was to always have an audience. The way this whole fucking compound was built to circle the arena made that very clear. Banking on his gut instinct that the bitch wouldn't hurt Beth, or Johnno and Fish, Finnegan, any of them, without spectators, Nate made his choice. *What if you're wrong?* his mind screamed.

He couldn't be wrong.

Wait. Roof. Finn was on the roof. From there, he'd be able to see where Beth and the others might be. Checking over his shoulder, Nate looked for anyone watching him. None. Sliding sideways out of the nook, he rushed for the open doorway of the concrete building beneath Finn's cage. Inside the door, he pressed himself against the wall, caught his breath, glanced around.

Jesus. It was the armoury. The building was full of goddamn explosives. *Why the hell was the door wide open?* His body tingled with awareness; he wouldn't be alone in here for long.

Nate moved further into the room, further into the darkness, towards the opposite end of the building. He reached a locked wooden door. His lungs deflated. He couldn't shoot the lock out, or they'd all be blown sky-high. Rattling the mechanism, he jumped backwards as the latch sprang open. The faintest glimmer of hope flared in his chest.

Edging the door open, the hinges mercifully silent, he slipped through the gap and almost lost his footing in the dim light, tripping on the stairs immediately behind the door.

Slowly, carefully, he made his way up the twelve steps, having to hunch, then crouch the higher he went. He reached the small trap door that lead to the roof. Pressing his hands flat against the steel, he pushed, the echo of Beth's screams urging him to hasten carefully. He couldn't fuck this up.

The crackle of a two-way radio made him freeze. A muffled male voice, young, agitated, and shouting in Pashto, yammered directly above him.

Fuck.

The slide of a bolt vibrating on his hands jarred Nate into action. With his body flattened as flush with the wall as he could on the hinged side of the door, he had a fraction of a second to get this right.

A size eleven boot with a calf muscle the width of his thigh stepped onto the first tread, then the next. The bastard would have to turn to keep balance while he pulled the door shut, it'd be Nate's only chance.

As the man dropped the lower half of his bulk into the hole, navigating the stairs by feel, Nate waited. The giant hunched to bring his shoulder down, and Nate launched onto the bastard's back, wrestling his pistol into the man's temple.

'How many on the roof?' Nate said in Pashto.

The man didn't hesitate. 'You will die,' he said, calm as a monk.

'Yeah, that's likely, but so will you.' Nate's tone brooked no confusion, even if his words were foreign. He jammed his gun further into the prick's I'm-not-telling-you-nothingneck, the movement distracting the man long enough for Nate to then slam the pistol into the side of his head and push the unconscious body far enough down the stairs that he had room enough to lever himself up onto the roof.

After confirming he was alone, Nate rushed to the rusted lever and pulley mechanism that held the chain suspending Finnegan. It was bolted to a steel and concrete housing.

'Finn.' Nate raised his voice just above a whisper.

'Finnegan.'

The whimper above him, and the faint whump whump whump of Finnegan's tail on the cage floor urged Nate's fingers to work faster. 'I'm coming, mate. Just hold on.'

Disengaging the lever's lock, Nate released the chain. He had to bring it down one link at a time, hopefully it'd be slow enough that no-one noticed. And he hoped to hell he then had enough time to get Finn all the way down while there was still mayhem on the ground to camouflage them.

'Please. Please, Zoreed. I can help you.' Beth's frantic shouts froze Nate's muscles.

She's still alive.

'I can help him. Let me help him.' Beth's voice was a mix of terror and steel. Nate slammed on the pulley lock, dropped to his belly, crawled across the concrete roof with his rifle, and peered over the ridge towards Beth's voice. He saw her in seconds, and immediately set his sites on the man at her side, moved his finger onto the trigger.

Beth on her knees, her hands bound behind her back was wedged in the dirt metres from a young child who was bleeding from his middle. Covered in mud, the kid looked like he'd been trampled in the rush.

Cradling the child was one of the men who'd hauled Beth from the arena, someone clearly close to, or in Zoreed's inner circle. Judging by the colour dropping from the kid's face, his sightless stare, he was in serious trouble.

'Let her.' Zoreed's voice boomed above the din from the adjacent corner. 'Let her help.' Nate's head snapped around to watch the matriarch emerge from a doorway, a hunting knife clenched in her hand. His finger pressed further into the trigger.

'You do not let him die.' Zoreed sliced the restraints at Beth's wrists. 'You fix him now.'

Nate's thundering heart filled his ears. If he took Zoreed out, any one of the lunatics surrounding Beth could retaliate and kill her. But if he didn't drop Zoreed, and the kid died, Beth would be shit out of luck anyway.

The only option was to get closer to Beth, and decide what went down next.

He had to get back down there.

Crawling back towards the centre of the roof, Finnegan's cage swayed above him. Nate's heart constricted. He had no idea what state Finn was in, but it wasn't good. He had to get him down. Had to get him down fast. *And then what?*

Even if Iskander made good with their plans and returned with backup, it'd still be at least two hours, or more, before there was any chance of anyone arriving. If at all. And the probability of getting more than one or two at best of them out of here alive, without help, was almost zero.

He had to try.

Scrambling back to the ledge, he noticed the rush of people had died down to an ordered haste, only the heavily-armed cohort remained, and were frantically inspecting every inch of the perimeter, including the rubble around the building the grenade had flattened. Nothing but grains, seeds and spices lay strewn amongst the debris. Nate felt a tiny sliver of relief. He couldn't be sure, but it didn't seem like there'd been any people inside. It was something.

Beth, the kid, and their entourage had vanished. Nate scanned the yard. The bloke that had been hovering over Beth stood outside the door Zoreed had come from, rifle cocked. It looked like it was the main house. Even if Beth got the kid through, saved his life, Nate had no doubt Beth'd still be dead before tomorrow if he didn't get her out.

Finnegan whimpered. Nate crawled back to the middle of the roof on his gut, checking the stairs again. *Jesus.* He had to get Finnegan, and make it to Beth and his men. It just wasn't an either/or kind of deal for him.

Checking the perimeter again, Nate launched forward, pulled on the rusted lever and started Finnegan's cage dropping down several links at a time. Orders were still being shouted beneath him, Zoreed's army taking up their positions, he hoped it was distraction enough from them looking up. His time was running out. The AK wielding search and destroy teams would close in on him pretty quick. He only had minutes. The cage descended and finally his boy came into view. Nate fought to keep his legs standing at the sight of his dog. He laid his gun at his feet to free his hands.

'Oh, Finn, mate, what have they done to you?' Tears smeared his cheeks, he buried his face in Finnegan's fur, rubbing his cheek across his dog's muzzle, rage quickly crowding in on his distress. 'Fucking bastards.'

Nate pulled away, and Finnegan's furry black head, soiled with blood, turned to Nate, his bright brown soulful Labrador eyes fixed on Nate's face, as he tried to drag himself along the cage. But one hind leg was tethered to the rear wall of the cage. He couldn't move. Instead, his matted and bloodied tail thumbed at break-neck speed, his spirit clearly still intact even though his body was so goddamn broken. 'Don't worry,

I'm here, mate.' Nate sniffed back the tears leaking from his nose. 'I'm taking you home.'

He'd kill the bastards who'd done this, and her. Zoreed. He didn't care if it was the last thing he did. Once Finn and Beth, and god help him, Johnno and Fish were safe. He'd take her out. Even if he had to come back by himself, he'd kill her for this.

Nate made quick work of the rusted lock on the cage, but just as he opened Finnegan's door, angry male voices boomed through the hole in the roof.

Fuck.

He could decipher two, maybe three voices. Once they saw the hulk sprawled on the stairs, they'd call for backup as well. His time was up. He snapped the cage door closed, couldn't risk Finnegan trying to get out to help him. He'd rip his leg off with that tether still attached. He ordered Finnegan to stay, and flattened himself against the pulley pylon to wait.

Shit.

He grabbed the rifle at his feet; the voices now at the top of the stairs.

Two men emerged onto the roof, their backs to him. *Idiots.* Neither looked behind them, too concerned by the cage now resting on the roof.

As they moved towards Finn, who was cowering in the farthest corner, Nate moved forward too. The two men were like a mirror image of each other. Twins.

'Kill the dog,' one said in Pashto.

The second one responded with an affirmation, and slid out a dented hunting knife from a crude hip-holster.

'Hey, arsewipes,' Nate drawled. He needed them away from Finn, the risk too high he'd be hit too if he fired at them now. They both spun on their heels, the knife-holder launching towards Nate, the other pulling his rifle into action.

Rolling sideways, Nate had the advantage of the entryway to the stairs being between them. Bullets sprayed in his direction. He sprang up onto his feet, the identi-kids separated, circling him. He moved closer to the knifer. If the other dick sprayed him with bullets, he'd risk killing his brother. So getting close was the best option Nate had.

Hurling himself onto the man's back, he punched into the side of the bastard's skull. The knife came close to Nate's face, he ducked, and cracked the side of the prick's head again, pushing them all towards the stairs with every action. If he went down, he'd take at least one of them with him.

Another man he hadn't seen leaped at him from the top step, rushed them both, but Nate caught it all too late. The thunk of the rifle butt upside his skull sent him spiralling into darkness.

Chapter 27

'Well, well, well, if it isn't the knight in shining armour all fallen from his horse.'

Shivering, Nate pressed his palm to his throbbing temple, peering at the figure with the familiar voice. It took a few seconds for his eyes to adjust to the light.

Outside. He was outside.

'Smashed you good, didn't they?' Major Black's chuckle rumbled around the darkness, Nate's skin prickled. Confusion invaded every cell.

'Dr Black?'

'I don't know why you're not dead yet,' he said, with an exaggerated sniff. 'Mind you, it's just a matter of time.'

Arena. They were back in the centre of the arena. The Major was shackled beside him, just out of reach. *What the hell?* The skin at the back of Nate's neck prickled. Not good. Nothing about this was good. Through the agonising pain pulsing in his skull, he tried to think. And he remembered. The bastard had raised an axe to Beth. 'Why the hell would you hurt her?'

'Ah, so you saw that little show, did you?'

'Where is she now, where's Beth?' Fury and fear burned hot in Nate's gut.

'Well, which question would you like me to answer first, Calloway?' Black swivelled, hunched his back, leaned in further towards his knees. 'Or perhaps, I just won't bother answering any at all.' He laughed again, the mirthless kind of noise reserved especially for mean bastards. 'Because, I know you're dying to know how it is that we're both here, right?'

'I know enough to realise that you're somehow up to your neck in whatever's going down here. And from what I saw, you'd willingly have them take Beth's life instead of yours, you gutless prick.'

'We all do what we have to, to survive out here, Sergeant, even you, you righteous fool.'

He let the taunt go, Doctor Black of no further interest to him right now, finding a way out of this, and to Beth, his first priority. Nate glanced around him. Johnno and Fish lay just beyond him, slumped in the mud.

Lawson followed his gaze. 'Yes, pity about them, isn't it?' he said, tilting his chin towards the men. 'And your friend, Sergeant Patterson, well, in the end, he wasn't really who I thought he was either.'

'What?' Nate hated himself for reacting. 'What do you know about Sergeant Patterson?'

'Well, basically, it boiled down to the fact he just didn't know how to do as he was told.' He tut-tutted theatrically; Nate wanted to wring his fucking neck. 'Really is such a shame the way things ended for him.'

'What the fuck do you mean?' Nate's shaking intensified, his thoughts lurching back and forth in his skull, nothing making sense. How did Black know Patto? *And what the hell was he referring to?*

They both flinched as many heavy footsteps rounded into the arena, marching towards them, with a blaze of torches bright as the frigging sun blinding them to whomever wore the boots crunching across the ground.

The front flank of people stopped metres from them, and the torchlights dropped. Nate counted four men, one with a news-crew sized camera with an enormous microphone perched on his shoulder. And then he saw them, Zoreed *and Beth.* 'Oh god, Beth,' he whispered.

Filthy, her hands tied behind her again, she looked ready to collapse.

Lawson lifted his chin to the women, looked up at Beth. 'Ah, Beth, surgery go well?'

She glanced at Lawson. Her face bruised, filthy and tear-stained was nothing compared to her split and swollen lip. Angry red welts streaked one bare arm, the sleeve from her shirt ripped away. In the torchlight, the blood staining her shirt across her other sleeve, shone like a glossy burgundy satin.

'He died,' Beth said, her chin quivering.

Bile seared Nate's throat.

She glanced sideways, her eyes landing on him, widening in shock. 'Nate?' Her voice hoarse, raw from god knows how much screaming, tore strips out of his heart.

'Doctor Harper.' He answered quickly, his fists clenched, begging to whatever entity out there might help, that she knew him well enough, could read him enough, to recognise his overt disinterest, and keep what they were to each other quiet.

Her brows knitted together briefly and released, her mouth moved to speak, but she stopped. Her shoulders hunched slightly as she briefly nodded back.

'Quite the reunion, isn't it?' Lawson said. 'All of us here, in the same place, close as peas in a pod again. Although I have to say, I much preferred our previous circumstances.' His gaze darkened, his eyes boring into Nate as he whispered, 'I should've put you out of your misery then, while I could.'

'Stand up.' Zoreed's voice boomed over Lawson's and Nate realised the marching feet hadn't stopped. Looking beyond the next line of torch-bearers his gut clenched. There had to be over sixty armed men and women encircling them. 'Bring the others,' Zoreed said.

Murmurs turned into jeers, turned into chants, as Fish and Johnno were dragged from the ground, stumbling. They were hoisted back to their feet when they fell, and then hauled up directly in front of Nate and Lawson. *Oh Jesus.* Nate's gut roiled at the sight of their torn flesh, their battered bodies. The men—his men—dropped like stones into the dirt, both lay where they fell.

'Sorry, man,' Johnno said through blistered and bleeding lips, his eyes fixed on Nate. Fish closed his eyes, tried to curl into a ball. *Oh Jesus.*

A growl snapped Nate's head sideways.

Finnegan.

On his feet in an instant, Nate launched for the bastard hauling his dog by a rope hitched way too tight at the base of Finnegan's skull. 'Let him go, you barbaric arsehole,' he roared. But with his hands and feet tied, the closest bastard only had to jab him with two well-placed fists and he dropped like a stone in his tracks.

Wheezing, Nate sagged as they dragged him back a step and threw him at the ground between Lawson and Beth. She too sat in the freezing mud, her ankles now tethered, tears streaking her cheeks, her lips quivering.

Nate watched helplessly as the bastard dragged his limping Finnegan, tied him up roughly, bound to a tree at the border of the compound's perimeter, with not enough length in the rope for Finnegan to do anything but lean upside the trunk or be choked.

Accepting defeat had never been an option in Nate's life, not even those worst days when he was a kid. But every fibre of his being screamed at him to accept this was it now. Iskander hadn't made it. Too much time had passed for their plan to have come off. Nate's heart shrivelled at the thought that the kid could be hurt, dead. Even the adrenaline firing around his body stuttered. Such a damn fine human, that kid.

He had to accept he was on his own, and no matter how hard he tried to deny it, he had to face the fact they were pretty close to screwed.

Nate sucked in a breath.

No, he damn well wasn't. While he had breath to suck in, there was still a chance.

Righting himself, pushing up on his elbows, he grunted his way up to sitting. Anyway, he sure as hell wasn't going down like a fucking coward face first in the dirt.

'So now our show, it begins,' Zoreed said, cueing the cameraman beside her to start filming. She addressed the crowd with such heavily accented English it took Nate a second or two to process what she'd said,

Zoreed started a slow repetitive clap, her fleshy palms and stubby fingers thwacking back and forth without rhythm. The swarm of people surrounding her followed her lead.

A group of men dragged in an enormous structure made of wood and rope.

Gallows.

His mouth felt like his tongue and lips had been replaced with swollen sandpaper.

She clapped again.

A second structure emerged, three women dragging it across the rocks and dirt. Swords. Two ancient looking broad swords laid flat on a wooden block.

The sour stench of tension and fear surrounded them all.

Zoreed sucked in a deep breath, her eyes sparkling with what he could only describe as fucking glee.

'You.' She pointed at Lawson. 'You will start.'

Two men hauled Lawson to his feet, slit the ties at his wrists.

'Wait! We had an agreement,' Lawson shouted, his tone nowhere near as assured as a moment ago. 'I gave them to you.' He pointed at Beth and Nate, his voice pitched higher. 'All of them. Me. I gave you your tickets to glory.'

Awareness stabbed into Nate's consciousness. *Jesus.* The bastard had sold them out, all of them. 'What the fuck did you do?' Nate shouted.

Beth's voice followed Nate's. 'Oh God, Lawson. What on earth was worth trading all our lives for?'

'Plenty,' he spat back, 'and you could've been on the right side of it all, instead, you shamed me and then ran off, with that.' He jabbed his chin in Nate's direction. 'So now, you get what's coming to you, you ungrateful, frigid bitch.' Spittle peppered his chin as he turned to face Zoreed. 'And I'll remind you, that if you kill me, no-one will get the next shipment to you, the big one. You will lose it all if I'm not there to receive it.' Lawson spoke to her like she was an elderly patient, hard of hearing.

'I do not need you, Major Lawson Black. You finished. I have new man,' Zoreed said, waving away his protestations with her hand. 'But I give you parting gift.'

'Wait, what do you mean? No-one knows all the details but me.' Lawson's words fell on deaf ears as he was dragged to stand centre stage of the arena.

Nate's brain still didn't want to connect the dots. *Deal? Shipment? Jesus.* The head of their hospital was a fucking drug trader ... a surgeon, who'd hawked the lives of his soldiers, his colleague? Sold them all out to sweeten a deal? Must've been some fucking deal.

The look on Black's face as he confronted the crowd told Nate the bastard still hadn't accepted he was as screwed as the rest of them now. Beth whimpered as Zoreed moved to stand beside her.

'My gift to you, Major Lawson Black, is, you pick who dies first, and,' she paused for effect, 'you pick who kills them.' She paused again, sweeping her gaze around the silent crowd. 'And you, Major Lawson Black, you will see everyone die. You go last.'

A snigger rumbled out of Lawson, a film of sweat layered over his face the only tell he wasn't as assured as he appeared. 'Oh that's easy then.' He pointed to Beth. 'I choose her. And she can kill him.' His finger jabbed in Nate's direction.

'No.' Beth's shriek so loud, so strong, had surprised murmurs rumbling around the perimeter. 'I won't do it,' she said.

'You pathetic, gutless prick,' Nate shouted. 'You need a woman to do a man's work, do you? Is that what you do in surgery too? Hide behind a woman's work? Should've known you're a pansy-arsed coward. You're nothing when you're not hiding behind a woman or a fucking mask, are you?'

Provoking the goddamn psycho with anything he could think of, anything that might rile him up, Nate kept up the abuse. It might buy them nothing but empty time, but he'd give anything a go that bought him even a second more of thinking time.

A purple vein pulsed at the centre of the prick's forehead. *Bingo! Strike one.*

'Alright then, since you feel so strongly, Sergeant Calloway,' Black said, 'I've got a better idea.' He clicked his fingers in the direction of the thugs that'd belted Nate when he'd launched for Finnegan. 'Bring the dog and the woman.'

'Wait,' said Zoreed, motioning for the cameraman to pause filming. No-one moved. 'I said one, Major Lawson Black.'

Lawson smiled in her direction. 'Trust me, this will be so much better.' His smile didn't reach his stone cold eyes. 'This way, he'll have to choose.' He pointed to Beth. 'Choose between his whore, and the dog. You've nearly killed yourself to get to this mongrel, be a shame to give it all up now, wouldn't it, Sergeant Calloway?'

A vice wrapped its way around Nate's chest and squeezed. Squeezed and squeezed and squeezed. Forced onto his feet and made to walk towards the centre of the arena, he gulped in air as starbursts of light flashed in front of his eyes. He tried to take in every element of his surroundings, in case, in case there was something. Anything.

But there was nothing.

No-one.

Johnno used what little energy he had to hurl abuse at the bastards from the dirt as Nate passed him. Nate caught his gunner's eye right before his life-light faded, his head falling like a stone into the dirt.

Beth screamed as they hauled her forward. Nate tried to turn but was punched in the back by the nose of two rifles. A yelp from Finnegan tore at him too. He roared at the perpetrator as Finnegan's brutalised body was hauled by his neck across the dirt towards where Black was seated.

He would not be made to kill either of them. He wouldn't.

The thugs shoved him into the dirt three feet from Lawson, whose hands, now in front of him, were gripping one of the swords. It'd been handed to the prick while Nate had been dragged closer.

'So, which heart are you going to stop first then?' the Major asked. Zoreed and the cameraman hovered close, serious, watching Nate intently. 'It's quite a thing to be the one to stop a beating heart. But you know that already, don't you, being a trained killer and all?'

'Yours, you gutless arsehole.'

Major Black shook his head, glanced at Beth and back to Nate again. 'Sad when you can't have what you want, isn't it, Sergeant?'

'Nate. Nate. Please, look at me.' Beth pleaded. 'Look at me, not him ... please, Nate.' He finally did, he glanced at his selfless, courageous Beth. 'I'm dead anyway,' she said softly. She'd stopped crying, was standing still, so still. So fearless. 'I'd rather you do it, not them. Please.' Her voice trembled on the last word.

A guard slit the tie at Nate's ankles.

'Oh this, this is just too much.' Black made retching sounds while the guard freed Nate's wrists, and the other, a few steps away, aimed the rifle at his head. 'You're making me want to vomit with all this desperate martyrdom, Beth dear.' Black bent forward, clutching his gut in an exaggerated gesture.

It was all Nate needed.

Snatching the sword, he whirled sideways and shoved it through the first guard, sending him hurtling into the second. Grabbing Zoreed a fraction of a second later, Nate faced off the wall of rifles as he held the sword beneath her chin, pressing the razor-sharp edge to her throat.

'Any one of you move, she's dead. I have nothing, nothing to lose.' His roar in Pashto filled the silence as he dragged her thrashing body with him towards the wall of the armoury.

'You make big mistake.' Her voice was low, the tone hard but without the edge, as he pressed the sword harder into her neck, crushing her vocal chords.

There'd be no way she'd be able to shout any orders now.

'I don't think so,' Nate growled. 'We'll see what—'

Beth's whimper, loud, desperate, stopped him, spun him on his heel.

Black had her hostage, a mirror image to how Nate held Zoreed. One of the other guards had Finnegan, his rifle cocked at Finnegan's temple, his knee on the dog's neck.

Like everything around them had pressed pause, the next moment happened in macabre slow motion.

Beth rammed her elbows into Lawson's gut, before diving towards the guard holding Finnegan.

'No, NO,' Nate roared as the bastard fired his shot at Beth, point blank. In the same moment, a deafening reverberation of machine gun fire exploded around them, and the perimeter of people started running.

Away from the arena?

The question in his brain, an automatic response to what he was seeing flashed neon, but Nate didn't give a damn about the answer. Something inside him shattered, broke. Hatred hazed his vision red. Dropping the sword, he hauled Zoreed into the armoury doorway, her body his shield, and then wrapped his hands around her throat. And squeezed. Squeezed and squeezed as he roared into her face. 'After I kill you, I will annihilate your family. All of them, every one. Every. Single. One.'

Shoving her sideways and into the stone wall, they struggled, her bulk ramming into him, her fingers scratching and pinching at his flesh. She was good, but he was stronger. As she weakened, and was nearing unconsciousness, he tightened his fingers around her neck, whispered in her ear, 'When I'm finished, it will be as if you never existed here.'

He watched the flare of anger spike in her eyes as she struggled harder, but he wanted it more. Her eyes closed slowly and she dropped forward, her head slumped at her chest. As she fell, Nate's own breath thundered in his ears, the angry, mean words his mother screamed at him from the bottom of a gin bottle rattled around his head like loose marbles. *Your father's family, my family, they're all a pack of murdering bastards. You can't escape your blood, kid.*

Nate released his hands from Zoreed's neck like her flesh had burned him. Flicking his fingers to the pulse point in her neck, he waited. It was faint, but there. He counted to ten, his fingers twitching, clenching and fisting, desperate to give her what she deserved, finish what he started. *Beth wouldn't want this. Don't do it.*

Sucking in lungful's of breath he swiped the sweat from his face, reason edging into his rage. There'd be no pain for her dead. And he wanted her to feel it. Feel what this hell was like. His loss, his grief, she'd have to feel it every day like he'd have to. He wanted for that, almost as much as he wanted Black to suffer with every single breath he ever took for the rest of his life.

Backing away from her, he dragged the pistol from Zoreed's waist belt, inched his head around the doorjamb, and almost dropped to his knees.

Soldiers. Australian soldiers. Rounding up men and women, pounding though the arena restoring order. *Iskander. The kid must've made it. Oh god, the kid made it.*

Nate dragged his hand over damp cheeks, staying hidden, sucking in lungfuls of oxygen, scanning for Beth in the mess of running bodies swarming across the ground where they'd just been standing.

'Hey.' He caught the attention of the soldier closest to him, just beyond the door. 'I need your help, mate,' said Nate. As the bloke turned, eyes he'd never forget met with his own.

'Betsy? Jesus ... is that you?'

The soldier whirled on his heel, protecting himself as he backed towards Nate. 'Yeah, man. It's me. Looks like you got yourself into a right mess, hey? Need this brother to come and save your nancy-boy arse again.'

'I thought you were dead?'

'Yeah, thought I was too for a bit. Gotta love that slim-line body armour though, mate. Fill you in about it all later.'

Betsy hoiked a pistol and a radio to Nate as he rattled off what was what, bringing Nate up to speed on the essentials as best he could in under a minute.

'Beth, have you got her?' said Nate.

Betsy shook his head. 'Negative. Sorry, mate. Black's gone bush with her. Hauled her up after she was shot, shimmied left and disappeared before we reached them. Our focus was on you, man. Bull and Richie are on him though. They're my best snipers. He won't get far.'

Nate nodded sharply. 'And Finnegan?'

'Shepherd's got him. Scooped him up. He'll get him to the medics as quick as he can.' Shepherd, another good bloke Nate had trained with. 'She saved him, your doc, she took one for Finnegan, mate.'

Nate chewed the inside of his cheek until the salty taste of blood made him gag. He swallowed convulsively just so he didn't hurl his guts up. After a moment, Betsy squeezed Nate's shoulder. 'We gotta move.'

'Get on the radio, tell them he's mine,' Nate said, turning his own radio on. 'Tell them that Black, the fucker who has her, no matter what, he's mine.'

'Yes, sir,' Betsy said and relayed the message.

'Roger that,' said Bull. 'We've seen him, and the woman.'

'Is she alive?' Betsy asked, released the radio button, the crackled return response simple.

'Can't confirm her status. Over.'

Nate didn't care what happened to him after this. If Beth was dead, he didn't care if he didn't see tomorrow. But right now, Black's arse was his, and no other bastard was taking him down. There'd be no bringing him in quietly. If she wasn't breathing, the only thing he'd be bringing the bastard is a bullet between the eyes.

'Let's get this done.'

Chapter 28

'Stand down, soldiers. I'll take it from here.' Nate's directive brooked no argument.

It'd taken the two snipers ten minutes to track Major Black and Beth, Nate and Betsy an extra eight minutes to catch up to them.

The thump of chopper blades thrummed in the distance, the rumble of their engines usually comforting to Nate, faded into the background, his focus zoned in on Beth's motionless body sprawled across the track just ahead of them.

'You checked her yet?' he said to Betsy's sniper mate.

'Yes, sir,' Richie answered. 'I'm sorry, she's gone, sir.'

Nate couldn't see, couldn't hear for the roar of rage, grief, guilt thundering through his skull. Black, a few metres from Beth, swivelled his bloodied torso and turned to face Nate, a smile cracking wide across his face.

'I win,' he screeched, hysteria ringing though his cackling. 'I win, Calloway. You lose.'

The two junior soldiers stepped forward, their rifles aimed at Black's chest.

'I said stand down, move out. Now.' Nate's roar drowned out Black's laughter.

'Yes, sir,' they responded together, stepping back, their guns still trained on Black's vitals, his laughter turning into hacking blood-strewn coughs. He'd been hit somewhere.

'Now back up, over the ridge,' said Nate to the men, his voice held the deadly calm of a snake ready to strike.

'Sir?' Bull said. Both men, sharp and cool, each glanced at Nate, their question for him clear, before returning focus to their target. When he didn't answer, they continued backing away as ordered.

'Ahh, Wolfman?' Betsy's warning tone rang clear as a bell from over Nate's left shoulder, as he edged closer to Nate through the scrub.

'You too, Betsy,' Nate said without looking at his friend. 'I said I've got this. Get back.'

'Yeah, that's not happening, brother.' Betsy's tone, as calm as Nate's, held none of the fury, but was just as inflexible.

'Do what you have to, Betsy,' Nate said as he started towards Black. 'But keep out of my way. I told you, he's mine.'

Black, the smug bastard, raised his hands in surrender as Nate approached. 'You got me. I give up,' he sneered.

'Sorry, what'd you say? I can't hear you. Explosion in my ears and all.' With his last word, Nate lowered his gun and threw his fist into Black's bleeding shoulder. The bastard's body hit the ground hard. Nate didn't waste time. Wrenching the man's right hand off the ground, he twisted as many fingers as he could grab and snapped them backwards.

Black screamed. Screamed and screamed and screamed.

'Calloway.' Betsy's voice, his warning, buzzed in Nate's ear like a fly he wanted to swat away.

'Fuck off, Betsy.'

Nate hauled Black to his feet and smashed his fist into the guy's nose, unblinking as the bastard's blood sprayed over his face. Black fell backwards, Nate with him. Straddling the bastard's heaving body he smashed his fist anywhere it landed. 'You killed her.'

Throat. Smash.

'My men. You slaughtered them. You sent men to die you've sworn an oath to protect, you fucking arsehole.'

Jaw. Smash.

'And my dog. You killed a defenceless animal, you fucking psychopathic arsehole.'

Smash. Smash. Smash.

'We're done here, brother.' Betsy hauled Nate skyward.

'I'm not done, get your fucking hands off me, Betsy.' Blood, snot and tears smeared his face, his hands, the flesh on his knuckles shredded. 'I'm not done till he's not breathing.'

Betsy shoved Nate onto his arse, wrestling with him in the dirt, laying a few punches of his own into his friend. With his strength almost gone, fatigue rolling in, his body shutting down, Nate struggled to keep Betsy off him. Bull and Richie moved forward again, kept Black in their sites.

'This isn't you, Wolfman.' Betsy wrestled Nate into a quasi-stranglehold, one good enough to make Nate's vision go grey at the edges. He angled his mouth towards Nate's ear, his volume low enough for only Nate to hear. 'He's fucked you over royally. He's taken from you. I get it. But don't give him the final word, let him ruin the rest of your life. Don't let him take your good, your decency, man. Cause then, you're never rid of him, can never shake his stink from you. Never. And he wins. *He* wins if you kill him.'

The fight in Nate disintegrated slowly, and Betsy eventually released his hold.

Nate rolled sideways coughing, sucking in oxygen. Betsy slid backwards, away from Nate, his breathing just as heavy.

Nate buried his head into the dirt and cried. Cried like he'd never ever stop. Cried until darkness closed in, and desperate oblivion dragged him under.

Chapter 29

'I can't believe you're, you're—'

'Breathing?' Beth finished for him, her abraded vocal chords made her voice foreign even to her ears. 'Damn slow heart rate, fools 'em every time,' she rasped.

'Yeah. The party trick.' He wasn't smiling as he reached for her hand, closed his own around hers and bent forward, pressing his lips to her cheek, infusing his warmth into her bruised skin. He stayed there for so long, when he looked at her again, he didn't hide the tears blurring his vision. 'You were dead.'

She swiped at his cheek, her hand lingering. 'No, I wasn't.'

He sniffed, cleared his throat. 'Beth.' His tone held an edge of something that scared her.

'What is it? What's wrong?'

'I'm flying out for Germany tomorrow. Problem with my lung. Apparently it needs sorting there before I can go home and be treated.' He said it all as if he was telling her he'd broken a toenail. No-one had let her see his records, but she knew he wasn't out of the woods for a full recovery yet.

'Good. You need the specialist care they can give you ASAP. And I'll be there soon too, we'll probably fly home together.'

He didn't look at her when he replied. 'About that, I don't think that's a good idea.'

'What?' The heart rate monitored blipped faster. 'Why not?'

He tunnelled a hand through his hair, pressed his back teeth together. 'I wanted to kill that bastard like I've never wanted to do anything before. I wanted to drain the life out of him, make it as slow and as painful as possible. I wanted to ... to torture him, Beth.' The anguish in his face squeezed at her heart.

'But, Nate, you—'

'Please, don't say anything, just let me finish.'

He looked so miserable, so desperate. She just wanted to reach up and pull him to her. But she didn't, she gave him the space to finish. 'Okay.'

'If Betsy hadn't pulled me off him, off that bastard Black, if he hadn't stopped me, I would've killed that prick with my own hands. And I didn't care, didn't give a shit about the consequences. Didn't care that it would've been cold-blooded murder. And, Beth, thing is, I'd do it again tomorrow. In a heartbeat, I can't even say I hesitate when I think about it. What the hell does that make me?'

The line these men walked, our soldiers, taking the lives of those they believed party to evil and gross wrongdoing, for the greater good, *in the line of duty,* that line, it was often a grey line. And the honour amongst them, the places they wouldn't go, the things they wouldn't do, even if they could, is what made them men not monsters. She'd seen into Nate's heart, and this man, he'd give his life before he'd trade his honour. He wasn't a cold-blooded killer.

'You wanted to take out a deranged man you thought played a part in killing Finnegan, killing other people you care about,' she said softly. 'Anyone, even a hard-arse psych would find that motivation plausible, reasonable. It doesn't make you a—'

'I can't, I don't...' He pushed the wheelchair away from her bed. 'I don't know that I won't do that again, Beth. I never, ever want to hurt you, or make you feel ashamed of me. I know what family means to you, and I ... what if—?'

'I know who you are, Nate Calloway,' she said, fear tightening her throat. She hadn't expected this. Hadn't expected anything like it. Was he saying goodbye? That just wasn't an option. 'And I love you. Every single part of you.'

He held her face with his eyes, his soulful, stormy eyes, and wheeled back to her, grabbing her hand so hard, like she might disappear if he let go.

'I've never felt what I feel for you, for another person, not ever in my life.' His words, hoarse, tore at her heart. 'And I will never forget that I was enough, enough for you to want to be by my side when there was everything to lose.' He exhaled on a shudder. 'But I can't ask you to do that in the real world, with me, like I am.' He stared so deeply into her eyes, she took a minute to find her words.

'Jesus, Nate, you're forgetting I'm a grown woman and can choose what I do and don't want for myself.' She didn't hide the desperation strangling her words. 'What this has proven to me is we can work through anything.' She pushed herself up in the bed. 'Surely you trust me enough to know I'll do whatever it takes?' Anger seeped into her shock, and she pulled herself further upright on the pillow. 'In fact, I'm insulted that you don't think enough of me to know I'm no flake when it comes to the tough stuff.'

'I'm sorry, Beth. I've made up my mind.' He pushed back from the bed, wheeled himself towards the door and out.

'Wait, Nate. Please.' If she could've she would have gone after him, but with her chest wired up like a circuit board, she couldn't move. She tried to calm herself, arguing with her panic that he was likely still suffering acute traumatic stress, that he wasn't thinking straight. *Yes, that was it.* He'd get over it, realise how ridiculous and selfish he sounded, and come around, come back to her, soon.

With pain in her chest that had nothing to do with the bullet wound just above her heart, Beth sunk into the bed, hoping, praying, that she was right.

He glanced towards her window, looked away, his slow and uneven walk continued in a straight line all the way to the plane. She watched as they helped him board for transport to Germany, closed the doors, the plane leaving exactly on time.

'Lieutenant Saunders, did you ask him to stop past before he left?' She hated herself for asking, but couldn't stop herself.

'Yes, ma'am, I did. So did Matthews, ma'am. Lieutenant Matthews went to see Sergeant Calloway this morning.'

'I see,' said Beth, clearing her throat.

'Sergeant Calloway did tell me he'd try, ma'am, but if he didn't make it in here before he boarded, to tell you goodbye.' Her nurse flushed pink, clearly uncomfortable at being the messenger. 'I told him I was certain you'd much rather he told you himself, ma'am.' Her nurse paused. 'I'm sorry he didn't make it in himself, Captain.'

'Thank you.' Beth could scarcely form words. 'I appreciate your help.' The sting of tears burned the back of her eyes. 'I'll be right for a bit I think, Lieutenant. Would you mind coming back later?'

'Yes, ma'am.'

Beth waited until she was alone before letting the tears roll freely down her cheeks.

No matter what he said, or how he packaged it up, it all boiled down to the fact that he didn't love her enough. Didn't love her enough to trust that she'd love him enough right back.

Chapter 30

Betsy's deep laugh echoed across the vines spread long and deep in front of them.

'Can't believe I'm in another bloody monkey-suit, swore I'd never wear one again,' said Nate, his smirk mirroring Betsy's as they clinked the necks of their beers together, both of them dragging in a long sip.

The guest's chatter and live R & B soul music drifted out of the fairy lit, white-fabric-draped barn just off to their left. The well-worn wicker porch chairs creaked as they settled in, enjoying the weathered, wide-board Jarrah deck all trussed up in Sunday best.

'Yeah, well, never thought anyone'd ever marry me either,' Betsy responded. They both chuckled softly, shaking their heads before a sad heaviness left them both silent. 'Longy's wedding, it was a good one, wasn't it?'

'Yeah, it was,' said Nate, swallowing down the lump blocking his throat. 'Hard to believe it was three years ago ... geez he was a funny bloke. You know what he told me that night?'

'Knowing Longy, he'd have gone on with some deep "the universe provides" shit. Right?' said Betsy with a smile.

'Yeah, something like that,' chuckled Nate. 'He told me I should try to keep a woman long enough to move on from the dark side of singledom.'

'Hey? What'd he mean?' said Betsy.

'Dunno really. He said something about loving a woman enough you wanna marry her, was like stepping into the light, and that once you'd been there, there's no way you'd ever go back to the dark side.' Nate took a long sip of beer. 'Some shit to do with we all need to find the light to our dark or something.'

'Bloody Longy, he was always spouting that philosophical crap.' Betsy took another swig of his beer. 'I reckon I know what he meant though. My life'd be nothing without Chelle.' Betsy stared out into the shadowy vineyard, a goofy smile lifting his mouth. 'Ahh Longy, he'd have loved tonight, the bloody sook.'

'Yeah,' said Nate, 'they all would have. Although, I reckon Johnno might've given you a run for your money with Chelle.'

Betsy's smile was sad. 'Christ I miss them.'

'I do too, brother.' The vines blurred as Nate looked out over them and across to the paddock. 'I do too.'

The unmistakable sound of Finnegan's panting along with his nails on the timber announcing his lopsided gait, interrupted their silence.

'Hey, Finn, come out to say g'day have you, wonder dog?' Betsy bent forward and ruffled the fur on Finnegan's head. 'I know I've said it before, but I still can't believe this guy came through.'

'Yeah, was touch and go for so long, but he's a fighter. It still takes him a bit of effort to walk, get around. But he does it. 'Specially if there's a ball involved.'

'Yeah, that ball'll do it.'

'You know, I thought for sure he'd be buried over there,' said Nate softly.

'Yeah, well you both have that same pig-headedness gene.'

'Yeah, yeah,' Nate said. 'Well, that gene's helped dig your sorry arse out of trouble a time or two.'

'That it has, that it has.' Betsy nodded, sipping from his drink. 'Gotta say, I'm glad you've dropped all that hob-nobbing 'round the countryside with your new grape growing mates long enough to host our little shindig.'

'Wouldn't have missed it.' Nate rubbed Finn's head. 'Anyway, got the business side all sorted now, can stay put here for a bit, see if I can build it all up to something worthwhile.'

'Geez, mate, if that wine in there's your low-grade stuff, I reckon you're on a winner. Mind you, what does a bloody camo-wearing-jock like me know about wine?'

'You've got a point there.'

Finn's alert stance stopped their laughter. They turned towards Nate's driveway, a two kilometre meandering road over to the right. The unmistakable rumble of an engine was heading up towards them. Nate shook his arm loose of his shirtsleeve, checked the time.

'Latecomer. Jesus, they've almost missed the whole bloody thing,' he said. 'You notice who didn't show?'

'Wouldn't have a clue.' Betsy downed the last of his beer. 'But I better go make sure my wife's happy as she deserves to be, and that *she* hasn't noticed someone hasn't showed up. You right to bring whoever it is across?'

'Sure. I can do that. And get that music sorted while I'm gone. I'm asking the band to change this bloody blue-grass-soul-guitartwanging whatever the hell it is, to something more this century soon as I'm back.'

'Don't you dare.' Betsy punched him playfully in the gut. 'She'll have your balls in her bag before you can cough, and then she'll have mine.'

'No, she won't, Chelle loves me, mate.'

Chelle was a great chick. She'd been part of the intel team that took down Zoreed and the rest of them. She and Betsy had hit it off instantly. Engaged after four months, they married ten months and twelve days after that. He was happy for his mate, a bloke he owed more than he could ever repay.

Whistling for Finnegan to join him, Nate ambled down his stairs and towards the driveway, checking over his shoulder that all was well at the barn as he left, slowing his pace so Finn could keep up.

'C'mon, wonder dog, let's see who's missed the party.'

He smiled as he walked. He'd sworn he'd never let anyone talk him into holding another wedding on his property, especially since the last bride who was here, Longy's gal, was now a widow. But how the hell could he say no to the bloke who saved him, and the woman who helped him do it?

Nate let his thoughts drift back to that hell day. He rarely visited the memories anymore, and Iskander filled his thoughts. The kid had made the raid, the whole rescue possible. He never gave up, never once believed he wouldn't make it. Even though Nate hadn't been able to get word to him, he followed their plans, made some of his own, and didn't let up on his mission until he'd made it. Back to his mum and grandfather, got the help they needed through Betsy's contacts, made it all happen. Nate smiled. Last letter he had from the kid, said he'd made plans to go to uni, be a doctor. Like Beth.

Beth.

Her face floated into his mind as he moseyed down the winding driveway towards the little red car ambling it's way up the last part of the hill. There wasn't an hour that passed when he didn't think of her, want to hold her. Wish maybe he'd made some different choices.

When he'd recovered, was first back home, Betsy, and even Chelle had stuck their bib in about her, told him to call her, see her, stop being a dickhead. He'd toyed with maybes, especially during this last month, given Black's hearing starts next week.

Angelis would be there too, Nate was thankful he'd made it. Nurses Matthews and Saunders, they'd have to make an appearance, Nate hoped to see them at some stage too. Thank them again in person for ... everything.

The other turncoat Fraser, his trial was slated after this one. He was being trialled separately because he'd rolled on bastards further up the line, cut a deal somehow. It was wrong, all so wrong. It was one of the reasons he'd chosen to get out for good.

Zoreed was awaiting prosecution for war crimes, drug trafficking and kidnapping. Well, that's what topped her list, he hadn't bothered to read any further than that.

When Nate could finally handle it, Betsy had filled him in on everything that'd gone down the year before the raid. He'd been working covert on taking down Zoreed and her associates, and had realised Patto was up to his neck in drugs and shit in the process. Betsy had tried to give him a way out, a way to do the right thing. But it was too late for Pat, he was in too deep.

Once Nate'd listened to it all, processed it, his first instinct was to see Beth, hit her doorstep, tell her everything. She deserved the closure too. He'd wanted to tell her he'd been seeing a shrink, and the shrink reckoned his sorry arse would stay the ugly side of okay for the rest of his life, that he'd be unlikely to lose his shit in a bad way, that he was safe.

He did try. To tell her in person.

He drove down to Sydney, to Clovelly, knocked on her door. She wasn't home. He'd called the number he had for her, disconnected. So he'd left, come back in the afternoon. Waited in the car. Felt like a damn stalker, but didn't want to miss her again.

She'd come home in the early evening. His heart had squeezed at the sight of her, kept it up till he couldn't breathe. She seemed happy ... enough, settled. Who was he to mess with that? Open closed wounds? It'd taken him an hour to do it, but he'd left. Let her go, it's what she deserved. Now it was too late to open that can of worms, wouldn't be fair. And anyway, the way these things worked, they'd probably be summoned for evidence on separate days, so it was unlikely he'd run into her next week, would avoid any awkward moments in some sterile corridor. And that'd be a good thing. Really. Yep, that door was shut, welded closed, and now, after all this time, it was best for everyone if it stayed that way. *Yeah, you keep telling yourself that...*

He still felt a total arse about leaving her without saying goodbye. He hadn't planned it that way, but when the time had come, he didn't think he'd get through it without caving, without begging her to forgive him for being a total idiot, and beg her to make a go of it, whatever happened.

'Fucking coward,' he muttered to himself, loud enough that Finn stopped, waited for a command. 'Sorry, mate, go on, all good.'

The car was finally on the bend just ahead of him, the lights from the barn had faded behind him, the music a lilting murmur wafting on the breeze. With only a half-moon to light the way, he picked his way from the edge of the grass, then across the driveway.

He turned slightly. 'Stay,' he told Finn as the car pulled up. He left Finnegan and wandered over towards the driver's door.

'Evening, Sergeant Calloway.'

'Beth?' He grabbed at the bonnet for support as she stepped out of the car. Finnegan started whining. 'Jesus, Beth?' He repeated her name like a complete dickhead. 'How, ah, what, ummm—'

'Betsy invited me, but I didn't want to make a scene, so said I'd come when all the formalities were done.'

Nate couldn't speak. His heart had leapt into his throat and strangled his words.

She closed her door and walked towards him, hushing Finn with quiet words, and the promise of a pat.

She stopped directly in front of Nate, the moonlight streaking her beautiful face, the breeze tugging at the loose honey-coloured curls framing her chin. It was like he'd only seen her, held her, made love to her yesterday. Like everything that happened after that never existed.

'I have to tell you,' she said, 'I was pretty gutted when you walked away and never looked back.' She cleared her throat, and he had the feeling whatever was coming next wasn't going to be pretty, but he deserved whatever it was and more. 'I was angry, confused, heartbroken really—' she exhaled unsteadily, '—but then, when you didn't try to contact me, or return my calls, I decided it was useless to want a man who didn't want me, so I let you go, let us—well the thought of us—go, and tried to get on with the next chapter of my life.'

Nate didn't know if he wanted to drop to his knees and beg her forgiveness, or drag her to him and kiss her breathless, then beg her to forgive him, right now, after, or ... wait. What if her being here had nothing to do with her still having feelings for him? Maybe this was just closure for her? Necessary before the onslaught of next week, having to face what happened at the trial, deal with Black and all that shit. Maybe she just needed to tie off at least one loose end, and this had nothing at all to do with her feelings for him.

'Beth, I...' He struggled with what to say to her. 'I can't believe you're here. Right here, standing in front of me.' She stared deep into him, biting at her lower lip. 'Jesus, I don't even know how to tell you how sorry I am,' he said simply. 'I was shit-scared I'd wind up hurting you, no matter what you said about being able to handle it, and I just couldn't have that after everything that happened to you. Because of me. You're the only person in my life who'd ever—' He still struggled to find the words to tell her what he felt. He searched her face, her expression almost unreadable. 'I just want you to be safe and happy.'

She dropped her gaze to her feet, crossed her ankles, and took a moment before she looked up at him again. 'Well are you ready to make good on that now?'

'What?'

'Safe and happy. Are you ready to make sure that happens for me? Cause it's my next chapter,' she said, the corners of her mouth tilted in a smile but her eyes stayed wary. 'And I'm not sure how my story ends, but I know I want you in it, Nate Calloway.' This time her expression was unmistakable. 'My story is with you. No-one else knows the words.'

He didn't hesitate, circled his arms around her waist and pulled her to him, her face a breath from his.

'Are you sure?' he said, pushing a strand of hair from her face, ignoring the stab of panic jabbing at his gut. 'Are you really sure, 'cause I'm never gonna be the good guy? Not always, anyway.'

'Let's see ... driving four hours to just miss a wedding ... is this the action of a woman unsure?' she asked, her smile reaching her eyes this time, her body relaxing a little into his arms.

'No, I guess not.' He cupped her chin, tilting her face to his. 'God I've missed you, Red,' he said against her warm, soft lips.

'I've missed you too, Wolfman,' she murmured back.

He kissed her. Long. Serious. Slow. Until she pulled back. And then he kissed the tip of her nose, her eyelids before sliding his lips along her jaw and back to her mouth.

'I've dreamt about this for ... since you left,' she whispered against his lips.

'Every day,' he echoed.

She wrapped her arms around his neck. His heart jolted, the knot in his gut alternating between tight and loose. He couldn't quite believe she was real. Here ... for him.

'I reckon Betsy and Chelle will have the binoculars out by now, sly buggers,' Nate said after a moment. He couldn't wipe the smile off his face, even given he was a little scared at how happy he felt. Beth, Finnegan, his friends, here. At his ... home.

'Well, let's go then,' Beth said, threading her fingers through his, calling Finnegan to her side. Finn snuggled between them, nuzzling their hands as they headed back towards the barn full of music. 'And as I recall it, you owe me a tour ... later.'

'That I do,' he said. 'I know the best place to start too.' He dragged her close, and kissed her slow, savouring her taste, hinting at what he *really* wanted to show her.

'Maybe you should show me that place now,' she said breathlessly, pulling back, locking her gaze with his, the heat in those gorgeous cognac eyes sending his heart rate into double time.

She didn't need to ask him twice.

Glancing up into the star-studded sky, he sent his silent cheers to Longy, his bloody red-haired, starry-eyed philosopher.

Thank you. Thank you. Thank you.

'C'mon.' Nate drew Beth closer to him as he changed direction and guided them towards the porch, to the French doors that opened into the master bedroom.

Lucky ... you're a lucky bastard, Calloway. Don't let her go.

He wouldn’t. Not ever again, ‘cause maybe, just maybe, he’d get used to living over here in the light.

Thanks for reading **Situation Critical.** I hope you enjoyed it.

If you'd like to know more about me, my books, or to connect with me online, you can visit my webpage www.amandaknightauthor.com, follow me on Twitter @AKnightWriter or like my Facebook page at www.facebook.com/amandaknightwrites.

You can also follow me through my publisher's page here www.escapepublishing.com.au

Reviews can help readers find books, and I am grateful for all honest reviews. Thank you for taking the time to let others know what you've read, and what you thought.

This book was published by Escape Publishing. If you'd like to sample some more great books from my fellow Escape Artists, please turn the page.

BESTSELLING TITLES BY ESCAPE PUBLISHING...

The Making of Henri Higgins
Elizabeth Dunk

He thought it was all a game ... until he grew accustomed to her face.

Henri Higgins is bored by everything – his life, his work, even the models he regularly sees socially (and privately). So when a close friend suggests a high-stakes, friendly competition, a 'fame' game, Ree leaps at the opportunity for a little shake-up in his daily routine. The rules are simple: the competitors are to take the first person that they meet at a certain time and make them as famous as possible within two weeks.

But Ree doesn't expect Elizabeta.

Elizabeta Flores del Fuego has a plan. An office manager by day, she moonlights at a number of creative Canberra businesses by night to learn all she can about the fashion industry and put her in the best place possible to help launch her beloved daughter, Angelina's design career. Cleaning the office of Higgins Publishing is just one of those jobs, but when Henri Higgins offers her a week's worth of work and a paycheque large enough to get Angelina Designs on its feet, it's an offer she can't refuse.

But Elizabeta doesn't expect Ree, and neither expect the lessons in love they're both about to learn.

Transfixed
Maddie Jane

Hot and flirty new romance from Maddie Jane about a woman who thinks she knows her limits, and the man who will help her see beyond.

Taking a business-for-losers course over the summer is Annie Cassidy's idea of hell. Her place as 'the looks not the brains' in her family is well-established, and she has no intention of ever entering a classroom again. Even if it means letting down her sister. Again.

Jilted professor, Dominic Grayson, reluctantly takes a job teaching an adult-learning summer class. It's a far cry from the university environment he's used to, and it's certainly not as stimulating as his regular job. Until Annie walks in and stimulates him in all the wrong ways. Avoidance seems the best option, but when his sister challenges him to see more than just her long legs and distraction techniques, Dominic can't refuse.

As the summer heats up, lines start to blur: between student and teacher, friend and lover, until neither Dom nor Annie know where they stand. And when it seems like Project Annie is doomed, can either of them see beyond a summer fling into something real?

Entwined
JC Harroway

Your true family is the one you choose...

When nurse Jess Bellamy returns to her hometown for a cousin's wedding, she hopes to completely avoid her ex and first love, Morgan Price. But Morgan is the best man, and the groom's best friend, so try as she might, Jess can't avoid him. Teenage Morgan, she got over. Grown up Morgan is infinitely hotter, infinitely more successful, and infinitely harder to ignore.

When they re-kindle the explosive physical connection between them, Jess hopes they've burned it out of their systems. She left everything behind five years ago after her father's funeral, including Morgan, and she's leaving again in two days. She had good reasons for going, and good reasons for staying away.

But as Morgan and Jess explore their searing passion during that lost weekend, Jess is tempted by what might have been and haunted by the ghosts of what was. She has two days to decide whether to keep her secrets or keep the only man she's ever loved.

She's The One
Bronwyn Stuart

In the game of love—and TV—you play to win or you lose your heart.

Millionaire Banjo Grahams originally signed up for *She's The One* drunk as a skunk and willing to do anything to bed Australia's most beautiful women, but when he sobers up he realises he could lose much more than his reputation if he goes through with it. Unable to back out of an ironclad contract, he makes a deal with the network boss to rig the show, picking the lucky bachelorette ahead of time and guiding the season to meet his own ends and keep the board happy.

When her father tells Eliza Peterson she isn't going to produce *She's The One,* but appear as a one of the contestants, she is livid. Competing for some guy on reality TV is no way to earn his—and the network's—respect and show them she is capable of producing shows of her own.

But for all the planning and staging, somehow the show takes on a reality of its own, and the goals of Eliza and Banjo fall away from something neither of them expected—love.

ESCAPE
publishing
A novel approach

Made in the USA
Las Vegas, NV
23 February 2022